RISING FROM THE DEPTHS

THE KRAKEN #5

TIFFANY ROBERTS

RISING FROM THE DEPTHS

A broken woman in need of healing. A stubborn kraken seeking redemption.

Two years after a bloody battle nearly tore his people apart, Kronus finds himself plagued with guilt and without a place to truly call home. And when he saves a blue-eyed human from a razorback, his world is once again turned upside-down. Though he once opposed relations with her kind, he is undeniably drawn to Eva's pain, loss, and inner strength. He will do anything to protect her - and to possess her.

Eva had a perfect life. But a few seconds of blood and terror took everything away. Left disabled and alone, she sinks deeper into despair every day - until the ochre kraken who saved her forces his way into her life. She wants nothing to do with the overbearing, gruff, and pushy Kronus...at least at first. With neither of them ready to let go of the past, how can they hope for a future together?

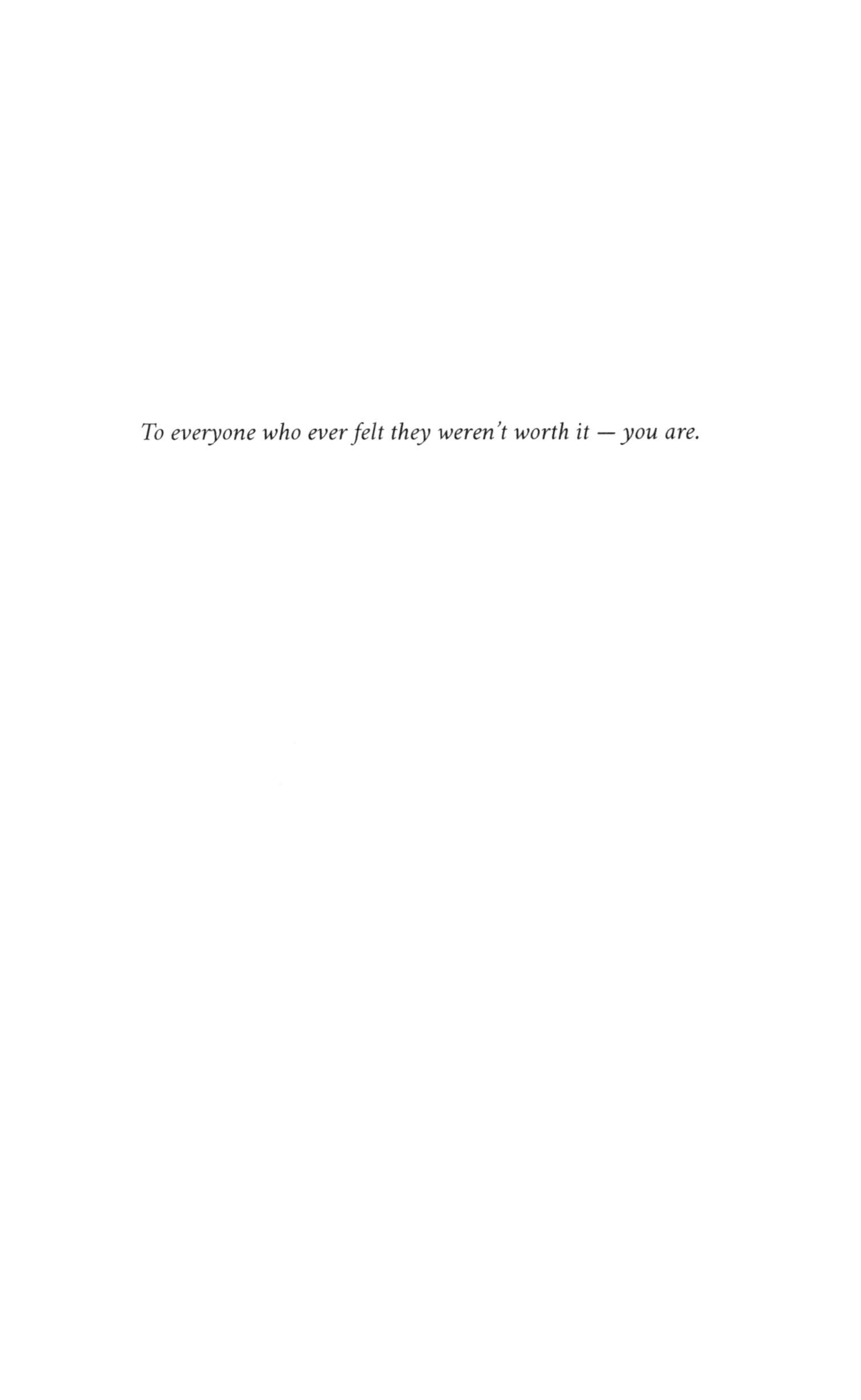

To everyone who ever felt they weren't worth it — you are.

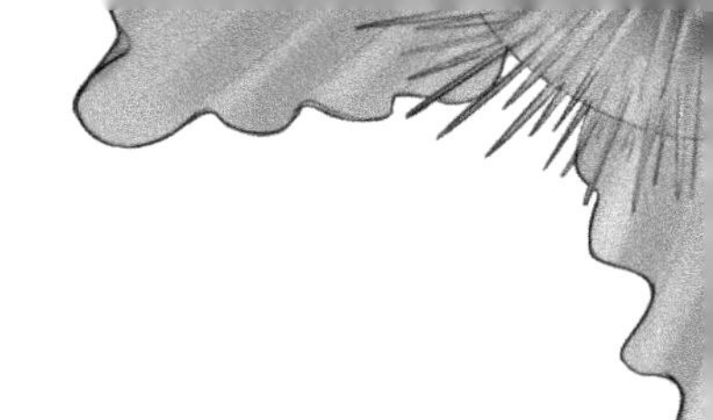

CHAPTER 1

"Do we really need *them* tagging along?" Ozcar asked, jabbing a thumb toward the small group of kraken males gathered on the dock nearby.

Breckett, the burly, hairy-faced man standing within arm's reach of Ozcar, didn't glance up from the rope he was coiling. "They're part of The Watch as much as you or me."

The surrounding water sparkled under the morning sun, casting bright, undulating light on the fishermen as they prepared their boats and equipment. The day was already warm. Nine months ago, it would have bothered Kronus; his years beneath the waves and within the controlled, consistent climate of the Facility hadn't prepared him for the weather on land, but he'd since adjusted to the fluctuating, more extreme temperatures on the surface.

"We've been taking care of our own for three hundred and sixty years," Ozcar argued. "We didn't need them through any of that, and we don't need them now."

Kronus clenched his jaw to hold in the words that nearly spewed from his mouth; they wouldn't help the situation.

It is us *who do not need* you.

The other kraken — Vasil, Brexes, and Charos — exchanged glances with one another, their tentacles writhing restlessly on the dock's surface.

Many of The Watch's humans at least attempted to be friendly to the kraken, but some, like Ozcar, made no secret of their distrust and suspicion. It didn't matter to the latter group that the two people had lived together in peace for well over a year. Kronus understood their feelings. When they looked at the kraken, they saw inevitable violence, saw the looming destruction of their way of life, saw *monsters*.

Part of Kronus felt the same way when he looked at humans.

He adjusted his hold on his harpoon gun, ensuring it was directed away from Ozcar — more to deny himself the temptation than put the human at ease. He shifted his attention to the gentle water off the dockside.

"Funny how some of you kids talk about how things used to be like you have any idea," Breckett grumbled, tossing the coiled rope into his boat. "Fishing's the best it's ever been, and this town is at its strongest in decades."

"That's because of this mass migration," Ozcar said. "The coast is teeming like never—"

"Don't tell *me* like never before." Breckett's skin reddened beneath his thick facial hair.

Conflicts between young and old, between past and present, were familiar to Kronus. But he had no desire to reflect upon his own experiences; there was work to be done. Out there, in the open water, he could forget everything else for a while and focus on what mattered — the hunt.

He could focus on helping his people.

"This is unheard of!" Ozcar declared. "These numbers, in these concentrations—"

"It's happened before," Breckett said, "and it will again."

"These migrations are regular occurrences," said Vasil, drawing all eyes to him.

Ozcar's face reddened; Kronus doubted the younger human's frustrations were quite the same as Breckett's.

Monsters weren't supposed to have a say.

"Every fifteen or twenty years," Vasil continued, "mature mirrorfins gather along the coast to breed, and it attracts all manner of sea life."

"And our nets can handle it, just like always," said Ozcar. "We don't need *them*."

"We need them now more than ever, looking out for us," Breckett said. "Making sure we all get home."

"Unless you believe your nets and little boat will hold against a razorback," Kronus said, staring at Ozcar. "You are welcome to take that risk. We are not the only predators lured by this migration."

Kronus turned his attention away, ignoring Ozcar's stammered response. He watched the sunlight glittering across the ocean's surface. He'd spent his life below, watching shafts of light create dancing webs of delicate shadow on the sea floor. Even after nine months in The Watch, it felt strange to witness everything from land, especially beside the beings his ancestors had reviled and warred against.

Human voices called his gaze toward the shore. The dock was flanked on either side by swathes of beach visible only when the tide was at its lower phases — as it was now — over which stood tall, curving cliffs.

They were dressed in what Kronus understood to be *underclothes* — scant garments that covered only what humans considered their most intimate parts. A common enough sight; the beach near the kraken dwellings outside town had grown popular for many of The Watch's humans, who often wore similar attire when they swam.

Though this beach was faster and more convenient to access from town — a quick walk down a ramp rather than a hike through the jungle — Kronus couldn't help but suspect another reason for these humans to have come here.

This place was far less likely to have kraken present.

The humans waded into the water as a group and swam away from the shore, laughing and splashing as they moved.

Kronus ran his eyes over the carefree humans — two males and three females, all appearing to be in their prime. Joy such as theirs had never been expressed among the kraken before Macy, Jax's human mate, had come to the Facility. Kronus still considered the behavior somewhat foolish; adults had no business frolicking like younglings. But their smiles and good humor produced a feeling in him which had become increasingly familiar over the last two years. It manifested as a hollowness in his chest and gut, sometimes so powerful it seemed his body would collapse in upon itself.

He refused to acknowledge it for what it was — envy.

One of the human females glanced his way and briefly caught his gaze before speaking to her companions.

The humans' playfulness and laughter faded as all five looked at Kronus, brows low. They exchanged hushed words and disgusted expressions. It was nothing new to Kronus; the humans prone to cruelty or intolerance often seemed bolstered by a sense of righteousness that left them unmindful of any consequences.

And what repercussions would they have faced, anyway? The kraken who'd chosen to dwell in The Watch did so with full knowledge that the humans didn't typically resolve their disagreements through violence. It was frowned upon in human rules and traditions, and even though humans still fought one another from time to time, a kraken battling a human would be seen in an entirely different light. The damage a kraken could inflict upon a human in a physical confrontation was immense. The still-building relationship between the two peoples would not likely endure the strain caused by such an event.

Most humans seemed accepting. That had to be enough for now.

Heat suffused the deepening hollowness inside Kronus as the humans continued to stare at him. Their humor had taken a cruel twist; they were not laughing out of joy but at his expense.

All of them except one…

A petite female with lightly tanned skin and warm brown hair kept her gaze on Kronus as her companions, still talking and laughing, turned their attention away. He found himself unable to take his eyes off her. Her features, like those of so many humans, were at once gentler and more defined than any kraken's, in large part due to her eyebrows and nose. But her face was unlike any Kronus had ever seen.

Something about her held his attention — the light in her eyes, the curve of her pink lips, or the hair brushing against her unblemished skin. Perhaps it was because she alone had not looked away, because she alone seemed to see *him*.

One of the males swam to the female and wrapped his arms around her. She blinked and shook her head, breaking eye contact with Kronus, before turning to face the male. He drew her close, and they pressed their lips together in a *kiss*.

The heat in Kronus's chest flared and spread throughout his body, making the surface of his skin itch. He turned his head away from the humans in the water. Their mating habits and relationships meant nothing to him; he'd come to The Watch only because the Facility, the place where his people had lived since their creation, could no longer be a home to him.

Kronus was not worthy of that place anymore. He couldn't look at its walls without remembering *everything* — the betrayal, the pain, the loss.

The other kraken remained nearby, but Ozcar and Breckett

had moved into their respective boats. Breckett worked alongside another older human, Wade, to secure the rigging of their vessel. Most of the other fishermen had also moved into their boats.

Vasil was staring at Kronus. Quiet Vasil, as observant as Arkon but always outside everyone's notice. Though he'd been one of the kraken captured by hunters two years before, Vasil hadn't broken under the mistreatment he'd suffered at their hands — unlike Neo. Neo, who'd—

No. There is no point in following that line of thought.

Vasil flicked his eyes toward the humans in the water. When he returned them to Kronus, the question within them was clear — *are you with us?*

Clenching his jaw again, Kronus tightened his grip on his harpoon gun. He had a duty to fulfill. He had people to protect and feed, even if they all weren't *his* people. Once that was done, he could return to his house atop the cliff, to the thoughts that often consumed him when he was alone.

Holding Vasil's gaze, Kronus nodded.

EVA RAISED an arm to shield her face from the wave of water Blake sent her way, which dampened her hair as it splashed over her. She laughed and returned fire, which resulted in peels of laughter from Samuel and Blake and giddy shrieks from Hailey and Addison.

A sense of lightness permeated Eva. She'd never imagined her life could be so perfect. While she missed her family, who still resided in Emmiton, her move to The Watch had been worth it. Just being here, in this moment, with her friends beneath the warm, bright sun made it all worthwhile. She didn't have a care in the world, and she was joined to the most handsome man she'd ever seen.

When she glanced at Blake, she found his gaze already upon her. He winked and ran his tongue along his upper lip. Her own lips curved up as lust sparked within her. She could easily imagine the titillating thoughts coursing through his head — similar thoughts were flashing through hers. There'd scarce been a day during which they'd kept their hands off each other since their joining.

"It's *so* good to have the day off," Addison said, tilting her head back and closing her eyes as she treaded water.

"Are you serious?" Hailey smacked the surface of the water, splashing Addison in the face. "Even on work days, you're always slacking off!"

Addison sputtered, wiping the moisture from her face. "Sam," she whined, "are you going to let her talk to me like that?"

Samuel swam up behind her, grinning. He leaned his head forward and brushed his lips over the shell of her ear. "Well, she *is* right."

Addison scoffed and turned, slapping his shoulder. "Jerk!"

Samuel laughed and swam away.

Blake snickered. "Have to agree."

Addison's face fell into a comical pout. "I don't know what Eva sees in you, Blake, much less why I still put up with Sam!"

"Aw, come on now, Addy," Samuel crooned, returning to her side and slipping an arm around her. "You know I don't judge you. It'd be hypocritical, since I join you on a lot of those *breaks*."

Addison's face flamed red. She sent a spray of water up into his face.

Eva smiled as she watched her friends. Though she'd been in The Watch for less than a year, they'd taken her in as family from the beginning. Blake, of course, had had a lot to do with that. He'd introduced her to them as soon as they'd come into town together; they'd met in Emmiton when he'd come to buy hides from her father, and he'd decided early on that she was the one for him.

"Ugh, check out what's looking our way," Hailey said.

Eva followed Hailey's gaze with her own. Fishermen were working all along the dock, but her friend wasn't referring to them; she was staring at the kraken. There were four of them, each a different color, each taller and broader than the nearby human males. Even from this distance, twenty or twenty-five meters, she could see the subtle movement of their tentacles on the dock.

She'd caught her first glimpse of their kind the same day she'd come to The Watch. The creatures were terrifying, but intriguing. All she'd known before that day was from stories that had drifted to Emmiton on the lips of far-roaming traders, stories about intelligent, *talking*, many-limbed creatures from the sea. That was all the kraken had been to Eva and her family — stories. Most of the kraken seemed to remain on the outskirts of town, where they worked, but there always seemed to be a few mingling with the humans, often working alongside them.

Her eyes locked with those of the ochre kraken. There was a stern set to his features, his brow low and his lips downturned. The golden sunlight lent a uniquely beautiful vibrancy to his color.

"What do you think they're thinking?" Addison asked.

"Probably thinking they have a chance with you," Samuel said, kissing her shoulder. "They can think again."

"How can *anyone* stand to be touched by those things? They're disgusting," said Hailey. "It's probably like being touched by a bunch of worms, all cold and slimy."

Addison gagged. "Stop it! That's a mental image I do *not* need."

Sam and Blake laughed.

"It's such a waste," Hailey continued. "I had my eye on Randall Laster when he came into town with his rangers a few years ago, but now he's with one of *them*. I mean, *how* can he stand touching that, much less fucking it?"

"They can impregnate human women, too," Blake said. "They're breeding with our kind."

"That's even worse! It's unnatural. Just the thought of one of those things squirming inside me makes me want to vomit." Hailey's revulsion was clear in her tone, though it seemed exaggerated.

Eva kept her attention on the ochre kraken as her friends continued to talk. He held her gaze unwaveringly. Awareness flickered in his eyes, as though he *knew* what her friends were saying despite the relatively low volume of their voices and the distance between them. A pang of guilt struck her, though she didn't necessarily disagree with her friends; the kraken were…inhuman.

Her gaze roamed over the male. Though she couldn't make out the subtler details, the differences between kraken and human were stark and unquestionable — the most obvious of all being the eight tentacles each had in place of legs. The appendages were lined with suction cups along their undersides and seemed to be in constant motion; they were wholly alien.

Something splashed behind her, and an arm snaked around her waist an instant later, turning her and pulling her against Blake's large, hard body.

"Doesn't matter," Blake said. "They won't get you. You're already *mine*."

Eva shifted her focus to the man holding her, her newly joined husband. The conversation she'd missed didn't matter; she was his, and she harbored no worries about the kraken.

He leaned forward and pressed his lips to hers. Smiling, Eva loosely draped her arms over his shoulders and returned the kiss, brushing her fingertips over his short blonde hair. Blake grinned against her mouth as he lowered his hands to the backs of her thighs and guided her legs around his hips. His palms slid along her skin, and he groaned as she locked her ankles, anchoring herself in place. He removed his hands only to continue treading water.

"I love your legs," he said into her ear, voice low. His tongue flicked out to lick her lobe, sending a tingle of desire across her skin. "Especially when they're wrapped around me."

Eva tightened her legs, pressing her sex against the hardened length of his cock through their clothes. She drew her head back and arched a brow. "Here? Now?"

Blake's grin widened. "Just looking at you. You're perfect."

"Don't soil the good name of this town by being such a horny bastard, Blake." Sam teased. He rose out of the water, dropped his hands on Blake's shoulders, and shoved both Blake and Eva beneath the water.

She barely managed to snap her mouth shut before she went under. The sound of water — somehow quiet and deafening at once — filled her ears.

Eva released Blake and kicked to the surface. She shook her head and wiped her eyes, sputtering and spitting salty water. "Damn you, Sam!"

Blake resurfaced with a great splash and charged after Samuel, who swam away laughing.

"Such a hypocrite," Addison chuckled.

"No kidding," Eva said. "I can't count how many times I've caught you and Sam during your *breaks*."

"They get down and *dirty* in those fields," Hailey said with a smirk, "and I don't just mean their hands."

Eva laughed along with her friends as Sam and Blake wrestled and splashed, but her laughter was cut short when something brushed against her leg. She started, reflexively pulling away, and immediately thought herself a fool; it was nothing but a fish.

Addison looked at Hailey. "When are you going to—"

She abruptly plunged under the surface.

"Oh, that was just mean guys," Hailey said, turning toward the last place they'd seen Blake and Sam wrestling.

They were both still there, wearing confused expressions.

Eva's eyes widened.

Bubbles floated to the surface over the spot Addison had vanished. Suddenly, the water was stained red with an ominous, slowly spreading crimson cloud.

"Addison!" Eva screamed. She spun about, scanning the water, but there was no sign of her friend. Fear slithered down her spine, sinking its icy claws deep to spread its chill through her entire body.

"Addy!" Samuel yelled, swimming toward Eva. "Where is she?"

"She disa—"

Hailey screamed as something bobbed to the surface of the crimson water. Eva's stomach lurched. What she was seeing wasn't real; it *couldn't* be real. It just…couldn't.

She's not dead. She's not dead. She's not dead.

"Get to the beach!" Blake yelled from somewhere behind Eva; his voice sounded far off.

"No!" Samuel bellowed, reaching for Addison. She floated face down on the surface, her skin shredded and bloody.

A huge, dark shape rushed up from below to intercept him. Eva caught a glimpse of the monster as it crested the surface — a huge mouth with long, curving, pointed teeth; a powerful body covered in pale blue skin; dark spines protruding from the top of a thick head. Its mouth came down on Samuel, clamping over his shoulder, and man and beast disappeared amidst churning water.

Hailey screamed again. Eva turned her head to see Blake swimming, already more than halfway to shore. Somehow, that cut through the fog of terror gripping her mind, inflicting a deep sting; she shoved it aside. Panting and trembling in fear, Eva hurriedly swam to Hailey.

She caught hold of Hailey's wrist. "W-We need to go." Eva tugged until Hailey tore her gaze away from the bloody, frothing water.

A great commotion rose from the dock; boots pounding on its surface, shouted, panicked orders, and several splashes, but she couldn't focus on any of it. She needed to get to land with Hailey. She kept her eyes on Blake as he dragged himself onto the beach.

Only twenty meters to go.

"We'll make it, Hailey. Keep swimming," Eva said, pushing her body harder than ever before, kicking and paddling with every ounce of strength she possessed.

"We're going to die," Hailey cried, voice high and shaky.

Something shifted in the water behind Eva; she was pushed forward as though on a sudden wave. A second later, immense pain burst through her as huge teeth clamped down on her calf. She screamed. The last thing she heard before she was yanked beneath the surface was Blake's voice distantly calling her name.

Water filled her ears, nose, and mouth, suffused with misty blood. She fought against the pull as she was dragged deeper, which only increased the agony ripping through her. The creature holding her was a dark blur amidst the bubbles and crimson fog. She kicked its face with her other foot, but it only tightened its jaws and shook her, its teeth shredding flesh and muscle and crunching bone.

Black spots dotted her vision, and her chest and throat burned as she clung to the last bit of air in her lungs. She needed desperately to take a breath, but the surface was so far away.

I'm going to die.

Tilting her head back, Eva looked up at the shafts of gold-tinged light shining down from above. Despite the crimson staining the water, there was an undeniable beauty to that light. It wasn't a terrible last sight.

Another dark shape entered her vision, approaching with great speed. Just before she closed her eyes, the shape drew close enough for her to make out its color — an earthy orange that seemed entirely out of place here amidst the otherworldly light and wisps of blood.

CHAPTER 2

Kronus charged forward, driven by instinct — females were in danger, and it didn't matter if they were human or kraken.

Without slowing, he slammed the point of his harpoon into the eye of the nearest of the two razorbacks — the one with its jaws closed around a female's leg. The beast thrashed and rolled, releasing the female, but Kronus grabbed hold of it with hand and tentacles, anchoring himself in place. Crimson water churned around him. The surface and its sparkling light tumbled above and below with dizzying speed.

He squeezed the trigger.

The gun fired with a *whump*, and the harpoon burst through the other side of the razorback's head. The creature's struggles intensified, and fresh blood flowed into the water around it. The razorback bent its long body, gouging Kronus's back with the spikes on its tail, but the pain was distant and unimportant.

Kronus held fast; the creature was at least five times his length, but he would not relent. He tugged his knife out of the sheath strapped to his left forearm and hammered it into the razorback's head repeatedly. The rhythm of his frantic stabs nearly matched the speed of his racing hearts. He didn't stop until its struggles ceased.

Finally releasing his grip, he swept his gaze over the scene. The second razorback was fleeing with two harpoon shafts jutting from its left flank. Chunks of flesh and gore floated in the bloody water, along with four of the five humans who'd been swimming.

Brexes and Charos moved to pursue the surviving razorback, but Vasil, who was just ahead of the pair, halted them with a flash of yellow across his skin. He moved his tentacles in a series of signs.

Tend the wounded.

Kronus looked upward. The female he'd freed from the razorback had kicked to the surface. Blood misted from her left leg, tracing a wavy path beneath her due to the gentle back-and-forth of the tide. He darted up, emerging in front of her.

She fought to keep her head above the water, drawing in quick, rasping breaths between sputtering coughs. Her eyes were wide and frantic.

"Hailey!" she called out weakly.

Kronus wrapped an arm around her waist from behind and pulled her against his chest.

She struggled, swinging her hands wildly and kicking at him, her desperation lending her strength enough to nearly break his hold.

"I have you, female," Kronus growled. "You are safe."

She turned her head and met his gaze; this was the woman who'd stared at him, the one who'd seemed more curious than disgusted. Her eyes were a blue so bright they put the cloudless sky to shame, but her dilated pupils were almost large enough to swallow the blue completely. Her skin was pale — far paler than it had been only moments before.

The female twisted to face him, taking his cheeks in trembling hands. "M-My friends. Please! We n-need to save my friends!"

Kronus swam toward the beach. "The others will see to your friends."

"But the beasts!" She strained against his hold, throwing her body weight against his forward momentum. "They're still out there!"

He grunted and pushed ahead faster. Several humans had already gathered on the sand — including the male who'd kissed this female — and more were scrambling along the dock, their panicked shouts carrying over the water. The light brown-haired female had gone limp and quiet, though his sensitive skin could feel the tremors coursing through her body along with her frantic pulse.

Once the water was shallow enough, Kronus swung his tentacles beneath his torso and rose, slipping an arm beneath the female's knees to scoop her up. It was only then that he noticed the damage done to her leg. Beginning less than a hand's width beneath her knee, her flesh and muscle were mangled, pieces hanging from shattered bone by thin tendons and strips of shredded skin. Blood poured from the wound.

Humans rushed toward him, but he paid them little mind. He was familiar enough with their kind by now to know that such a wound was potentially fatal. She needed immediate attention.

Stop the bleeding.

He raised a front tentacle and wrapped it around her left thigh just above the knee, coiling it tight. She clung to him, but little strength remained in her fingers. He met her gaze.

The woman's eyes were glossy, and her breath was even shallower than before. "My friends. Please," she whispered.

"They will get your friends," Kronus responded.

She drew herself forward, entire body shaking, as though

she meant to dive back into the water. "We have to go to them. Have to-to help them…"

"We have to help *you*. You are wounded, female. Be still."

She fell back against his arm, and her eyelids fluttered closed. Her hands fell away. Panic sped Kronus's hearts. Her blood trickled over his tentacles, its metallic taste distinguishing it from the sea salt coating his skin.

"Eva!" a male human shouted.

Kronus lifted his gaze to see Eva's male standing before him, eyes wide and face pale.

"Eva," the human repeated, reaching forward. He paused when his gaze fell on her leg. Somehow, his face paled further. He turned away abruptly and heaved, doubling over as he emptied his stomach onto the sand. Still retching, he flicked his gaze toward the female's face only for it to dip back to her mangled leg. He shook his head and stumbled back, looking away from her.

He shoved his fingers into his hair, grasping the short strands. "*Fuck!* I can't. I can't look. Fuck, Eva. *Fuck!*"

Kronus scowled at the male. By their earlier interaction, this weak human and the female in Kronus's arms were mates, and the male had failed to protect her in any capacity. Eva was a female, a precious being, to be protected at all costs. Though Kronus knew humans didn't necessarily view it the same way — their kind had ample women, while kraken females were quite rare — this male's behavior struck him as cowardly.

He placed a hand on Eva's neck. Her pulse was rapid and weak beneath her cool skin.

When he looked up, he realized he was surrounded by humans, all of them speaking hurriedly to one another and to him. He clenched his jaw, and it took a great deal of willpower to keep himself from tightening his grip on Eva. The sea was at his back, but the humans were so close, and there were so many of them. His lungs burned, and his throat was constricting. Fury ignited in his gut; he'd fight his way through them if they didn't back away and give her room to breathe.

Breckett forced his way to the front of the crowd, his mouth lost within his bushy beard, eyebrows low.

"Set her down, Kronus," Breckett said. "Doc's on his way, and you've got a good hold on her, but we need to get a tourniquet on her leg before she loses any more blood."

Kronus still tasted her blood on his suction cups, still felt its fading warmth on his skin. He found himself suddenly reluctant to relinquish his hold on her. He was stronger than all of them; he could protect her.

She is wounded, and there is nothing I can do about it.

The thought was a sobering one. With a wary glance at the other humans, Kronus lowered himself and gently laid Eva on the sand.

"Keep that tentacle in place," Breckett said as he reached down and unclasped his belt.

Eva caught Kronus's wrist with one of her hands, squeezing weakly. She opened her mouth and spoke, but her words were too soft, her voice too broken, for him to understand. Her eyes shone with a desperate gleam.

Kronus held her gaze. He doubted the fear on her face was caused by concern for her own safety now anymore than it had been in the water. Despite suffering a grievous injury, she was worried about her friends foremost. That was something to be admired amidst this carnage.

Breckett leaned over Eva and wrapped his belt around her thigh above Kronus's tentacle. He slipped the end through the buckle and wrenched it as tight as he could, well past the last notch.

"Can you make a hole here?" he asked, easing the belt slightly and indicating a spot with one of his blunt fingers.

Kronus nodded. Eva's grip remained loose on his wrist as he moved his hands to the belt and punched a hole in the leather with a thumb claw. Breckett hurriedly slipped the metal prong through the new hole and secured the belt.

A pair of humans worked their way through the crowd and laid something on the ground beside Eva — two long, thick poles with some sort of cloth between them.

"Help me get her up," Breckett mumbled, carefully slipping his arms under Eva's armpits.

Kronus took hold of her right leg behind the knee and grasped the outside of her left thigh. Together, he and Breckett lifted Eva from the sand and settled her onto the cloth. Kronus forced himself to release his hold on her quickly for fear he wouldn't be able to let go otherwise. She needed aid he could not give.

The humans who'd brought the device each took an end, using the poles as handles, and carried Eva away.

Rising, Kronus looked over the gathered crowd; Eva's male was nowhere to be seen, and none of the humans were staring at him any longer. Their stunned faces were directed at something behind him.

Kronus turned to see Vasil, Brexes, and Charos wading to shore, each carrying a limp human.

The crowd eased back, allowing the kraken to lay their burdens on the sand. Two of the humans were dead — a male and a female, the former with one arm torn off at the shoulder and the latter with a massive chunk of her torso missing. The third, the one Eva had been pulling toward land, was still alive, sucking in rapid, shallow breaths.

She hadn't suffered bites like the others; the puncture wounds on her chest, which oozed dark blood, had undoubtedly been caused by the hard spines that earned razorbacks their name. Her body convulsed when she coughed, forcing fresh spurts of blood from her wounds and her mouth. A wet, gurgling sound rose from her chest as she breathed.

Several humans hurried forward. Vasil backed away,

granting them space to drop to their knees around the injured woman. The four kraken eased into a small group and watched as the humans struggled to staunch the woman's bleeding.

Moments later, a final, labored exhalation escaped her.

"Razorbacks should not be so close to shore," Charos said softly.

"Nor should they be in pairs," added Brexes.

"A mated pair, perhaps," said Vasil, staring at the dead woman with a sorrowful light in his eyes. "Drawn to shallow water by the migration."

Kronus lifted his gaze. Beyond the crowd, the two men were carrying Eva up the ramp leading from the dock into town. Would she survive her wound, or had he reached her too late? If he'd acted faster, perhaps these people wouldn't be dead. Perhaps…

Two years ago, he wouldn't have cared. Dead humans were of no consequence so long as the kraken were safe and prosperous. He lowered his gaze to the bodies laid atop the bloody sand.

Wasn't this what he'd advocated? Wouldn't this have been the result of what he'd wanted when Macy, the first human to have entered the home of the kraken people in hundreds of years, had been brought into the Facility? Dead humans. Even if he hadn't intended direct violence, he'd argued to have her exiled, to leave her at the mercy of the sea — as good as death, for a lone human. And all that he'd done afterward — all the words he'd spoken, the hatred he'd spewed — had inspired a group of his people to act upon his implied threats. To call for the deaths of innocent females and younglings.

But after everything that had happened, after the bloody battle in the Facility...

"We need to get back into the water," Kronus said, turning to face the other kraken.

"That was all of them," said Brexes. "All that remains out there are pieces."

"And a dead razorback," Vasil replied.

Kronus nodded. "We need to get it out of the water before anything else gets to it. We cannot allow that much meat to go to waste."

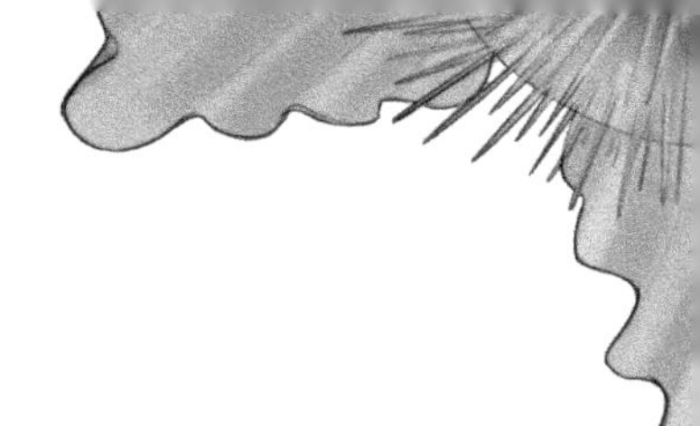

CHAPTER 3

A HEAVY SENSATION PRESSED UPON EVA WHEN SHE WOKE, weighing down her body. She felt strange, groggy, disconnected, as though she were floating on the border between dreams and reality. It was an unpleasant sensation that left her confused and anxious. Voices came and went, voices she didn't recognize, all muffled and far-off like she was hearing them underwater.

Awareness came slowly as the fog receded. It was quiet by the time she could open her eyes; she flinched and squeezed them shut immediately, blinded by a bright light.

How much did I drink yesterday?

She lifted a hand, which felt ten times heavier than normal, and rubbed her eyes. Her mind was still fuzzy. She couldn't recall drinking wine the night before, but she had the dry mouth, headache, and muscle pain of a terrible hangover.

Why does my leg hurt so much?

I must have banged it against something.

If that was the case, she must've been pretty drunk to have forgotten. The pain was sharp enough to suggest a serious bruise, if not a fracture.

Eva dropped her hand to the side of the bed and reached for Blake.

Her arm dangled off the edge, hanging in air. He wasn't there. The rest of the bed wasn't there.

"Blake?" she rasped, her voice cracking. She opened her eyes to slits. The light wasn't so bad this time, but it didn't seem right. Their room was never this bright, and they always kept the windows covered, blocking out the morning sunlight. Grunting against the effort, she lifted her head to look around.

The room was small. A counter ran the length of one wall, with numerous covered containers lined up atop it. A large potted plant was tucked in the corner. The ceiling was pure white, but the walls were covered in vibrant greens, purples, and browns that depicted the jungle surrounding The Watch. There were two plain chairs nearby, a standing tray with wheels, and several machines on either side of the bed.

This wasn't her bedroom. She was at the clinic.

"Blake?" she called again.

Why wasn't he here with her?

Eva slowly pushed herself up, wincing and gritting her teeth against the pain radiating from every muscle in her body — her left leg especially. A wave of dizziness struck her. She stilled for a moment, breathing slowly, and tried to concentrate, tried to remember.

Why am I here? Why am I so weak?

Carefully, she turned, swung her legs over the side of the bed, and pushed herself off the edge to stand.

The world tilted around her. She hit the floor hard, her hip taking the brunt of the impact, but again it was her left leg serving as the main source of her pain. She cried out and grasped her thigh, just above the knee, digging her fingers into her flesh.

But her fingertips met cloth instead of flesh.

A bandage?

Twisting, Eva sat up and looked at her leg.

The room around her faded into a dark blur, and a high, faint ringing drowned out all other sounds. All she saw, her only point of focus, was the end of her left leg — a bandaged stump just below the knee. Her calf, her ankle, and her foot were *gone*.

There was movement at the edge of her vision, and it was only then she realized her mouth was open, and she was screaming. It burned her lungs and throat, and all at once, she could hear it, deafening and filled with terror. Someone was speaking to her, but she couldn't make out the words through her scream.

Panting, Eva lifted her leg and reached forward to touch the space her calf should've occupied as though this were an optical illusion and the rest of her would just appear. Her hand passed through empty air.

This is a dream. I'm not awake. This is a nightmare.

This is a dream.

A nightmare.

Wake up!

WAKE UP!!!

Gentle hands settled upon Eva's shoulders as someone kneeled beside her.

"Eva?" the woman said. "You're safe, Eva. You're at the clinic, and you're safe. I don't know if you remember me, but my name is Aymee. I need you to calm down, okay? You're hyperventilating. Take some deep breaths."

"No," Eva breathed, shaking her head. "No. No, no, no, no. I'm not awake. This is a dream."

One of the hands on her shoulders slid down to rub her back, but Eva was barely aware of it. Her entire body shook, and her heartbeat thundered in her ears. Tingles raced over her skin. The light in the room was dimming, and darkness encroached on the borders of her vision.

"Dad!" Aymee called over her shoulder before turning her

face back to Eva. The motion of her hand on Eva's back didn't falter. "Shh," she soothed. "Breathe for me, Eva. Slow, deep breaths."

"My leg! What happened to my leg?" Eva demanded.

Heavy footsteps approached, and another pair of legs entered Eva's peripheral vision. There was a masculine curse. "Let's get her back into bed."

"Eva, this is Doctor Kent Rhodes, my father," Aymee said. "We're going to lift you and get you back onto the bed, okay?"

"No! I just want to wake up!" Eva yelled, struggling against the hands that carefully grasped her and lifted her off the floor. Her achy, weakened muscles could not overcome Kent and Aymee; they settled her atop the bed and held her down. "Please let me wake up!"

"Give her a sedative, Aymee, then check her leg," Kent said.

Tears filled Eva's eyes and blurred her vision. She wailed and fought to free herself, but Kent kept her firmly in place.

"I know you're confused and frightened, Eva," he said, his voice warm and gentle, "but we are taking care of you. We have to sedate you, so you don't cause yourself any further harm, do you understand?"

Eva looked up into his blue eyes. "What happened to my leg? Where's my leg?"

Something cold pressed against her neck. There was a click, a pinch of pain, and a hiss. Eva flinched.

"The damage was too extensive, Eva," Kent said, sounding farther away with each word. "We had to amputate it to save your life."

Fingers brushed over the skin of Eva's thigh as Aymee peeled back the bandages, but Eva refused to look. She blinked away her tears, keeping her eyes on Kent's. "What...what happened? Why? This...this isn't real. Please tell me it's a dream. Where's Blake?"

Her gaze drifted away from Kent, wandering around the

room as though her husband would be there. Her mind — and her senses — were growing fuzzy.

Not so fuzzy, however, that she didn't notice the troubled glance between Aymee and Kent.

"Blake is… He's working in the tannery," Aymee said.

"He came by to check on you earlier. I'll send someone to let him know you woke up," Kent said.

Aymee frowned deeply; she seemed about to say something more about Blake, but she shook her head. "You just need to focus on resting, okay, Eva? That's the only way you're going to recover."

"How's it look?" Kent asked.

"The skin hasn't torn, thankfully," Aymee replied. "The supplies Arkon helped me get from the Facility are definitely better quality than anything we've had here before. You wouldn't think it's only been four days."

"Four days?" Eva asked, her words slurring. Her eyelids — along with every other part of her body — felt suddenly heavy. "What's only been four days?"

"You've been asleep for a while, Eva," Aymee said. "You lost a lot of blood, and we've kept you sedated to make sure you were getting the rest you need."

"What…happened?"

"You don't remember?" Kent asked.

Eva shook her head. She'd been in the water with Blake, Addison, Hailey, and Samuel, enjoying a day off. They'd planned to swim and lounge in the sun…but she couldn't remember anything after they started swimming.

"There was an accident," Aymee said. "We can talk about it when you're feeling a little better, okay?"

"What…?" Eva murmured.

"Rest, Eva. We'll find Blake, and you can ask questions when you wake up."

Eva's eyelids drifted shut against her will.

"She really can't remember anything?" Aymee asked softly.

"It's a natural response to trauma," Kent replied. Eva felt his hands lift away, but her body was leaden and unresponsive. "She may remember, in time…or she may never get those memories back."

What happened? Tell me what happened!

But her mouth wouldn't work, and no sound emerged from her throat. She gave up her fight and let oblivion claim her.

ARTIFICIAL LIGHT DOMINATED the room when evening came. The sun had set some time ago; whether it had been minutes or hours since, Eva could not say. Time was immeasurable as she sat in the clinic bed with her back propped against the pillows.

Aymee had been there to administer a pain-relieving shot upon Eva's second awakening; the medicine wasn't a sedative, but now Eva wished it had been. All she could do was sit and stare at what her mind refused to accept as real. She had hoped and prayed it was all a bad dream, that nothing had happened, but no amount of wishing could change the reality she faced.

Her legs were hidden beneath a blanket, but the cloth was draped over her stump, outlining it clearly. She could still sense the rest of her leg, could still imagine her toes wiggling upon her foot, could even *feel* it.

But it was…*gone.*

Eva reached down and bunched up the blanket in her hands. Her stomach churned, and her heart constricted. Before she could consider what she was about to do, she whipped the blanket aside.

She wore no pants to conceal her legs; with the blanket moved, there was nothing to hide the truth — no calf; no foot; no wiggling toes. Only a bandaged stump just below her knee. She lifted her leg and bent her knee, ignoring the agony it caused. Tears filled her eyes as she lowered her stump to the bed.

The door opened, and Eva turned her head to find familiar eyes upon her.

"Blake," she breathed. Her tears fell at the sight of him. She didn't know why he hadn't been there before, but he was here now, and that was all that mattered.

Except…something was off.

He stood in the doorway, his gaze moving from her face to her exposed leg. He paled and looked away.

Why wasn't he rushing to her side to hold her, to touch her? To tell her everything would be okay?

"Blake?" Her tone begged him to look at her.

He did, but only briefly. Clearing his throat, he stepped into the room, closing the door behind him. "Doc said you were asking for me."

"Of course I was. Why wouldn't I?"

Come closer to me. Hold me, Blake!

"I know. Sorry, I just…" He exhaled loudly, glanced at her, and sat in one of the chairs against the wall, lowering his gaze to the floor. "How, uh… How are you doing?"

Eva stared at him silently. She couldn't comprehend what was going on. Why wasn't he next to her? Why was there so much *distance* between them?

"I lost my leg, Blake," she said blandly.

Blake swallowed. "I know. I know. *Fuck!*" He bent forward, dropped his elbows to his knees, and shoved his fingers into his hair.

"What happened, Blake? I can't… I don't remember *anything*. Please, just tell me what happened."

"How the hell could you forget any of *that*?" he snapped, looking back up at her.

Eva flinched, eyes wide. In all her time with him, he'd never raised his voice, had never spoken to her so harshly.

He leapt to his feet and paced anxiously, keeping his gaze averted. "How could you forget that thing tearing Addison apart, or ripping off Sam's arm? Your own *fucking leg?*" His face had taken on a sickly pallor.

An image flashed through her mind, a chaotic mess she could barely decipher — churning crimson water with tangled blonde hair floating on its surface. *Addison's* hair.

Eva swallowed the bile rising in her throat.

"Where are they?" she croaked. "Are they okay?"

Blake spun toward her. His eyes were rounded, pupils tiny, and his lower lip quivered. "Where *are* they, Eva? *Dead!* They're fucking dead! Sam, Addy, and Hailey are *gone.*"

He turned and stormed away from her, hanging his head.

Fresh tears streamed down Eva's cheeks. Something cold and heavy closed around her heart. She hadn't known, hadn't remembered. *Still* couldn't remember. How terrible a person did that make her? What sort of monster *forgot* the deaths of her friends?

Blake shook his head. "If you hadn't…"

Eva sniffled and wiped the moisture from her eyes. "Hadn't what?"

His shoulders rose with a deep breath. He swung his head toward her, but still didn't look at her. "If you hadn't said we should go swimming, they'd still be here. We could've done *anything* else, but you wanted to go swimming, and now…"

"You're blaming *me?*" Disbelief mixed with her hurt, overwhelming her.

Blake closed his eyes and turned his face away. "I…I can't do this, Eva."

Eva's heart pounded, and her breath came quick and shallow. Her entire body trembled. "Can't d-do *what?* Blake, what is going on? Why are you *being* like this?"

"You need to rest," he replied, walking toward the door.

"Blake! Where are you going?"

"I have to…clear my head. I have an early day tomorrow." He pulled the door open and hesitated as he was moving through. For an instant, it seemed as though he'd look at her, as though he'd come back inside, and this ongoing nightmare would finally end.

But he continued through and closed the door quietly behind him. Despite his gentleness, the sound of the latch clicking into place possessed a weighty finality that sent a chill through Eva.

CHAPTER 4

Kronus looked up from the table only briefly to glance at the orange-and-purple sky. A salt-kissed breeze flowed through the open windows, refreshingly cool after another hot day. Even when it was stiflingly warm outside, he usually left the windows open just to hear the waves sighing against the nearby shore, to smell the ocean mist in the air, to remind himself that even if he wasn't *home*, the place he belonged was never far away.

He dropped his gaze to the piece of wood in his hand. A pile of curled shavings had gathered on the table beneath it, and the shape he'd subconsciously sought had finally emerged. He eased the blade of his knife against the wood and coaxed away another shaving, smoothing the curve of the little figurine's shoulder.

It was a human female, slightly less crude than his prior carvings but nothing like the detailed trinkets he'd seen one of the fishermen, Wade, produce. Kronus had carved dozens of creatures — most of them sea dwellers — to pass the time here. The other kraken socialized with one another frequently, and children's playful shouts and laughter often sounded from the nearby homes, but Kronus was content with his solitude.

No, not *content*. Perhaps *comfortable* was the more accurate word.

Holding his palm flat, he studied the little figure atop it, forcing himself to note all its flaws, all the spots requiring refinement.

For years, Kronus had dismissed another kraken, Arkon, as being foolish for pursuing similar creative endeavors. All the kraken had, save for Jax the Wanderer, the one who'd changed everything by rescuing a human female during a storm. What would Arkon think if he knew Kronus had been shaping blocks of wood into crude figures?

Arkon's opinion wouldn't have made a difference, but Kronus had a feeling the other kraken would've been enthusiastic and supportive despite Kronus's past behavior. That was a hard truth to accept.

Every truth revealed over the last two years had been hard to accept.

Kronus had spent his time in The Watch clinging to whatever distractions he could find — working with the fishermen, venturing into the outskirts of the jungle to find suitable wood for burning and carving, and cooking food; they were all things he wouldn't have done were it not for the humans. Each task was a little escape from the memories ceaselessly roiling just under the surface. Every task granted a brief reprieve from the hardest truth of all — the truth of *himself*.

He adjusted his hold on the wooden figure and set the knife to it again. It was best not to follow those paths of thought, best not to reflect upon why he'd shaped the wood into the form of a human female.

He'd done his part already. There was no reason for further concern, no reason to think about *her* anymore.

Gritting his teeth, he slid the blade along the outside of the figurine's thigh, slicing away a tiny ridge left by his prior shaping. He continued to smooth the imperfections along the leg, frowning as he found new ones to correct. The gradually building tension in his hands was lost to him until it was too late. The blade sank deep into the wood, splitting off a large chunk. He halted the knife and tried to ease it back before causing further damage.

The blade slipped. With a *snap*, the figurine's leg broke off at the knee.

Kronus stilled but for his trembling hand. After seeing to the dead razorback on the day of the attack, he'd given in to Breckett's gruff insistence and gone to the clinic to have the gashes on his back tended. While Aymee had sealed Kronus's wounds, she'd mentioned that they'd had to amputate Eva's leg just below her knee.

The deaths of the three humans and the grievous wound Eva had suffered crashed down on him again, as they had so many times over the last five days. He released a harsh breath through his siphons as his chest constricted. Dropping the carving and setting down the knife, he grasped the edge of the table and shoved it away before taking his temples between forefinger and thumb.

All he'd wanted in The Watch was a fresh start, a chance to distance himself from his past mistakes, an opportunity to move on from his guilt. What had happened to Eva and her companions was not his fault, and he had no reason to feel responsible for it. He had no reason to care beyond three of the four victims being females.

And yet Eva had remained a steady presence in his head. Images of her flashed through his mind constantly — her steady stare, brimming with barely restrained curiosity before the attack; her panicked, wide-eyed expression as Kronus had taken hold of her; the contrast of crimson against pale sand. Sometimes, he thought he still felt her cold, weak, desperate grip on his wrist and tasted her blood on his suction cups.

He looked at the one-legged figurine again. He'd never

meant for it to be Eva, but it had become her despite his efforts and intentions.

Kronus needed something else to occupy his mind. Night had not quite fallen, and it would feel all the longer if he couldn't shift his thoughts away from Eva, if he couldn't find peace or—

There was a knock at the door.

He drew himself upright abruptly, hearts booming. A warm tingling sensation spread across the surface of his skin. He stood for several moments with hands raised, ready to fight, before he realized his skin had shifted to an angry red.

The knock sounded again. Though loud in the relative quiet of his den, it conveyed no threat; there was an odd hesitance to it.

Kronus lowered his hands and reverted to his normal color as he moved to the door. Keeping his body back, he extended a tentacle and grasped the latch. He opened the door warily; he was unaccustomed to visitors, and he was completely taken aback by who stood outside.

Aymee's dark eyes met his, and she smirked. "Surprised to see me, I take it?"

He glanced past her, ensuring that she was alone. "Why are you here?"

"You know, it's usually customary to greet someone or invite them inside when they come to visit."

Drawing in a deep breath, he willed his hearts to slow. "Hello. Why are you here?"

Aymee stared at him silently for a moment, her face void of expression, but then she snorted and broke into laughter. "Still haven't forgiven me for punching you?"

Kronus's brows dropped low, and he scowled. "I have no patience for games." He shifted himself forward, grasped the door handle in one hand, and pushed the door closed.

Aymee stepped forward and pressed her hand against the

door, stopping it before it shut completely. "Okay, I'm sorry. No messing with Kronus, got it. I came because I thought you might want to know that Eva woke up yesterday."

A pulse of warmth flowed through him, speeding his hearts again. "And?"

"Are you going to open the door, or are we going to talk through it?"

Sighing, he backed away and pulled the door open again. Aymee stepped inside. Whatever playfulness had gleamed in her eyes a few moments before was gone now.

"Is she all right?" he asked, voice low.

"She's...not so good. Mentally, that is." She glanced around the room, then met his eyes again. "She doesn't remember what happened."

How could anything like that be so soon forgotten? Every instant of the battle in the Facility was emblazoned in his memory with chilling detail, and he somehow knew those memories would linger with him until he died, and the sea reclaimed him.

"Is that a...*human* condition?"

Aymee tilted her head. "It's a *survival* thing. My dad and I read up on it last night in the files from the Facility. When someone — human or kraken — experiences something trau-matic, the brain shifts into survival mode and focuses *everything* on making it out of the situation alive. That doesn't leave much to make memories, and the memories it does keep usually get locked away as another means of protection. The mind can only take so much before it breaks."

Did that mean Eva didn't remember Kronus, either?

It does not matter whether she does or not.

But that didn't prevent a sense of disappointment from spreading through him.

"So she is broken, then?" he asked.

"No, she's not, but..." She looked away from him with a frown.

"But you fear she will be?"

"She has no support, no one to help her through this."

"She has a mate, does she not?" he asked, recalling the male human who'd fled the water ahead of the other humans and had turned away from Eva when Kronus brought her ashore.

Aymee lifted a hand and ran her fingers through her curly hair. "Blake is struggling with issues of his own. I don't think he's in any state to help her heal right now...if he ever really was to begin with. He's visited the clinic twice, and when he came yesterday, he left her in tears, and she wouldn't tell me why."

Kronus clenched his jaw and dropped his gaze to the floor. He could not understand a male acting that way toward a female. Kraken males did everything they could to protect and provide for their females, even knowing the female could cast them aside at any moment. But this human had fled. He was unworthy of having a mate. Unworthy of Eva.

The ends of Kronus's tentacles swept back and forth across the floor; he stilled them, annoyed at both himself and the way this *Blake* had behaved.

Aymee sighed heavily. "Sorry, I didn't mean to dump this on you. I just wanted to let you know she's awake. Physically, her recovery is proceeding astonishingly well, but the rest..." She tilted her head and regarded him. "How is your back? You haven't been back to clinic to have it checked."

"It no longer bothers me," he replied. Once the danger had passed and the excitement had died out, the gashes on his back had been quite painful, but kraken healed much faster than humans.

Aymee nodded. "Good." She moved back toward the door. "Thanks for letting me in."

He drew in a breath, about to snap at her, but whatever harsh words he might've spoken died on his tongue. She'd done nothing to warrant cruelty. He met her gaze and offered her a nod instead.

She hesitated as she stepped out, glancing at him over her shoulder. "If…if you *wanted* to, you're welcome to visit her at the clinic. She might not remember what happened, but you were the one who saved her life, and knowing that might help her a little."

Aymee delayed for a moment longer, as though awaiting a response from Kronus. When he offered none, she slipped out and closed the door gently behind her.

Kronus turned away from the door and moved to the table, bracing his hands at two of the corners and dipping his head. He had no reason to visit Eva; it wasn't his place, she wasn't his problem. He'd done his part. If she didn't remember him…it was all the better. He didn't want her gratitude, didn't want her attention, didn't want—

His eyes fell on the carving with the broken leg, its featureless face staring up at him. Its expression could have conveyed anything — sorrow, fear, judgment, pain, loneliness, anger. His mind dredged up memories of that strange time after he'd been banished from his home, utterly alone in the deep. Doomed to death if he entered the Facility, doomed to death if he was found by the kraken who'd once supported him in his efforts to expel the humans.

There'd been no one for him then. No support, no camaraderie.

He could guess at how Eva felt.

Kronus bared his clenched teeth, squeezing the edges of the table.

It was *not* his place. It was not natural for him to yearn for another glimpse of her clear, bright eyes, or to wonder at the feel of her long, shimmering hair or her smooth, tanned skin. She had a male, and if that male was inadequate, it was up to her to cast him aside and find another. She'd made her choice, and if it had been a poor one…

And how many poor choices have I made? How many bad decisions trail behind me, and yet I remain? If I was afforded another chance, if I have been offered forgiveness, why should she deserve to suffer alone?

Perhaps I could be her male. Perhaps I could show her what it truly means to have a mate.

Kronus had never seen the appeal of humans. They were strange looking, small, and weak, ill-suited to thriving on a world like Halora. But Eva had caught his eye. There was a beauty to her, an appeal, that he could neither understand nor define. Something about her drew him. He'd glimpsed a strength in her — not of body, but of spirit. In her most terrified moments she'd tried only to help her companions. Even as she'd weakened from loss of blood, she'd tried to fight his hold, to go back for the people she cared about.

That was a selflessness to be admired regardless of her species.

He slid his hand over the surface of the table, brushing a finger against the wooden carving.

No, it wasn't his place to go to Eva, but he *wanted* to.

CHAPTER 5

Eva stared down at the tray of food in front of her. There were eggs, toast, and slices of winefruit; all the things she ate most mornings, the things she made for herself and Blake all the time. But she couldn't bring herself to take a single bite.

"Eva, you need to eat something," Aymee said, glancing up at her as she finished rebandaging Eva's *stump*.

"I don't want anything."

Aymee sighed, picked up the booster gun, and placed it against Eva's thigh. Eva held still through the injection. She was used to the shots. Their brief sting was nothing compared to the persistent pain in her leg, which was dulled by the medication but never really went away.

There was a soft knock on the door before it opened. Kent poked his head through and offered Eva a kind smile. She didn't miss the pity in his eyes.

"Blake is here," he said.

Eva's heart leapt, and she stared at the door as though she could see through it.

He's here! He's here for me!

Aymee covered Eva's legs with the blanket and stepped away

from the bed to place the empty booster gun on the counter. "I'll come back later, Eva."

Kent withdrew from the room. Aymee followed, pausing in the doorway to glance back at Eva. She opened her mouth, hesitated, then closed it and stepped into the hall.

Muffled voices drifted to her from the hallway. Though she couldn't make out the words, she recognized Blake's voice among them. She grasped fistfuls of the blanket to keep her hands from shaking.

Soon, the door opened wider, and Blake slipped through, closing it quietly behind him without turning toward her. He kept his back to her for a time, silent; a sense of dread filled Eva.

Nothing had changed since his visit the day before. She tightened her grip on the blanket, willing him to speak, to look at her.

"I had time to think," he said, his voice shattering the silence like a sudden boom of thunder.

"To think about what?"

He turned to face her. His hair was neatly combed today, and his clothes looked freshly cleaned. He took a step toward her. Just *one*. The two meters between them might as well have been two million.

Tears stung Eva's eyes. "Why are you doing this, Blake?"

His gaze dipped to her legs but did not rise to meet her eyes. Hands fisted at his sides, he inhaled deeply. "I can't do this, Eva."

"Do *what*?" Hurt and confusion warred within her. "You're not doing anything!"

"Us!" he yelled, glaring at her.

Every bit of oxygen fled Eva. She stared at him — the man for whom she'd left behind everything she'd known to be with, who she'd joined as husband and wife — and didn't recognize him. "W-What do you mean?"

"I just... *Nothing* is going to be the same after this, Eva. You're...crippled. Our lives would be too different, and I'd have to take care for you all the time. That's not the life we planned. Not the life I want. And I just…I can't look at you anymore."

Eva's eyes widened, and ice slithered through her veins. Each of his words sank into her heart like a nail, driven hard by his tone, by the look in his eyes. And it was those last words that hurt the most — so much disgust had colored his voice as he'd spoken them.

"What…What do you mean you can't *look* at me, Blake? What does that mean?"

"Damn it, Eva, I don't have to explain—"

"Yes, you do! You're my husband, and I'm your *wife*. You're supposed to be here for me, not…not… What are you saying?"

He scowled and raked his fingers through his hair. "I can't stand to look at you, Eva. When I do, I just see the others. See… blood in the water. I see the woman you *were*. And I can't deal with that. It's too much, okay? It's too much, and…"

"We can get through this, Blake. Together. Please," she begged, "stop putting distance between us."

"It's too late, Eva. We're done."

"What?" she breathed. She must not have heard him right; she couldn't believe those words could have come out of his mouth.

"We're done," he repeated more firmly. "Whatever life we'd have after this isn't one I want. I'm not going to throw years away taking care of you. I need to be able to move on, to find my happiness. So, we're done."

"You mean you're running away, like at the beach." The words came unbidden, and it was only as Eva spoke them that she saw the fragment of a memory — Blake already halfway to the shore before anyone else had been able to react, Blake standing on the beach while she was surrounded by churning, bloody water.

Blake recoiled, his face instantly losing its color. Eva didn't care. Fury burned within her.

"How dare you blame me for this and talk about how your life is ruined, how you need to find *your* happiness, when *you* were the one who ran away without looking back?" She trembled with hurt, betrayal, and anger. "I don't remember much of what happened, Blake, but I *know* you left us out there. And I can forgive that, but if you run away now, if you run *again*..."

"There was *nothing* I could've done," he said in a low voice, lips barely moving. "Nothing but die for no reason."

Tears fell from her eyes. Had she ever meant anything to him, anything at all? "No reason? *I* wasn't a reason? I'm not saying you should have died, but you didn't even try. You left me! You left all of us, and you didn't even hesitate!"

"That's not fair, Eva!"

"Neither is anything you've said or done!" She threw her arm out toward her leg. "I lost my damned *leg*, Blake! How is that fair? Our friends are dead! Is *that* fair? And you told me the other day that it was *my* fault. Don't talk to *me* about what's fair."

He turned his face away from her, shoulders rising and falling with deep, harsh breaths. "Clearly you're emotional right now. You'll understand it's best for both of us, eventually. I've already moved on. You'll get there, too. There are a lot of other people in this world. I've...already met some."

For a few moments, Eva's chest and throat were too tight to produce a sound, too tight to draw in even the smallest breath. She couldn't acknowledge what he'd said; she was still asleep, still having a nightmare. "Why are you being like this?"

Blake walked to the door, grasped the handle, and pulled it open. He paused before walking through, briefly pressed his lips into a tight line, and met her gaze. "I rescind my vows to you. We are joined no longer."

Without awaiting a response, he left, not bothering to close the door.

Everything within Eva — the maelstrom of agony, loss, and

rage — exploded. She screamed with everything she had. Swinging her arms, she knocked the tray of food away, sending it clattering to the floor, and screamed again, but it could not ease the hurt eating away at her heart and constricting her chest.

KRONUS HAD JUST ENTERED the clinic when Eva's male, Blake, walked into the hallway from one of the rooms. The human's eyes hardened, and his brows fell low as he met Kronus's gaze.

A female's ragged scream filled the corridor with agony and grief, making Kronus's skin crawl. Blake flinched but did not look behind him. When something banged and clattered in a room down the hall, the man jumped and hurried past Kronus, giving the kraken a wide berth, darting out of the clinic as the female screamed again.

Kronus rushed down the short hallway and entered the room from which the screams had originated. A metallic tray lay overturned on the floor, with a trail of food scattered nearby. Eva was sitting up in bed, streams of tears glistening on her cheeks. The devastation in her expression reached into Kronus's chest and clamped down on all three of his hearts at once.

She turned her face toward him and sucked in a sharp breath. Recognition lit in her bright blue eyes.

"*You,*" she rasped.

Kronus held her gaze, unsure of how to respond. His interactions with humans were infrequent and terse; he didn't know how to decipher the nuances of their expressions and body language with any true accuracy. Her tone implied she was unhappy to see him, but that seemed an oversimplification.

"Why did you have to save me?" she demanded, pulling herself closer to the edge of the bed. "Why didn't you just let me die, too?"

"It was too late to save the others," he replied. "You were the only one who had a chance."

"This is your fault!" she screamed. "I told you to help *them*. I *begged* you to! Why didn't you save them?"

"They were already dead." He nearly added *and that was not my fault*, but couldn't bring himself to say the words. Could he have been faster? Could he at least have saved the female Eva had been trying to lead to shore? "You are not. I've no desire for your gratitude, but I believe it is a natural reaction to having one's life saved."

Rage flashed in her tear-filled eyes. "Get out! Get out of here you...*monster*!" She pointed to the door. "Leave!"

Kronus gritted his teeth. He wasn't sure what he'd expected when he decided to come here this morning, but this...this was not it. This supported Aymee's assessment — Eva was in a bad place. A dark place.

A lonely, desperate, tortured place.

"I said *get out*!" she screeched. Leaning toward him as though to emphasize her words, she thrust a hand down to the railing, but her palm slipped. Her torso lurched over the bed rail, and she tumbled onto the floor, landing heavily.

Kronus moved to her without thought as she cried out in pain, spreading his tentacles to sink low beside her.

It was only then that he noticed the clean bandages wrapped around the stump of her left leg. Her right leg continued from the knee into a shapely calf and a dainty foot — nothing like the tentacles of his people, but oddly appealing — while the other simply *ended*.

And for humans, limbs did not grow back.

Wrenching sobs wracked her body. "I should have died with them."

"But you did not," Kronus said, slipping his arms beneath her.

She pounded a fist against his shoulder and flattened her other palm on his chest, pushing him. "Don't touch me!"

He released air through his siphons and rose off the floor as she continued to hit him and struggle against his hold. "I did not save you just so you could give up and die afterward," he grumbled.

When her nails bit into his flesh, he bared his teeth and growled. Despite her weakened state, she was making a surprising effort to fight him off. What would it take for her to turn that spirit toward *living*?

"Let me go!" she screeched.

He obeyed, dumping her onto the bed. She bounced once, grasped the rail, and moved to pull herself up again, but Kronus halted her with a firm hand on her shoulder. He pressed her back down. She shrieked and clawed at him, swung her fists and cursed in words he understood and words he did not.

Hers was a familiar anger; it reminded him of his own deep-seated rage after the battle in the Facility had ended. He'd hoped to die during that fight, had expected to die afterward, but the same kraken who'd banished him beforehand had chosen to be merciful. Part of him resented their mercy. How much easier would it have been to die?

"What is going on?" Aymee demanded, striding into the room.

"It's his fault!" Eva yelled, thrashing atop the bed.

Kronus grunted as her assault on him intensified. He leaned over the bed and, with more difficulty than seemed possible, caught her wrists in his hands and pinned them to the bed at her sides. He coiled two of his front tentacles around her knees, locking them in place, and settled some of his weight over her middle to prevent her from bucking her hips.

She closed her eyes and screamed, the sound so loud and piercing that it was more painful than all her scratching and hitting.

"Shit! Hold her still!" Aymee rushed to the counter.

"I *am*," Kronus growled through his teeth, turning his head as though it could provide him some relief from Eva's noise.

Aymee hurried to his side, pressed a small injector gun against Eva's neck, and pulled the trigger. Eva's eyes flared open wide, and her scream faltered. For an instant, she pushed up against Kronus with renewed strength, and he feared she might slip free of his hold.

Then she sank onto the bed, her body giving up the fight as she closed her eyes again and cried. Her anger had vanished, leaving only raw grief and misery.

"He left me," she said between sobs. "He...left me alone. Left me...on the beach..."

Her head lolled to the side, and the remaining tension in her body eased. Cautiously, Kronus eased off her, first releasing her wrists, then shifting his torso upright before withdrawing his tentacles. He hadn't realized just how ragged his own breath had become, just how thunderously his hearts had been beating.

Had he done the right thing in saving her? The answer came without delay.

Yes.

"What happened?" Aymee asked. "We were in the middle of a procedure with another patient when she started screaming."

Kronus frowned, staring down at Eva's now relaxed features, which were framed by tousled hair. "I need to visit her male. Blake. Where does he dwell?"

"What? Why?"

"Her male," he repeated, looking up to meet Aymee's gaze. "Where can I locate him?"

"He was just...here." Her eyes rounded, and she shook her head. "No, Kronus. No challenges, no fights, no *violence*."

"He turned away from her when I pulled her out of the water," he said, dropping a hand to the metal railing on the side of the bed and squeezing, "and you said he has only visited her here twice. The last time, he left her in tears, and this time was even worse. He needs to learn that his behavior is *not* acceptable."

Aymee's eyes dipped to Eva, and her brows fell.

"*This* was her breaking," Kronus continued.

"You're right, but hurting Blake isn't going to help Eva get better."

"It will be a start."

Aymee raised her hands and waved her palms toward the floor in a placating manner. "No. You need to leave him alone. Trust me in that, okay? If you really want to help, if you really want to make a difference…*she's* the one who needs attention."

Kronus tightened his hold on the railing; the metal groaned within his grip. "I am ill-suited to mending broken humans. But I *can* break her male. That is what I know."

"I can't let you do that, Kronus. However much of a coward he might be, he's not in his right mind at the moment, and you beating the tar out of him is only going to get people riled up. Especially the ones that don't want your kind here. She just… needs time. And more than that, she needs *someone. Everyone* needs someone."

A strange light entered Aymee's eyes as she stared at him; it was deep with meaning, weighty and dire, and he felt her gaze upon him like it was a physical touch.

He shook his head. "I am not that someone, Aymee."

But I want *to be...*

She tilted her head slightly. The tiny change of angle only made her stare heavier.

Kronus looked back to Eva and released a long, soft sigh. His forearm stung where her nails had raked his flesh, but he could not deny the wrongness of this. Her peace had come only as the result of a drug. She deserved better. Even if he didn't know *her*, he understood that much.

As he turned away, his gaze met Aymee's briefly. He didn't

respond to the disappointment creasing her brow, didn't acknowledge the pleading frown into which her lips had fallen. He left the room without looking back.

What did it matter if Aymee wanted him to help? Eva clearly wanted nothing to do with Kronus, and the decision, as always, fell to the female.

CHAPTER 6

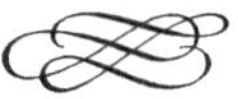

Aymee seemed surprised when Kronus approached her the morning after his visit to the clinic and inquired about Eva's condition.

"She's...not good," Aymee said. "She's despondent, barely eating, and isn't talking much. I think she said all of four words after you left yesterday."

He didn't know what *despondent* meant, but Aymee's tone would've been enough by itself to make her point clear.

They parted ways. For Aymee, it was one of the rare days during which she wasn't working in the clinic, helping in the fields, or baking with her mother — she would be spending her time with her mate, Arkon, and their youngling, Jace. Kronus had volunteered to help keep watch on the bay while plans were made to organize hunting parties and clear razorbacks out of the coastal waters; it was not thrilling work, but it was important, and it would give him a task upon which to focus.

He gruffly asked Aymee about Eva again the following evening. The only thing to have changed was Aymee's concern, which had clearly increased.

Kronus's sleep was restless that night. He tried to explain it away by reminding himself that he'd suffered many nights of broken slumber over the last two years, especially since he'd come to The Watch, but he knew there was more to it this time. Eva lingered in his head, dominated his thoughts, and kept his mind racing. Any attempts to steer his thoughts away from her eventually circled back around to Eva.

By the time the first light of dawn touched the sky on the third day since his visit with Eva, Kronus was ready to get out of bed. Lack of sleep had only made him think of her more. He needed a distraction, needed a new focus.

He ate some smoked fish — one of the human cooking techniques he'd come to appreciate — and selected a fresh chunk of wood from the basket he kept in the corner. After opening the land-facing window to allow in both the gray dawn light and the relatively cool morning air, he positioned himself at the window sill and set to work with his knife. Wood shavings piled on the sill as the sun slowly rose over the jungle. Kronus's hands scarcely slowed their movement, but it became increasingly clear that he had no direction. Wade often muttered about discovering the shape waiting in the wood; this piece refused to reveal its secrets.

No, that wasn't right. The problem was Kronus's own inability to see it.

The sun was a bright disk hanging just above the trees when Kronus gave up and set the wood down amidst the shavings. He cleaned his knife, returned it to its sheath, and closed the window.

It was nearly time to meet the others, regardless. There was no sense in lingering in his den and falling victim to his own thoughts.

After strapping the sheathed knife to his wrist, he headed outside. The air was already warm, but the hint of ocean mist on the breeze granted a whisper of coolness. Kronus drew himself along the path that had been worn into the grass that grew all over the ridgeline. His den — *house*, to the humans — was the last in a line of dwellings constructed on the cliff, over-looking a stretch of beach below.

Younglings were playing outside — Sarina and Eros, the half-human, half-kraken offspring of Macy and Jax, giggled as Rhea's daughter, Melaina, chased them through the taller grass. Jace, Aymee and Arkon's son, stalked behind Melaina as though ready to pounce on her; that she was twice his size seemed to matter little to the youngling. He was a natural hunter despite his youth. Several human children had joined in the games, seeming to make no differentiation between themselves and the kraken.

The children laughed and darted around Kronus as he passed. He slowed his pace to avoid a collision and shook his head. Once, this situation would have annoyed him, and he'd have given their mothers a reproachful glare. But this was not the Facility, and many of the old ways were gone; this was where these younglings denned with their families, and — even if he wouldn't admit it aloud — it lifted his hearts to see them happy at play.

They were the future of his people. They were the ones who would eventually inherit Halora. If they were safe and content, there was hope.

Macy was outside with Rhea; the females, one human and one kraken, greeted Kronus as he neared. Both their friendship with each other and their forgiveness of Kronus were unlikely, and yet here they all were.

He was surprised at his disappointment as he continued along the path into the jungle — Aymee hadn't been outside. Was she already at the clinic?

I should stop there and check on Eva.

No. That wouldn't accomplish anything. He was expected at

the dock. There was work to be done; Kronus had given his word, had pledged his aid. He wouldn't back out of that obligation.

Kronus remained on the path as it cut through the pastures where odd land animals fed on grass and weeds, and soon entered the town. The lighthouse stood vigil above everything, a silent guardian for a place that was anything but silent — The Watch was bustling, just as it was most mornings. Many humans woke with the dawn, though some — like the fishermen before the migration had changed their routines — rose even earlier.

He wound through the now-familiar streets, grateful that relatively few people bid him a good morning, and finally descended the ramp toward the dock. He stopped at the small storage room built into the cliffside at the base of the ramp and retrieved a harpoon gun and a few spare harpoons before continuing onto the dock. The whole structure swayed with the gentle motion of the seawater upon which it floated; it was built in segments that allowed it to rise and fall fluidly with the tide.

Kronus glanced to the side. Today, the water touched the cliffs on either side of the dock. The beach where he'd laid a bleeding, desperate Eva on the sand, where the bodies of her companions had lain motionless beneath a clear, sunny sky, was completely submerged by the high tide.

Vasil stood beside Breckett's boat, coiling a length of rope around his elbow and palm while the grizzled human checked the boat's rigging. When Kronus neared, Vasil offered a nod in greeting. Kronus returned it.

"Just in time!" Breckett boomed. "Well, a bit early, but we may as well get to it. Wade's sailing with his boy, Camrin today, since Camrin's lady, Jenny, has the day off to watch their little one, and—ah, you don't need to know all that. We've got traps to check today. That's what matters."

"The other boats have escorts?" Kronus asked.

"Yes," Vasil replied, passing the bundle of rope to Breckett. "Brexes, Charos, Jax, and Arkon. Dracchus has a small group patrolling the bay."

"You two are welcome to ride with me, if you don't want to swim all the way out to the first traps," Breckett said.

Vasil lowered himself to gather his gun and harpoon off the dock before grasping the side of the boat and drawing himself into it. Once he'd set his equipment down, he swung his gaze to Kronus. The light gray kraken wore an expectant look on his face.

Kronus held his place, hesitant to join them. He was accustomed to swimming; under the surface, he could lose himself in monitoring his surroundings, and communication was limited to signs and flashes of color. But in a relatively small boat, surrounded only by the water's surface and the open air — both of which seemed to stretch on endlessly — he'd have little to distract him from his thoughts apart from conversation. Would that be enough?

"Oh, come on," Breckett urged gruffly. "We won't bite." His gaze fell to Vasil before returning to Kronus, and a hint of a grin became visible within his facial hair. "Well, *I* won't. It's you quiet ones we've got to worry about."

Vasil arched a brow in question, and Breckett chuckled.

What harm could come of it? Perhaps companionship would prove to be what he needed to finally move his thoughts away from Eva. Nothing else had worked over the last few days. And if Kronus felt out of place amongst them — which he already did — that was just one more thing to keep his mind occupied, wasn't it?

Kronus extended his front tentacles, grasped the boat railing, and pulled himself into the vessel. Once his rear tentacles had a hold, he placed his weaponry along the bottom and eased himself down nearby. The movements of the water felt more pronounced than they had on the dock. It was a small thing, but it was of comfort to him — a gentle reminder that the sea was within easy reach should he require it.

Breckett saw to the ropes securing the boat to the dock, put his boot against the edge of the platform, and shoved off. He turned toward the mast and manipulated the boom. Within a few moments, the sail caught the wind, and Breckett guided them smoothly out of the bay.

The air over the open water felt different — cooler, breezier, somehow purer. Kronus relished its feel against his skin; it could not compare to swimming, but it had its own charm, offered a unique sense of freedom.

Conversation was sparse; the three passengers seemed content to enjoy the morning. But the way the sun sparkled on the water reminded Kronus of another morning not long before — when he'd rescued Eva from the razorback.

How much bloodshed had he seen in his lifetime? How many creatures had he killed to provide food for his people, how many kraken had he killed to protect females and younglings when Neo led his group in an attack on the Facility? He shouldn't have been affected by more blood, especially not human blood.

But the attack on Eva and her friends continued to haunt him.

Kronus released a relieved sigh when they reached the first of the bright yellow markers floating on the surface. He and Vasil gathered their harpoon guns as Breckett lowered the sail and slowed the boat, drawing alongside the marker. The human handed Vasil a small sack — its fishy smell suggested it was fresh bait — and the two kraken dove into the water, beginning their descent.

The sea life was sparse until they neared the bottom; the ocean currents guided the migrating schools of fish to other points along the coast, but the resulting relative lack of predators made this an ideal area for various bottom-feeding creatures to thrive — especially hardshells, which the fishermen called *Halorian lobsters.*

While Vasil sank to the bottom to inspect the first string of traps, Kronus scanned their surroundings. The water was perhaps six body-lengths deep — deep enough for prowling razorbacks, even under normal circumstances.

Would Kronus have noticed the razorbacks in the bay before the attack if he'd been in the water sooner? Could the kraken have saved four lives instead of one?

Kronus cast aside those questions. Regrets could not change what was already done; he knew that better than most. But he also knew those same regrets could shape the future. They could be lessons, if he allowed them to be; lessons about what was right, what was just, what was honorable.

Vasil grasped the rope connecting the traps to the float overhead and tugged it down several times. A few moments later, the line went taut, and the traps rose off the sea floor. High above, the boat bobbed with Breckett's efforts as he hauled the trap up. At least six hardshells were inside the wood-and-wire cages.

Kronus and Vasil moved to the next set of traps.

Small fish, seemingly unconcerned with the kraken's presence, drifted lazily between dancing shafts of sunlight nearby.

What would Eva's hair look like under the morning light? Human hair seemed to lose much of its shine when wet; would hers remain light brown or favor the glowing gold of sunrise when it was dry?

He snapped his head from side to side, hoping to shake away those thoughts. Despite his best efforts, his mind returned to her repeatedly. He should have gone to her again over the last few days, shouldn't have allowed her outburst to drive him away. She was lost, but it was not too late for her. She could be found again. She could come back from the dark place into which she'd sunk.

After checking the second bundle of traps, Vasil flashed yellow, catching Kronus's attention. He signed quickly.

You check the others. I will watch.

Vasil kept his coloring natural, his movements unhurried, but there was something in his eyes that unsettled Kronus despite its lack of malice — a knowing gleam.

Offering no argument, Kronus nodded and swam to the next set of traps. He went about his work absently; though he willed himself to focus, his mind refused to remain on task. Images of Eva's blue eyes flitted through his memory; blue eyes filled with pain, sorrow, and despair, devoid of the joy and curiosity with which they'd shone when he first saw her.

When the traps had all been checked, Vasil and Kronus returned to the boat. Vasil and Breckett hauled up the final string of traps together, opened them, and dumped the hard-shells they contained into a waiting basket that was already half-filled with the creatures. Kronus rebaited the empty traps, and Breckett lowered them into the water.

Soon, Breckett was directing the boat along the coast toward the next trapping area.

"You seem distracted," Vasil said.

Kronus didn't have to look up from the water to know Vasil's eyes were upon him. He clenched his jaw and fought the reflexive color change threatening to overcome his skin. "I am *fine.*"

Vasil was silent.

Growling, Kronus swung his gaze to the other kraken. Their eyes locked. Vasil maintained his silence, his muted coloration, and his scrutiny.

"It is none of your concern," Kronus spat.

Breckett cleared his throat, but the two kraken did not break eye contact with one another.

"We work together and hunt together," Vasil finally said. "Your ability to focus *is* my concern, because I am depending upon you for support, just as you depend upon me."

"And when have I ever wavered in my duty?" Kronus demanded. "Everything I have done has been—" he snapped his mouth shut before he finished. His hearts pounded against his ribs, and his skin had taken on a reddish hue.

This wasn't the time or place.

"For our people," Vasil said softly.

"What?" Kronus grasped the boat railing to ease the trembling of his hand.

"You have done everything for the good of our people. You were wrong in much of what you said and did, but I believe you acted — at least most of the time — for the benefit of the kraken." Vasil betrayed no outward sign of agitation or distress; Kronus found himself suddenly resentful of the other kraken's calm.

"I did not request your thoughts on those matters." Kronus's claws sank into the wood and his tentacles writhed in agitation as he turned back toward the water.

"But you have it now, regardless."

"This behavior is unlike you, Vasil," Kronus warned. "Make your challenge if you intend violence, or else shut your mouth."

Vasil's heavy gaze lingered on Kronus, a weight that made his skin itch. But he would not scratch, would not shift in place, would not display any sign of discomfort or weakness. Part of Kronus longed for a challenge, for a battle like he'd not fought in two years, for the sting of an opponent's strikes and the thrill of his own blows connecting with flesh.

More than that, he wanted to leave this boat and return to The Watch. Whether it was to retreat to the isolation of his den or visit Eva at the clinic he could not say.

"Have you kept up on the girl you rescued, Kronus?" Breckett asked. By his tone, he simply hoped to steer the conversation away from the sudden tension between the kraken, but the question struck Kronus like a slap across the face. It was too relevant to the thoughts that had been consuming him.

Kronus's jaw muscles ticked. "Yes."

"And…how's she doing? I heard Doc had to take off her leg."

"Poorly, and he did." Kronus folded his arms across his chest.

"Ah."

The rigging creaked and jingled, and the ocean sighed softly all around, lapping at the boat's hull. The silence between the three males deepened, and as it did, the surrounding air seemed increasingly thick and charged with an unsettling energy. That energy built in Kronus's chest, slowly winding around his hearts and lungs to make everything feel tight and constricted. He was no stranger to guilt and regret, but why should he experience those emotions *now*?

Realization came to him when he forced himself to look at Vasil again, who wore a deep frown as he stared at the sea. Though Vasil had been somewhat intrusive and assertive, he and Breckett had both been attempting the same thing — friendliness. For kraken, solitary beings by nature, such relationships were new. Only Jax and Arkon, who'd been considered oddities among their people, had been anything like friends before human influence changed the way many kraken viewed their own society.

Kronus had never experienced friendship himself; his instincts were torn even now between the kraken longing for solitude and the human desire for companionship.

"Her mate left her," he said, clenching and relaxing his jaw, "and she is unwell because of it."

"Her mate left *her*?" asked Vasil.

"That little piece of—" Breckett cut off his own words with a grunt. "I haven't met the girl more than a few times in passing, but she always seemed pleasant. Her folks are from Emmiton, I think. She came here to be with Blake. He was a troublemaker when he was younger, but I thought he'd grown out of that. It's harsh, but I always thought he was the sort who needed to have his ass kicked a few times to straighten him out."

Kronus glanced at Breckett. The human's thick brows were low over troubled eyes, and his mouth was lost amidst his bushy beard, which was usually a strong indication of his displeasure.

"I was told not to harm Blake," Kronus said.

Breckett laughed, but the sound lacked humor. "Doubt Kent would be able to put him back together again after you were done. We've got plenty of men in town would be happy to teach Blake a lesson after doing something like that, though."

The idea of Blake suffering was satisfying to Kronus, even if he couldn't inflict that pain himself. But what mattered more — causing pain to Blake or diminishing Eva's?

Kronus dipped his head as thoughts swirled through his mind. There were connections to be made, there was a solution here, he just needed to puzzle it out. He'd leapt to violence many times, had issued many challenges, and had ignited fury in others to incite them to fight their perceived enemies with passion and ferocity. None of that would be helpful in this situation. This solution was different.

"You care for the female," Vasil said.

Kronus's eyes widened as he lifted his gaze to Vasil. "I simply do not wish to see my efforts go to waste." His voice was too harsh even to his own ears.

Vasil frowned, brow creasing.

The concern on his face sparked something in Kronus's chest, and the feeling swept through Kronus with all the strength of the ocean slamming into shoreside cliffs.

He knew what he needed to do, knew it with more certainty than he'd ever experienced in all his life.

He twisted to look back at Breckett. "She doesn't need to see Blake hurt, even if part of her wants it. What she needs is to know The Watch will support her, even when her mate will not."

Breckett's eyes softened, and he nodded. "We can do that."

And more than that, she needs someone. *That someone who will stay with her no matter what.*

Fortunately, Kronus was nothing if not persistent.

CHAPTER 7

Eva dreamed of churning red water and terrified screams. She dreamed of Addison's shredded body bobbing on a sea of blood. She dreamed of *them*, her friends. They haunted her sleep and her waking hours alike, and all she could do was lay in pain, silently mourning them.

New, broken memories came to her every day, but she had no way of knowing which, if any, were real. She couldn't rule out the possibility that her mind was simply filling in the gaps with imagined flashes from her nightmares.

The door opened; Eva stared blankly at the ceiling. There were only two people who came to check on her, and they only did so because it was their duty. Deep down, beneath that bitterness, Eva knew Aymee and Kent cared, but they weren't the people she wanted to see. Everyone who she wanted to visit were too far away, or had abandoned her, or were…dead.

"Look what I brought!" Aymee's excited voice filled the room. "We can sit you down and take you for a ride outside. It'll be fun!"

Eva closed her eyes as though it would magically transport her somewhere else. Anywhere else.

Aymee sighed heavily and approached the bed. She settled a hand on Eva's shoulder. "It's been ten days, Eva. You *need* to get out of this bed."

Eva turned her face toward the wall.

A strange, soft sound drifted to her from the hallway, like something was slithering over the floor.

"You're here." Aymee sounded both surprised and confused.

Who is here?

"I didn't expect to see you back after last time," Aymee continued.

For a moment, Eva wondered if Blake had come back to apologize for all the hurtful things he'd said, for all that he'd done.

"What is *that*?" Kronus asked.

"It's a wheelchair. I was trying to coax Eva outside for some fresh air."

"Will fresh air help her?"

"Yes. She's been in that bed since she was brought here. She refuses to leave it."

In the brief silence that followed Aymee's words, Eva heard that light, raspy sound on the floor again, softer than before.

Tentacles.

Oddly, the realization wasn't followed with a wave of revulsion.

"I will take her," Kronus said without a shred of doubt in his voice.

Like hell you will.

"Are you sure?" Aymee hesitantly asked.

"Yes."

"Be careful with my patient, Kronus."

He made a deep grunt that offered no reassurance whatsoever.

Eva opened her eyes and listened to Aymee's retreating footsteps in disbelief. Aymee was just leaving her to *him*? To this creature?

Kronus moved slowly around the bed to insert himself between Eva's eyes and the wall. She rolled onto her left side, giving him her back. Not having to look at him was worth the discomfort in her leg.

"Aymee says you need fresh air, female."

Eva pressed her lips together. She felt him lingering behind her, his presence a well of heat that made her skin tingle, and she scooted herself a little closer to the edge of the bed to get as far away from him as possible.

It didn't help when he suddenly leaned forward and slipped his arms beneath her body, lifting her off the bed as though she weighed no more than a feather.

She tensed for a moment before trying to jerk away from him. "Don't touch me!"

"You need fresh air," he replied, his hold unbroken despite her struggles. He pulled her against his chest and moved around the bed toward an odd-looking chair with wheels attached to it.

The blanket slid off her and she twisted in his arms and kicked her legs. She shoved against his shoulders and struck him with her fists, but he shrugged off the blows like she was a cranky infant throwing a tantrum.

"Put me down," she demanded, panting, body already weakening from the exertion. Her left leg throbbed; fiery pain burned from her stump to her hip.

She knew she should've been more specific when he sat her in the wheelchair. Eva tried to rise, but Kronus grasped the armrests and leaned over her, caging her in with his body.

"You are going outside, Eva. You can give in and relax, or you can keep fighting until one of us is too tired to continue." He dipped his head a little closer. "And *I* will not tire first."

Eva leaned back in the chair, putting as much distance between them as she could, but there was no escape. She looked up at him, her eyes widening in startlement. This was her first true, up-close look at a kraken.

The humanity in his face was made more alien by his inhuman features. He had tube-like growths where his ears should've been, and his nose was wide and flat. There was no hair anywhere on his ochre skin, which had a bumpy texture she'd never noticed from afar — though her brief brushes with it had been like velvety caresses. His jaw was well-defined, his full lips set in determination, and his brow was low over his eyes.

It was those eyes that arrested her attention beyond all else, that caught her and refused to let her go; she feared she'd never be free of them no matter how hard she fought. There were swirls of molten gold, bisected by pupils that were narrowed into horizontal slits. His gaze was heavy, heated, and intense.

His eyes dipped, and his brows shifted infinitesimally.

Kronus lowered himself slightly and dropped his hands from the armrests. They brushed along her outer thighs as he swept them toward her backside, and Eva inhaled sharply as a jolt of excitement ran through her. Breathing shallowly and suddenly helpless to move, she watched as he plucked up the ends of a strap and buckled them over her middle, securing her in place.

"Why are you doing this?" she asked quietly, staring at his large hands and their claw-tipped fingers.

"Because someone needs to." He pushed away and paused as he was rounding the wheelchair. Without saying anything else, he took the blanket from the bed and draped it over Eva's lap, covering her thighs — which were largely exposed due to the simplistic gown in which she was dressed. He took his place behind the chair.

A moment later, he was rolling her down the hallway toward the clinic's exit.

"No," Eva said. "I don't want to go out."

He didn't slow their steady pace. "But you need to."

Eva caught her lower lip between her teeth to cease its trembling. She wound her hands into the blanket, clutching the fabric between her fingers.

Just before they reached the door, he spun the chair around. She glanced over her shoulder as he released the chair with one hand, opened the door, and pulled her through backwards.

The first thing she was aware of was how *bright* it was outside. Ten days indoors had heavily skewed her perception of sunlight, and she had to squint for a while before her eyes finally adjusted. The air bore a hint of the sea that didn't seem to carry into the clinic. She hadn't realized how much she'd come to appreciate that scent since she came to The Watch, and she inhaled it deeply now.

But when she closed her eyes, that scent brought her back to the beach. Brought her back to that day.

Her grip on the blanket tightened. "Take me back inside."

"Why?"

"I don't want to be out here. I just…want to be left alone."

"Few of us get to have what we want," he replied as he turned the chair away from the clinic and pushed her forward.

"I hate you," she said, unable to keep the tremor from her voice as tears filled her eyes.

There was a slight delay in his response. "Good. At least you feel something."

At least she felt *something*? She felt *everything*. Not a day passed during which she didn't feel the ache of loss in her chest, the heartbreak, the shock and lingering disbelief. Her friends were gone. Her own physical agony was a constant reminder that she was no longer whole. There was no numbing what she felt, no running from it.

Eva remained silent and kept her gaze downcast as Kronus wheeled her into the town center, a large, paved square bordered by some of The Watch's larger buildings. It was late enough in the morning for most folk to have moved on to their daily duties, but there were still a few people walking outside. Eva made sure not to look directly at any of them. She'd only find pity in their eyes.

That's all *this* was. Pity. She was a burden *someone* needed to take care of, and Kronus had volunteered.

They crossed the town center and took a right turn at the next intersection, following the new street toward a corner. The turn moved them out of the buildings' shade, allowing sunlight to fall on Eva's head and warm her hair.

She closed her eyes, shutting out her surroundings, and tipped her head back. She'd forgotten how good it felt to have sunlight on her skin. All her life, she'd lived in the sun — she'd helped her father with his traps in the jungle, had hiked the mountain trails around Emmiton with friends, and had sometimes worked the fields, always glad to help, glad to be outdoors. Though she'd occasionally assisted Blake with tanning hides and leather after coming to The Watch, she couldn't stomach the smells and much preferred the open air.

The chair turned again, left this time, and the road became rougher. Eva opened her eyes. "Where are you taking me?"

Kronus didn't answer. He pushed her along the dirt road, which was flanked on either side by lush vegetation, until they reached a wide area of pastures filled with livestock. He turned the chair toward one of the pastures and halted in the middle of the road, surrounded by animals making low calls and feasting on the grass.

"Why are we here?" she asked.

"These beasts are odd-looking and have a foul odor," he said, "but I find their company preferable to that of most people around here. I thought you might agree."

Eva turned her head and glanced up at him. He was looking at the animals ahead of them, his expression solemn. Frowning, she faced forward again.

I find their company preferable to that of most people around here.

There was so much weight to those words that, for a moment, she saw past her own pain and wondered what lurked within him. She suddenly recalled the callous remarks her friends had made. She wasn't innocent herself; she'd called him *monster*.

Guilt assailed her.

"Why are you here, then?" she asked softly.

"Because most people would find the company of these animals preferable to mine."

"I mean why do you stay in The Watch? Why not go… home?" Eva's question seemed to strike her harder than it did him; was that what awaited her? A long, painful recovery culminating in a tearful journey back to Emmiton, undoubtedly made more difficult by her injury?

He drew in a deep breath and released it slowly. "I am no longer worthy of my home."

Eva's brows lowered.

A krull — a long-necked, four-legged beast covered in violet fur with a splash of red beneath its jaw, and long, slender horns — raised its narrow head and looked their way. Its jaw worked in a steady rhythm as it chewed grass.

"Why do you say that?" she asked.

"For reasons that do not concern you."

"Then why bring it up?" she asked, her frown turning into a scowl.

"You asked me."

She glared back at him. "And you started the conversation."

He returned the glare, undeterred by her expression. "I am *trying* to be *nice*."

"Well firstly, you're doing a terrible job, and secondly, I didn't ask for you to. I didn't ask for this at all!" she snapped, crossing her arms over her chest and facing forward.

He drew in another deep breath. Tension radiated from him as he turned the chair and wheeled her farther down the dirt road, away from town. "What we want and what we need are rarely the same," he said in a low voice.

"Then why are you bothering? It's clear you don't want to help me."

He stopped abruptly enough that Eva's hands reflexively grasped the armrests, and if it were not for the strap holding her in, she might have fallen to the ground. The blanket slid off her lap, catching on her foot.

"I would not be here if I did not wish to be," he said. "I...do not know how to deal with your kind."

Eva frowned. "Wouldn't it be the same way you deal with your own kind?"

"Kraken think differently. We largely prefer solitude."

"Why would you prefer that?"

Something brushed against her right leg; startled, Eva glanced down to see one of his tentacles stretching forward to clasp the blanket. He lifted the blanket and leaned over her, taking it in his hands to drape over her lap. His scent hit her then, a blend of land and sea — the salt of the ocean mingling with earth and stone, wholly masculine. It was surprisingly pleasant.

"It is our way," he said.

Eva tilted her face up toward his, and he looked down to meet her gaze. "That's a lonely way to live."

His eyes shifted to the top of her head, and before she realized what he meant to do, he raised a hand and brushed his fingertips over her hair. After only a moment, he withdrew his hand and straightened his torso. Grasping the chair's handles, he turned Eva back toward town.

He didn't reply to her, and Eva said nothing more. She sensed there were many things Kronus didn't want to talk about, though she also had the impression that he didn't talk much to begin with. He seemed so...withdrawn. Was that simply his personality or had something happened to make him that way?

Their return to town was unhurried and quiet. Strangely, Eva felt little discomfort despite the silence between them, despite his standoffishness. When he pushed her back onto the paved road, he continued straight, along the street that ran behind the town hall. It was busier now as the midday meal approached, but it wasn't the increased number of people that made Eva's heart pound; the leatherworker's shop was on this street, and there was a familiar figure standing out front.

Blake's laughter was deep, carefree, and boisterous, the same as it had always been. She watched his head tilt back, watched the rays of sunlight catch upon the golden locks brushing his brow, and watched the flash of his white teeth. He said something Eva could not hear, and his words were punctuated by feminine laughter.

Eva tore her gaze from Blake to look at the woman in front of him. The woman's posture was languid, her body leaned casually toward him as though she'd reach out and put her hand on his arm at any moment.

But the woman didn't reach for Blake; *he* reached for *her*. He tucked the woman's hair behind her ear and brushed the backs of his fingers over her cheek.

Eva's heart stopped, and her breath fled her. Her chest tightened, flooding with raw pain. This wasn't… This couldn't be Blake.

But it was. She knew him, had known him intimately for months.

Struggling for breath, Eva gripped the armrests. "Take me back. The other way…the way we came. Take me back now."

She realized that Kronus had already stopped the chair. They remained there, in the center of the street, for many seconds, and the only sound Kronus produced was the soft squeak of his hands squeezing the chair's handles.

"*Please*," she rasped, tears blurring her vision.

With a frustrated growl, he turned the chair around. Neither of them spoke as he retraced their earlier path. Eva didn't notice the buildings around them, the people, the sunlight or the sky. The wheels rolled steadily beneath her, trembling when they hit the occasional rough patch, and she didn't care. As long as she was away from there. Away from Blake.

Soon, they were back at the clinic. Kronus wheeled the chair to her bed and moved to her front. She didn't resist as he scooped her up and held her against his chest. For a fleeting instant, she had the urge to clutch him, to bury her face against his velvety skin and sob until everything went black, but she resisted. His muscles were rock-solid beneath that soft skin and bristling with tension, but he was nothing but gentle as he laid her atop the bed.

Eva turned her face away from him and closed her eyes. He hesitated for a moment before withdrawing his arms, palms brushing over her gown to spread heat across the skin beneath. He draped the blanket over her and lingered beside the bed.

She longed for him to say something, to say *anything*, to give her words she could cling onto. Anything so she didn't feel so... dead inside, so utterly alone.

"I will return tomorrow," he finally said. The soft slithering of his tentacles over the floor announced his exit.

When the door clicked closed behind him, nothing remained to hold back her tears. She let them flow freely, silently, until exhaustion finally claimed her.

CHAPTER 8

TRUE TO HIS WORD, KRONUS RETURNED TO THE CLINIC THE NEXT morning. Aymee was in the front room when he arrived. She greeted him with a smile that quickly faded as she explained that Eva seemed *worse* since yesterday.

He frowned and looked down the hall toward Eva's room. He knew little of human ways; though they spoke the same language, they often seemed to use the words differently, and their manner of thinking was often beyond his understanding. But he knew why she'd fallen in spirits. It was for the same reason he'd gone to sleep angry and had woken even angrier.

Blake.

Though Aymee's counsel against harming Blake was wise, it had taken all Kronus's willpower to prevent him from attacking the human the day before. His fury had only intensified as time passed — especially during the night, when his sleep had been fitful and often broken and he'd been left with nothing to do in the dark but listen to the ocean and think.

He entered Eva's room to find her laying in the same place, in the same position, as he'd left her the day before.

"Time to go," he announced.

She didn't respond. Nor did she react when he picked her up and moved her into the wheelchair; no cursing, no fighting, no anything. She remained as limp as a fresh corpse, barely holding herself upright after he strapped her in.

Aymee's brow creased as Kronus wheeled Eva toward the exit. She opened the door for him, and her gaze was troubled as it briefly met his. He had an odd sense that, despite her skill in treating ailments, Aymee was just as uncertain of how to help Eva through this as he was.

Eva was silent as he pushed her around town, ignoring his few clumsy attempts at starting conversation. He was careful to avoid the street on which they'd seen Blake the day before. If she noticed that, she made no indication of it. Though the sky was clear and blue, and the sunshine was pleasantly warm, she kept her gaze downcast throughout.

Kronus gritted his teeth hard enough to make his jaw ache. This was worse than her outburst the first time he'd gone to see her. He would've welcomed punching, kicking, and clawing if it ended this *nothingness*. Why was she an empty shell now when just yesterday she'd seemed on the verge of reclaiming a little bit of herself? Did Blake truly hold such power over her?

Reminder of Blake twisted Kronus's insides into knots and poured fire into his gut. Kraken males saw it as a privilege to be selected by females, no matter how fleeting those pairings often were. But from the little Kronus knew about human relationships — learned mainly through human-kraken couplings like Aymee and Arkon or Macy and Jax — humans committed to their mates with the intention of spending their lives together.

Why would anyone throw that away? Such stability, such security, had never been commonplace amongst Kronus's people. The Facility had provided them shelter since the uprising centuries ago, but nothing had been guaranteed. Why give up a lifetime with a mate when so many male kraken wanted nothing more than to be chosen by a female for even a day?

Frustrated, concerned, and uncertain, he brought Eva back to the clinic. If Aymee or her father were still there, neither made their presence known as Kronus took Eva to her room and moved her onto the bed.

It was only then that she finally moved of her own accord, rolling onto her side to face away from him.

Kronus's hands fell to the bedrail, and his tentacles writhed over the floor. Nostrils flaring, he covered her with the blanket. What had happened to the progress she'd made? What had happened to the inner strength she'd displayed when he pulled her out of the water? This didn't look like recovery; it looked like slow death from the inside out.

She was broken.

Reaching across the bed, he took Eva by the shoulder, rolled her onto her back, and took her chin in his other hand to force her face toward his. Eva's eyes widened as he leaned over her, stopping his face less than a hand's span from hers.

"I will return tomorrow," he growled, "and you will be *here* with me. Do you understand, human? *This* will continue no longer."

She held his gaze for a few moments before turning her eyes away. Kronus clenched his jaw. His attention dipped to her lips; would she react if he *kissed* her, like he'd seen so many humans do? Her pink lips looked soft and warm, and he'd wondered about how kissing felt. The kraken who were mated to humans all seemed to enjoy it.

He lowered his head further. Desire kindled within him, shoving aside his frustrations. A little closer and he'd feel her mouth against his, taste her upon his lips, and take her breath into himself. His cock pressed against the inside of his slit, aching with sudden need.

He released his hold on her and drew back before giving into temptation.

"Tomorrow, Eva," he promised, voice husky.

She shifted onto her side again just before he left.

WITH ELBOWS LEANED against the edge of the table, Kronus turned the little carving between his fingers. His eyes kept drifting to the figure's broken leg no matter how hard he tried to direct them elsewhere. Each time he looked at it, he turned the figure a little more, as though the slight change of angle would somehow make it appear different.

Heavy pounding on the door startled him out of his thoughts. He shifted his gaze to the window, noting the deep orange of the sky; the sun had nearly set. How long had he been at the table, lost in contemplation? It had still been afternoon when he picked up the carving.

He dropped the figure, pushed himself upright, and moved toward the door as the pounding repeated. The noise grated on him, nearly making the tips of his tentacles curl. Grabbing the handle, he tugged the door open.

"What?" he growled.

Aymee stood on the other side, eyes wide, brown, curly hair in disarray, and shoulders heaving with ragged breaths. "Is Eva here with you?"

Her disheveled appearance cut through Kronus's annoyance, allowing confusion to fill its place. "No. Why?"

"She's not at the clinic, and her wheelchair is gone. I thought… I didn't see you come, but I thought you might have taken her for another walk…" She swallowed. "She's gone. I don't know anyone else who might've come to visit, unless Blake…"

"I know where she is," Kronus said. He latched onto the doorframe with his tentacles and pulled himself through.

Aymee stumbled out of his way. "Where?"

"Go back to the clinic. I will bring her there." He hurried toward the rocky path leading down to the nearby beach.

"Kronus, where are you going?" Aymee called behind him.

He didn't answer; there wasn't time. Eva's words echoed in his mind.

Why didn't you just let me die, too?

He scrambled down the path and dragged himself across the sand as fast as he could. Instinctually, he knew the land route was a shorter distance, but he was far faster in the water. *To the abyss with the razorbacks.*

Kronus dove into the surf without a backward glance. The water, which was stained red-gold by the setting sun, shimmered liked liquid fire. His tentacles lashed forward, digging into the wet sand to pull his body forward until he was deep enough to swim. His hearts pounded like peals of thunder in his chest as he sped along the coast.

His muscles burned with exertion by the time he rounded the cape atop which the lighthouse stood, but Kronus pushed harder, faster, drawing upon reserves of strength he hadn't known he possessed. Though his life had been in danger on countless occasions, this seemed the direst, riskiest, most important situation of his existence.

Far ahead, the underside of the dock materialized out of the ocean haze. He swam closer to the land, sweeping his gaze along the shallow coastal water, but saw no sign of Eva. That was a small relief. He pushed to the surface.

Once his eyes adjusted to the open air, his vision fell on the stone stairs bridging the dock platform to the beach. Eva's wheelchair lay on its side at the base of the steps. A trail of disturbed sand led away from the chair toward the water.

And Eva was at the trail's end, crawling slowly toward the sea on her belly.

This was where it had happened, where her life had been forever, irreversibly altered.

Kronus ducked underwater and darted forward, clawing at the sand to drag himself up onto the beach once he reached the shallows. He rose out of the water and hurried toward her.

Eva was at the water's edge when Kronus reached her. Extending an arm, she buried her fingers in the wet ground and pulled herself a little closer to the sea. A little closer to dying with her friends.

A rage sparked in Kronus. He took hold of her beneath her arms, and she yelped as he lifted her up, swung her away from the tide, and dropped her on her back in the softer, dry sand. Her eyes met his, and for an instant, she stilled.

Then she opened her mouth and screamed. It was the most primal, agonized sound he'd ever heard — and it called to the despair deep within him.

She moved to sit up, but he lowered himself over her, caught her wrists, and pinned them to the ground as he restrained her kicking legs with a few of his tentacles. She bucked and writhed beneath him.

"Let me go! Just let me go! I should have died with them." Eva's shoulders shook with her sobs. "Y-You h-h-have no right!"

"You did *not* die with them," he snarled, "and if they would have wanted you to, they were no friends to begin with."

Tears spiked her long lashes and flowed down the sides of her face as she yanked her arms. "It's not your choice!"

"Your friends died for no reason," he said, not relinquishing his grasp on her, "because that is how the sea works. Do you wish to die for no reason, too? Or are you as much a coward as Blake?"

She looked up at him, the blue of her eyes stark against the irritated red surrounding them. Strands of hair stuck to her face. "They're gone, and he left me. I have *nothing*. No one."

A deep, rumbling growl rose from his throat. "You have me!" he shouted. He released one of her arms and wrapped his free hand around her throat, forcing her chin up so she looked at him, at *only* him. "You have *me*," he repeated quietly. "And I refuse to let you end yourself. I will *make* you fight."

Lowering his face closer to hers, Kronus brushed his thumb along her jaw. "If you would throw away your life, then I will claim it as *mine*."

Fresh tears welled in her eyes before she broke into another wave of raw, gut-wrenching sobs, her struggles suddenly ceasing. Each of her shuddering exhalations pierced his hearts anew.

Kronus pushed himself back and slid off Eva, releasing his tentacles' hold on her legs. He gathered her against his chest, and she threw her arms around him, clutching him tightly. Her thighs straddled his waist, and both her breath and her tears were warm against his neck. The bite of her nails into the skin of his back sent a thrill through him despite the situation.

He coiled a pair of tentacles beneath Eva, granting her some support, and slid another around her waist. His suction cups sampled her scent and flavor where they touched her bare flesh, serving only to awaken a craving in him for a deeper taste.

He meant what he'd said — she'd forfeited her choice by her actions. As far as Kronus was concerned, Eva was *his*. His mate. And he'd do everything to keep her safe from the world, even if it meant protecting her from herself.

Remaining silent, Kronus ran his claws through Eva's hair until her cries tapered into small hiccups and shuddering breaths, until her hold loosened, and her body relaxed against him. He drew his tentacles close and pushed himself up, shifting an arm to cradle her backside. She rested her tear-moistened cheek against his shoulder as he carried her to the steps and up onto the ramp, leaving the wheelchair where it lay.

The sky was deep violet everywhere save on the horizon over the sea, where the last bit of sunlight slowly died. The streets were quiet. Most of the lamps had been lit — some electric, many more burning oil — granting The Watch a gentle, welcoming glow despite the encroaching darkness. If any of the few people Kronus saw thought it odd for him to be carrying a one-legged human female, none were bold enough to express their opinion.

Aymee rushed to meet him the moment he entered the clinic, reaching up to press her fingers to Eva's neck. "Where was she? She's so cold. Get her to the room and tell me what happened."

"Nothing happened." Kronus moved down the hallway to the room Eva had been staying in.

"What do you mean *nothing*? She's covered in sand and—"

"If something had happened, Aymee," Kronus snapped, "she wouldn't be here right now. She will be fine."

"Don't you take that tone with me," Aymee growled. "I'm her doctor, I deserve to know what—"

"I'm okay," Eva said softly, tightening her hold on Kronus.

For once, Aymee was silent.

Kronus glanced over his shoulder to see Aymee staring at Eva, mouth hanging open. He turned away, clenching his jaw to suppress a smile, and gently settled Eva on a chair near the bed. He had to carefully pry her arms off his neck to withdraw from her.

"You need rest," Kronus said, "but Aymee will help you clean up first."

Eva's eyes met his. A sheen of moisture lingered within them, but no more tears fell. She was disheveled — her hair was a mess, the skin around her eyes was puffy, grains of sand clung to her everywhere, and she looked exhausted.

But there was a light in her eyes again, faint yet unmistakable.

She was *alive.*

She was beautiful.

"I...yes," Aymee said, stepping forward. "Let's clean you up and get some fresh sheets and clothes." She looked at Kronus, brows raised, waiting for an explanation that wouldn't come.

"I need to retrieve her wheelchair," he said before swinging his attention to Eva. "I will return shortly. Aymee will stay with you until I am back."

"Where *is* the wheelchair?" Aymee asked as he rose and moved toward the door.

"The same place she was," he replied.

"And where was that? Damnit, Kronus! I want answers!"

But he was already out of the room, and the answers were not his to give. He exited the clinic without slowing; the less time he spent away from Eva, the better.

CHAPTER 9

Eva awoke more alert than she'd been since the day of the attack. There wasn't a spot on her body that didn't ache, but she had a strange sense of lightness. Though guilt and sorrow lingered within her, curled and coiled around her heart, they were muted by something new, something bright — hope?

That little light was tiny compared to the remaining darkness, but it was undoubtedly there, waiting for her to tend it.

Running her fingers over the crisp bedding, she inhaled its fresh scent. Even *she* felt clean and refreshed for the first time in a long while.

Shame suffused Eva as the events of the night before came back to her in a rush; her behavior was the reason for the change of sheets and clothing, for the bath she'd received.

She shifted atop the bed, intending to sit up, and accidentally put pressure on the end of her amputated leg. Lips drawn back in a grimace, she hissed and dropped herself onto the bedding. Though the near-constant pain clearly signaled the point at which her leg now ended, it often felt like her foot was still there.

A warm, strong hand settled on her right leg, and she flinched from the touch.

"Should I call for Aymee?"

Eva started at the deep voice and swung her gaze to Kronus, who stood next to the bed. His touch was a hot brand on her thigh, searing through the blanket to thrill the flesh beneath. She glanced down at his hand. It was large, and each of his long fingers was tipped with a wicked claw. Thin webbing stretched between each of those fingers, and she could see tiny, faint veins running through the seemingly-delicate skin.

Had he stayed with her all night? The thought made her feel strangely warm inside. Why did Kronus care so much while the man she'd been joined with, her *husband*, had abandoned Eva during her greatest time of need? This kraken, this stranger, one of the beings she'd judged and dismissed as inhuman, cared more about her than Blake ever had.

She trailed her gaze up Kronus's arm, over powerful, defined muscle to linger on the dark stripes that began at his biceps and ran to his shoulders.

His hand flexed, squeezing her thigh. "Eva?"

"No. I'm fine." She forced her eyes to meet his. "Why are you here?"

"Eat." He lifted his hand away and pushed the rolling tray table to her.

Eva's stomach growled, suddenly hollow, as she looked at the plate of food atop the tray. For the first time in days, she was *hungry*.

She picked up one of the hard-boiled eggs and took a bite. Her next bite finished the egg off. The other egg followed, accompanied by toast and winefruit. Only when a single slice of fruit was left on her plate, and her stomach felt as though it might revolt, did she glance up at Kronus.

He held her gaze, and she stopped chewing the mouthful of

sweet fruit. Seconds ticked by. She swallowed the food in her mouth, and still he stared.

"Finish," he finally said, dipping his chin toward the last piece of fruit.

Her brows fell as she picked up the last slice. Even a single bite more seemed too much now. "You still didn't answer my question."

Kronus remained silent. Frowning, she returned the fruit to her plate and pushed the tray aside.

Taking hold of the tray, he wheeled it away and turned back to her. "You are going to walk today."

Eva paled. "That is cruel."

"It is the truth. Nothing more nor less."

"I can't walk!" She gestured toward her left leg. "It's *gone*."

Kronus moved to the side of the bed and held out a hand. As she looked up at him, she realized for the first time just how big he was; she knew the kraken tended to be larger than humans, but somehow — despite him carrying her several times — she hadn't really registered the difference.

"You *will* walk, human."

"That's easy for you to say when you have eight legs, or tentacles, or whatever they are! I have one!"

"That is one more than none."

Eva's patience was suddenly worn quite thin. "Why are you here?"

"So you have someone to be mad at," he replied, leaning forward and slipping his hand under her back. He lifted her into a full sitting position as easily as he might've folded a piece of paper and turned her so she sat on the edge of the bed.

"What?" she asked, taken aback.

He paused, meeting her gaze again. His hands settled on her hips, and he leaned closer still. "If anger is what drives you for now, I am here to be its target. Because I am not going to allow your self-pity any longer."

Eva didn't want to do this. She *couldn't* do this. "Aymee!"

Somehow, Aymee heard her through the closed door, which opened not a moment later. Aymee stepped into the room with a pair of crutches.

Eva stared at the crutches in horror. "You're *allowing* this?"

Aymee propped them against the bed. "Not only allowing it but encouraging it. You need this, Eva, and Kronus has agreed to help you."

"I *can't.*"

"Have you tried?" Kronus demanded.

Eva gripped her left thigh. "Kronus, I can't do this."

His skin flashed red. "You can, and you will," he said, voice dropping low. "Only after you have fallen down and pulled yourself up a thousand times will I accept that you cannot."

Tears of fear, pain, and frustration filled her eyes. She looked to Aymee, silently begging the woman to put a stop to this, to just let her be, but Aymee offered only an encouraging smile.

"If you need me, I'll be nearby," Aymee said gently, making her way to the door.

"You can't leave me with him!"

"You're in good hands, Eva."

Eva stared at the open doorway in disbelief. This was real. It wasn't a dream, or a nightmare, it was her life. Movement at the edge of her vision called her attention to the crutches.

One of Kronus's tentacles had slithered over the bed, slipped through the gaps beneath the arm-pads on both crutches, and lifted them. Removing his hands from her hips, he passed the crutches into his left hand and held them upright at the bedside.

"Come, female."

Eva shook her head. "No."

"If you prefer to walk without these sticks, I will make you do that instead."

Eva pressed her lips together and gritted her teeth. "Fine."

Kronus backed up slightly, allowing Eva some space as she

tossed the blanket aside and scooted her bottom to the edge of the bed. Her bare right foot settled on the cool floor. She scowled down at her stump.

Shifting his position, Kronus grasped her left bicep and tugged her off the bed — onto her foot.

Eva gasped, balance wavering. "No! No, I'm not ready!"

"Lying in bed will not make you ready." The solidness of his hold maintained her balance, prevented her from pitching too far forward or back. He extended his other arm to hold the crutches in front of her. "Do you know how to use these?"

"No."

Suddenly Kronus was before her, a wall of ochre skin and sculpted muscle. He guided her hand to his shoulder; she wasn't sure why until he released his hold on her. She dug her nails into his skin, clutching at him to keep her balance. Days in bed with little to no food had weakened her and left her shaky.

She wasn't sure she *could* do this, whether she wanted to or not.

Kronus separated the crutches from each other and, without ceremony, shoved their padded ends under her arms. He directed her right hand to the grip further down the crutch before moving her left hand off him and repeating the process. Without his support, she was forced to spread her weight between her foot and the crutches.

"Now what?" she asked.

He backed away from her; it was her first opportunity to watch his entire body move, to study the strange gait created by his tentacles simultaneously pulling and pushing to drag him over the floor. The muscles of his middle bunched and stretched, and Eva found herself staring. The defined muscles of his abdomen were suddenly quite appealing.

Kronus stopped in the doorway. "Walk."

Eva blinked, dragging her gaze up to meet his eyes. "How?"

"Just *move*," he growled, his skin flaring red once more, but it wasn't so quick to revert to its normal color. "You have three legs now instead of one, and you still continue this whining?"

"You are such an *ass*!" she snapped. How *dare* he? He had no idea what she was going through, what she'd lost. He had no right to judge her!

She lifted one of the crutches and moved it forward. The cushion pressed into her armpit uncomfortably. She shifted her weight onto the crutch, lifted her leg, and immediately tipped to the side.

Her heart lurched, and she squeezed her eyes shut, body tensing for the inevitable impact.

Strong hands grasped her upper arms, halting her fall. She opened her eyes and tilted her head back to find Kronus in front of her again. What was the appropriate response? Gratitude, laughter, tears? She didn't know how to feel.

"The sticks are your leg," he said in a low voice, standing her back up. "*Together*. Do you understand?"

"Why are you doing this?" she asked again. "Why do you care?"

"Because I do. Now *walk*." He pulled away again, tentacles stretching and contracting as he returned to the open doorway.

"Why are you so damn *bossy*?" she demanded even as she obeyed his command.

Using both crutches at the same time provided much better balance, but she was still weak from lack of exercise and food, and wobbled one way or another many times. Each time, Kronus was there to catch her. Over and over he spat that same word — *walk* — and whenever she neared him, he moved farther away, leading her on the slowest, most pathetic chase around the clinic she could imagine. Eva cursed him the entire way.

She grew more accustomed to the crutches with each

passing minute, but walking with them became increasingly taxing as her limited strength waned.

Eva stopped in the clinic hall, limbs shaking and perspiration dampening her hair. She couldn't keep her limbs from trembling. "Enough!"

Kronus swept his gaze over her from head to toe and back again and nodded once. He moved close to her, placed a steadying hand on her back, collected the crutches from her weary arms, and passed them to a tentacle. She sagged against him, and he bent slightly to scoop her into his arms. Moments later, he had her back in the room, settled on the edge of the bed with the crutches against the wall nearby. She hated him for his mobility, hated him for how easy it was for him.

He captured her chin firmly between his finger and thumb and tilted her face up to meet his gaze. She glared at him and grasped his wrist. He'd been nothing but rude and pushy, and she wasn't in the mood to take even one more of his damned commands or insults.

"You did well, female," he said softly. His golden eyes shone with gentle praise, gleamed with pride.

Pride for *her*.

Something within Eva broke. Her heart quickened, and she couldn't look away from him. His pulse thrummed beneath her fingers, matching the speed of her own. He shifted closer and lifted his free hand, brushing hair away from her cheek with the backs of his fingers. His skin had changed color again — a faint maroon tint.

One of his tentacles slid over her foot and coiled up her calf. Eva's lips parted, and her eyes flared. His suction cups, each of which lightly kissed her skin as they moved, sent tingles through her; they were at once stronger and softer than any lips could've been.

Desire filled her, unbidden and undeniable. Her breasts felt suddenly heavier, the tips of her nipples hardened beneath the gown, and heat suffused her as his touch traveled higher. Her grip on his wrist tightened. She didn't know whether to push him away or pull him closer.

How could her body react so strongly to a kraken's touch? It was more powerful than anything she'd ever felt with Blake. How would those suction cups feel on other parts of her body? Her stomach, her breasts, her...*sex?*

Kronus's nostril's flared. He narrowed his eyes, and his pupils expanded from horizontal slits into rectangles. The tentacle around her leg rose higher still, settling on her thigh. The color of his skin slowly deepened from a mere tint to full-blown maroon as he released her chin to lay his fingers along her jaw. His gaze dipped to her lips. Tension radiated from his body, and his tentacles shifted restlessly on the floor.

When he leaned his head closer, she tilted her face toward him, sliding the tip of her tongue over her lips in anticipation. The moment felt right, despite everything that had led to it. Perhaps it was desperation, or a need to feel something, *anything*, beside pain and sorrow. Perhaps it was a need to feel like she mattered to someone, somewhere.

Another of his tentacles trailed over her left leg.

The sensation was so startling to the new, sensitive skin of her wound that Eva released her hold on his wrist and cringed away from him.

Whatever madness had overcome her shattered at that instant.

"Don't," she rasped.

Kronus drew back, his skin shifting to deep red before reverting, slowly, to its normal ochre. His hands and tentacles fell away, but she didn't miss how his fingers curled into fists at his sides. His chest swelled with a deep inhalation.

"Don't," she repeated, reaching for the discarded blanket at the end of the bed. She pulled it over her legs; it was a meager shield, but it was better than nothing.

Her chest was tight with emotion, her body still thrummed with desire, but it was too much. She wasn't…she wasn't *whole*. He'd touched her, *there*, where a piece of her was missing. Hiding beneath a blanket wouldn't bring her leg back, but at least she wouldn't have to look at it. At least she wouldn't have to be reminded that she was incomplete.

As though I can ever forget.

He darted toward her suddenly, moving with enough speed to make her jump back on the mattress. His clawed hand swung toward her. Before she could even squeeze her eyes shut in fear of the coming blow, he snatched the blanket and tore it away from her.

"This is *you* now!" he snarled, jabbing a finger toward her left leg, his skin pulsing crimson. "You do not have to like it, but you *will* have to accept it. You cannot turn away from this, you cannot pretend it did not happen, and I will not allow you to. Your krullshit ends here and now!"

Fury blazed within her, hot and explosive.

"You do not get to tell me how I feel!" she screamed, grabbing the nearest loose object. She twisted, swinging her arm, and used all her strength to hurl it at him.

Even with almost no time to react and less than a meter of distance between them, Kronus was almost fast enough to catch the pillow. His hands closed around it the same instant it struck his face. For a moment, he was still, *terribly* still, and then he threw the pillow across the room. He bared his teeth, eyes smoldering with anger.

Eva dug her fingers into the bedding as she glared at him. "You have no damned right!"

"This is you," he repeated in a low voice, his red skin belying his relatively controlled tone. "There was not any good reason for what happened to you, but it is *done*. Your scars are no cause for shame. You received your wound with honor and selfless-ness. *You* have no reason to hide."

For a moment, Eva was speechless, her features relaxing slightly. He raged, she could tell by the tension radiating from him, from his eyes, and the color of his skin, but his words were…kind, in their own way. Why was he still here with her? Why did he endure her pessimism, her anger, her ungrate-fulness?

Eva studied him as the silence stretched between them, their harsh breaths the only sounds in the room.

What did he mean that *she* had no reason to hide?

His words from the pasture came back to her in a rush.

I am no longer worthy of my home.

"What are you hiding from, Kronus?" she asked softly.

The muscles of his jaw bulged, making the cords of his neck stand out. His skin reverted to its normal coloring slowly; she had the sense that he was willing it to do so, fighting back whatever turmoil was within him.

"You have earned some rest. I will find Aymee and ask about your next meal." He turned away, gathered the pillow off the floor, and tossed it, along with the wadded blanket, onto the foot of the bed. That done, he moved toward the door, his upper body oddly stiff in contrast to the fluidity of tentacles.

Eva watched him go with a frown. When she could no longer hear the familiar drag of his movements from the hall-way, she looked down at her left leg and raised it. The bit remaining below her knee — little more than a nub — moved with ease. There was nothing to weigh it down; no shin, ankle, or foot to lift, and she could not help her emotional response to the sight. It was unnatural. Incomplete. She could *almost* see, in her mind's eye, what her leg had looked like before.

If she stopped and forced herself to consider it rationally, it was just a leg. A leg that happened to end quite a bit sooner than it used to. It was different, yes, but it was still the same thing it had always been.

She shifted her gaze to the crutches against the wall. Using them hadn't been easy, hadn't been comfortable, hadn't been pleasant, but…it had been better than nothing.

It had been a *start*.

CHAPTER 10

KRONUS RETURNED SEVERAL TIMES OVER THE NEXT FEW DAYS, rarely leaving Eva alone. He made sure she ate every bite of every meal and forced her to get up and move regularly. They bickered frequently — he issued commands she often defied, usually just to spite him. Despite the struggles, Eva pushed herself just as hard as he did.

The crutches became easier to use as she recovered her strength. Kronus responded to her increasing endurance by making her walk farther every time; when he decided she'd mastered walking around the clinic, he made her go outside. Though he didn't relent to her complaints about going outside, he never forced her beyond the street immediately in front of the clinic, and she appreciated that small courtesy.

He was always gruff with her, but his constant presence and willingness to catch her whenever she fell made it clear that he cared about her wellbeing — even if she couldn't figure out *why*. He refused to accept whining or self-pity. And though he often angered and riled her, Eva found herself looking forward to his visits.

The more time they spent together, the more she noticed his

little quirks — from the slight twist of his lips when something amused him to the subtle changes in coloration that flashed over his skin, signaling shifts in mood he otherwise masked.

The rest was more difficult to figure out. She'd realized after her first few prolonged conversations with him — if they could be called that — that there was far more information to be gleaned from what Kronus didn't say than what he did. He wasn't a fan of answering questions, and though it frustrated her, his evasiveness had soon begun to shape a picture of what went on inside his head.

If her inferences were right, Kronus was as lonely and broken as she was. Was that why he sought to help her? To find companionship, as terrible as hers might be?

Kronus's physical differences, while impossible to ignore, had almost become familiar to her. She didn't fear his claws or sharp teeth and was fascinated by his tentacles and their movement, which also changed subtly based on his mood...and she never forgot the way they felt against her bare skin.

She found herself often thinking back to their near-kiss, recalling the way he'd held her chin, the way he'd looked at her as though she were all he could see, and the little kisses from his suction cups as his tentacle had caressed her leg.

Though she had imagined his mouth meeting hers many times since then, she couldn't begin to guess how his lips would feel. Kronus seemed comprised of unpredictable contrasts. His skin was soft but the muscle beneath was rock-solid; his demeanor was gruff and irritable, but his actions were considerate; and he was large and almost brutish in appearance but moved with grace and confidence, handling her with the utmost gentleness. His lips looked soft and yielding, but would they prove firm and unforgiving instead?

She finally pried her eyes from his lips, raised a spoonful of stew to her mouth, and ate. As she chewed, she watched him. His attention was on the piece of wood in his left hand. His right hand moved a knife along the wood, shaving off bits and pieces to slowly shape something new. It was the third time she'd seen him at the task.

"My father used to carve like that," she said after swallowing her food.

"Poorly?" he asked without looking up. There was a small pile of wood shavings on the floor beneath him; Aymee's admonishments had yet to deter him.

"Why do you say that?"

Grasping the carving between two fingers, he held it up as though it supported his statement without further comment. It was a four-legged creature with a long neck and little horns that looked like they'd snap off at the most delicate touch.

"Oh, it's a perfectly good sheep," she said, barely keeping a straight face.

His jaw clenched for a moment. "It is a *krull*," he replied.

An amused sound escaped Eva. She returned her attention to the stew, hurriedly scooping another spoonful into her mouth to stifle her laughter. Kronus glared at her with low brows from the corner of her eye. To her surprise, one corner of his mouth tipped up slightly before he lowered his head and resumed his carving.

She chewed silently, watching his hands move. And they were nice hands. *Really* nice. Large, strong, with long lean fingers, and…

Eva swallowed and cleared her throat. "He used to carve little animals and people for me and my siblings when we were kids. We had an entire farm with enough people to make a village." She looked down into her half-empty bowl. "He's a trapper, so he spent a lot of time in the jungle. He'd bring home chunks of wood, and we'd all gather around him and watch him doing what you're doing now. My elder brother picked up the talent, but I didn't. I was never really any good with my hands when it came to small, detailed things. Probably because I always had trouble sitting still long enough to get anything done."

He was quiet for a time, and in that silence, she thought she could almost hear the faint sound of the knife moving over the wood.

"Your home is far from here, is it not?" he finally asked.

Eva frowned, set the spoon in the bowl, and absently rubbed her arm. Did she have a home anymore? She'd given up her childhood home to be with Blake, and the home she'd made with him was gone now.

But she hadn't left her family on bad terms; however hard it had been to move on, Eva's relationship with her parents and siblings remained intact.

"Yeah, it is," she said.

He exhaled heavily. "I know how difficult that can be. Your family may not be here, but I am sure they care for you very much."

His words helped a little. She missed her family terribly, and the reminder that they cared provided some comfort.

"What about you?" Eva looked up at him. "Do you have family?"

"Kraken do not...*did* not have family the way humans do."

She furrowed her brow. "I know you said kraken prefer solitude, but...surely you had a mother? A father?"

"I never knew my sire and was only with my mother until I was of age to hunt with the males," he replied. His hands stilled, and he lifted his face to meet her gaze. "Things are...different now for some of my people."

"Because of...us? The humans who joined with kraken here in The Watch?"

"Because of both your people and mine." He looked at the carving again, which he turned slowly in his hand. "Not all kraken welcomed those changes, just as they have not been welcomed by all humans."

"Well, it's a good thing you're not one of them, isn't it?"

His shoulders rose and fell with a deep inhalation. His color darkened, but the change was subtle enough that it *almost* seemed a trick of her eyes. "I was."

Eva stared at him while idly tracing the edge of the spoon handle with the tip of a finger. "Why are you here then, Kronus?"

"Why do you insist on knowing?" he growled. "Why is it so important for you to have an answer for that?"

Eva glared at him. "Maybe I'm just trying to get to know you, to understand you!" She pressed her lips together and took a slow, steadying breath. "You make it really difficult."

He narrowed his eyes at her, but his lips parted briefly as though in surprise. He regained his composure quickly and pointed to her bowl. "Eat."

She met his gaze and held it. "Make me."

Kronus set aside his knife and the carving and pushed himself toward the bed. His approach halted only when the door opened.

Aymee stepped inside carrying a large basket in her arms. Her eyes flicked between Kronus and Eva several times before dropping to the pile of wood shavings on the floor. She scowled. "Damnit, Kronus, I told you not to do that in here!"

"You act as though your people did not invent brooms," Kronus snapped.

"Then learn to use one!"

He extended a tentacle toward the pile, keeping his gaze locked with Aymee's.

Her eyes narrowed. "Don't you dare."

The end of his tentacle curled and drew back from the pile slightly — not a retreat, but the wind-up for a swing.

"Kronus, I swear, if you—"

His tentacle swept forward, scattering the wood shavings across a half-meter long portion of the floor.

Aymee's growl of frustration was drowned out by a burst of laughter; though Eva struggled to contain it, she only laughed harder the more she fought. Tears welled in her eyes, her chest ached, and Kronus and Aymee stared at her in shock, but it felt *good*.

Her laughter soon died down as she caught her breath and wiped her eyes with the back of her hand.

"Okay then," Aymee said, clearing her throat and battling away her smile before she looked at Kronus. "You're still cleaning it up."

"Fine," Kronus replied. His golden eyes didn't move away from Eva; they shone with a new light, one she hadn't seen before.

Aymee stepped farther into the room and set the basket onto the counter. All mirth slipped away from her features, and she winced as she spoke. "Blake came by today."

Eva's smile fled, and her heart thumped hard in her chest.

"Why did you not tell me? I would gladly have cast him out," Kronus grumbled.

"He didn't stay long. He wanted…" Aymee glanced at the basket. "He brought your belongings, Eva."

Eva stared at the basket silently.

So that was it. Everything she owned tucked away neatly in a basket, as easily cast aside as she had been. Her eyes burned with the threat of tears. The humor she'd experienced a moment before made this hurt even more.

Aymee sighed, glanced at Kronus with an arched a brow, and looked back to Eva. "I will be outside if you need me." She closed the door quietly behind her once she'd slipped out of the room.

Eva's attention returned to the basket, which was reduced to a brown blur through her welling tears.

"How does this make you feel?" Kronus asked in a menacingly low voice.

"I don't want to talk about it," she said, pushing aside the food tray and the half-eaten stew. She didn't owe Kronus anything. She'd never asked for him to be here.

Kronus inserted himself between Eva and the basket. His skin was scintillating with shades of red as he grasped the bedrail and leaned closer to her. "How do you feel, human? Sorry for yourself? Sad?"

Eva drew back and glared at him. "Leave me alone, Kronus."

"Did you lose your leg or your spine? You are pathetic," he sneered.

Her hand flew up and connected with his cheek before she even registered its movement. The crack of flesh meeting flesh resounded through the room, and his head snapped to the side with the force. Her palm stung from the impact.

She recoiled as he turned his face back toward her; she hadn't meant to do it, hadn't even thought about it.

There was a fire in his eyes, but it wasn't fueled by the fury she'd expected. Maroon rippled across his skin, mingling with the crimson. "Are you angry, female?"

"I didn't mean to—"

"Are you *angry*?" he growled, looming over her. "Are you angry about the way I talk to you? About the deaths of your friends, about the loss of your leg, about the way your mate abandoned you like you were a piece of refuse he'd grown tired of?"

Fresh tears, tears of anguish and fury, gathered in her eyes. She pressed her hands to his shoulders and shoved, but he didn't budge. "Why are you doing this?"

"Because anger is a tool, and you have failed to utilize yours to its full potential. Be angry, Eva. Latch onto it. He cannot harm you in your fury. Latch onto it and see how strong you are!"

"I can't!"

"If you couldn't, you would have died with them." He

reached forward and grasped her jaw. She could feel the pinpricks of his claws against her cheeks. "You fought for them. Now is the time to fight for *yourself*. You deserve better than what Blake has given you. And you will not lie down and take whatever krullshit he or anyone else tries to throw your way. You are better than all of them, and you will know it if I have to shout it at you every day for the rest of your life!"

Eva blinked, her tears falling as she stared into his eyes, searching them; they were filled with fury, passion, a hint of desperation, but above all a sense of *need*. His lips were pulled back, his sharp teeth bared, their white color a stark contrast to the red tones of his skin.

She reached out and cupped his jaw. "Why are you doing this for me, Kronus?" she asked softly, brushing her thumb over his cheek.

He nearly recoiled from her touch, confusion flitting across his expression — as though the last thing he expected was for his aggression to be answered with gentleness.

"Because someone must remind you of your worth even if you cannot see it yourself," he replied.

"Does anyone see yours?"

His brow furrowed, and the tension faded from his jaw as his mouth fell open. His eyes shifted from side to side without looking away from hers. "I have done things that cannot be forgiven, Eva," he rasped.

The rawness of his answer stunned Eva. She hadn't expected him to respond, hadn't expected this vulnerability in him. Perhaps she was looking into it too deeply, but she couldn't help feeling like he'd opened himself to her, if only in a tiny way, had shown his trust in her.

"Because they won't forgive you, or because you won't forgive yourself?" she asked, sliding her fingers over his jaw soothingly.

He closed his eyes and leaned into her touch. His hold on

her face eased slightly, and the pads of his fingers trailed over her skin with surprising delicacy despite the strength he possessed. Just as he seemed on the verge of leaning closer still, he lowered his hand and withdrew from her touch.

Kronus opened his eyes and met her gaze. "I am here for *you*, Eva. And I will not let you fall."

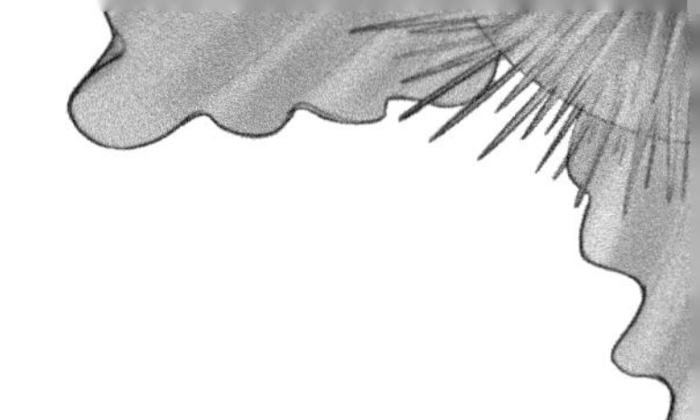

CHAPTER 11

KRONUS WAS GONE WHEN EVA WOKE THE NEXT MORNING. SHE looked around the room; the wood shavings had been cleaned up, the door was closed, and golden sunlight streamed in through the gauzy curtains. Eva frowned as she sat up.

It was strange not having him beside her, whether he was pushing her through exercises, forcing her to eat, or carving a piece of wood with an exaggerated look of concentration on his face. For days now, he'd been there when she went to sleep and when she rose. A pang of guilt struck her. When did he rest? Didn't he long for his home, for his own space? He'd stuck by her, pushing her to do better and refusing to let her wallow in self-pity.

I will *do better.*

He'd been right. She was *alive,* and it was because of him. Twice he'd saved her, and he continued to make her fight, continued to insist she was worth saving. It was time she showed Kronus that she *wanted* to live. That she was willing and able to fight for herself.

Deciding to take advantage of the privacy, Eva pushed herself to the edge of the bed, grabbed her crutches, and propped the pads under her arms. Sliding the rest of the way off the bed, she found her balance and walked to the bathroom.

Though it was a simple, plain room, it benefited from the clinic's status as one of the surviving structures from the colonization — there was a toilet and a sink with running water on one side, and a large showerhead on the other with a drain in the tile floor beneath it. A floral-patterned curtain provided the only color in the room. Sturdy-looking handles were bolted to the wall near the shower, and a seat jutted out from beneath them.

Eva relieved herself and quickly stripped out of the clinic gown. Her flesh pebbled at the chill in the air. She turned on the shower and stepped into the spray as soon as the water was steaming, leaving her crutches against the wall outside the splash zone.

The hot water sluiced down her body, and she nearly moaned at how good it felt. She'd been surprised by the easily accessed hot water the first time she'd showered here two days ago. Nothing in Emmiton had been maintained well enough to grant hot water on command; a warm bath meant building a fire first. Though most homes in The Watch had running water, she didn't know anyone who could turn on their faucets and have hot water on demand.

She'd asked Aymee about it, and Aymee had explained that more resources had been devoted to keeping the clinic running than any other building in town simply to ensure that the townsfolk had the best care possible over the long years since the first colonists landed.

Once she'd finished showering, she dried off, dressed, collected her crutches, and returned to her room. She was sitting on the edge of the bed brushing her hair when there was a knock at the door, which opened a few moments later. Aymee poked her head through, caught Eva's gaze, and grinned.

"I have a surprise for you," she said, stepping into the room.

There was a familiar, faint dragging sound behind her, and Eva watched expectantly for Kronus, her heart suddenly fluttering. Except it wasn't Kronus who entered the room behind Aymee. Though this kraken looked about as tall as Kronus, he had a leaner build, and his skin was blue-gray with dark stripes on his head, shoulders, and tentacles. He had a long, black container in his hands. Eva couldn't tell by looking at it if it was plastic or metal.

"Eva, this is my mate, Arkon," Aymee said, turning her head to smile at the male. The adoration was clear in her eyes.

A voice — Hailey's voice — echoed in Eva's mind.

How can anyone *stand to be touched by those things? They're disgusting. It's probably like being touched by a bunch of worms, all cold and slimy.*

But the kraken's tentacles weren't cold and slimy, and Kronus's touches hadn't made Eva think of worms at all. The kraken were just *people*, with likes and dislikes, with feelings that could be hurt just like her own. And they were capable of *love*.

Eva saw it as she looked at Arkon — the light in Aymee's eyes was reflected in his, and a warm, gentle smile played on his lips. Eva couldn't recall Blake looking at her like that during their time together. With lust, yes, but never such raw, pure affection.

She clutched the fabric of the gown over her heart. "Hi."

Arkon turned his attention to her. "It is a pleasure to finally meet you, Eva."

Eva furrowed her brow. "Finally?"

"Aymee has spoken of you often. We've been trying to come up with something to help you get back to some semblance of normalcy." He moved to the bed and set the container down atop it, facing her, and hurriedly unlatched the clasps. "Now, this was built using technology we do not fully understand and records that are centuries old, and it will likely require adjustment over time, but...I think it will prove useful to you."

The excitement in his words piqued Eva's curiosity.

Arkon moved aside and gestured to the container. "Go ahead, Eva. Open it."

She glanced at Aymee. The woman smiled encouragingly.

Scooting closer to the container, Eva raised the lid and peered in. It took her several moments to understand what she was looking at.

The object within was long and black, gracefully shaped. Its inside appeared hollow, visible through the intricate patterns forming it — twisting, spiraling shapes ran around the not-quite-cylindrical object, flowing in such a way that made it impossible to tell where they began or ended.

Were it not for the foot — which was no less graceful despite its relative simplicity — at the narrower end, she might not have realized it was a *leg*.

She looked up at Arkon and Aymee. "This is for me? You... did this?"

Arkon nodded. The smile he'd worn for Aymee had widened into a delighted grin. "I hope you don't mind the embellishments I made. They shouldn't compromise its structural integrity at all, but I did not find the original design appealing."

"You *made* this?"

"To be fair, I only designed it based on existing plans," Arkon replied. He leaned forward and carefully lifted the leg out of the container, presenting it to her on flattened palms. "It was made by a machine in the Facility."

Eva stared at the limb in his hands. "Facility?"

"It's an underwater building off-shore," Aymee said, stepping closer to Eva. "It's where the kraken are from. Where they were created, actually." She raised the end of Eva's gown just enough to uncover her left leg mid-thigh. Her fingers probed around Eva's knee, then down to the stump. "How does this feel?"

"A little sore, but not terrible." Eva returned her gaze to the artificial leg; she was completely floored by what they'd done for her.

"It's healing wonderfully. The boosters really helped." Aymee reached toward the container and removed a couple other items from within. She held them up for Eva's inspection. One of the items looked like an oversized sock, while the other was made of a rubbery material with a metal pin at the end. Aymee placed the sock on the bed and took the rubbery thing in both hands. "This is a liner. You'll wear this to keep the prosthesis in place."

Eva felt like she was in a dream as Aymee crouched in front of her, gently lifted Eva's left leg, and eased the liner onto the stump and up to Eva's thigh.

"Wear this over your leg to make it a snugger fit," Aymee said as she rolled the sock on over the liner. "Millie, one of the weavers, is going to have a few more of these ready for you in a few days."

"As I said, we will have to make adjustment as time progresses," Arkon said. "The musculature of your leg will alter as you grow accustomed to it, so it will take some tinkering to get everything to fit properly for the long term."

Aymee glanced up at Eva and grinned. "I kind of…scanned and measured your leg while you were sleeping for this one."

Eva didn't know what to say. The lengths to which they'd gone for her — Kronus, Aymee, and Arkon — left her speechless.

Arkon handed over the prosthesis, which Aymee slid into place.

Aymee rose and held out her hand. "Let's get you standing."

Eva took it and slid off the edge of the bed. As soon as her weight pressed down on the prosthetic leg, there was a click. The pressure on her stump was strange but not entirely uncomfortable. Using Aymee as balance, she lifted her left leg, and the prosthesis rose off the floor. Tears stung her eyes as she lowered her foot.

"I...I don't know what to say." Eva looked up at Aymee and Arkon, smiling. "Thank you."

Aymee's smile widened, and, though it seemed impossible, Arkon beamed with *more* excitement. His tentacles moved restlessly beneath him and his eyes were bright.

"Try walking," he said.

Leaning on Aymee, Eva took a tentative step forward, then another, and another. She kept a tight grip on Aymee's hand as she walked slowly around the room. Her gait was clumsy; being unable to feel her left foot reminded her of the times she'd sat on her leg for too long and made it go numb, of those moments when all she could feel of her leg was dead weight before the pins and needles struck. It would take time to adapt her stride to the prosthetic leg's movement, but she was *walking*. Her lack of grace made no difference.

Eva turned her head and stilled; Kronus filled the doorway, one of his hands curled around the doorframe. His brow furrowed as his gaze swept over Aymee and Arkon, but the confusion smoothed from his expression when he looked at Eva. For the first time since she'd met him, Kronus smiled — not the smug half-smirk he sometimes wore when he was amused, but a real, genuine smile that sparkled in his golden eyes.

Feeling suddenly shy, Eva turned toward him, placed her free hand on the bed rail for balance, and lifted the hem of her gown to reveal the prosthesis. "What do you think?"

"You are walking," he said.

"Arkon and Aymee made it." She lifted the leg off the floor and extended it. "It's amazing!"

"A little practice, and she'll be walking without any help," Aymee said. She gently removed her hand from Eva's and stepped aside as Kronus entered the room.

He approached Eva slowly, his eyes not once leaving hers until he was immediately before her. His tentacles spread wide, and his torso dropped low. Carefully, he cradled the back of her prosthesis in his palm, tucking the heel against the inside of his elbow, and trailed the fingertips of his other hand over its patterns.

Were she to close her eyes and concentrate hard enough, Eva might've been able to imagine how his touch would've felt against her real limb. The thought sent a warmth through her that coalesced low in her belly, and she found herself wishing he was touching her right leg instead.

"I recognize Arkon's work," Kronus said, lifting his gaze to meet hers, "but this leg belongs fully to you."

Eva's cheeks flushed, and she smiled. "You like it then?"

Kronus nodded. He guided her foot back to the floor, withdrew his hands, and rose. "More importantly, *you* like it."

Her smile widened, and she turned her gaze to Aymee and Arkon just in time to catch the startled glance they exchanged.

"You…you met with the others this morning to discuss the situation with the razorbacks, did you not?" Arkon asked, turning his attention to Kronus. "Do you have any news?"

A sliver of fear raced down Eva's spine at the mention of razorbacks.

Kronus seemed reluctant as he shifted his gaze to Arkon. "A few more sightings along the coast, but even one sighting is more than there should be. Dracchus is organizing hunting parties from both The Watch and the Facility to stalk the spawning areas for razorback along the coastline. For now, it is still unsafe to travel the water without an armed group."

"Guess we'll need to organize an escort," Aymee said, frowning. "Macy is going insane with worry about our trip back to the Facility as it is."

"W-Why would you go then?" asked Eva.

"Thana is nearing her birthing time. She normally assists the other female kraken during their births, but she wanted me to be there to help when her child comes." Aymee glanced at Arkon and smiled softly. "Kraken females have difficulties getting pregnant, so it's an exciting thing, and I want to make sure she has all the aid she needs for a safe delivery.

"Which brings us to our next topic of discussion." Aymee stepped closer to Eva and took her hand again. "I think you're ready to leave the clinic."

Eva felt the blood drain from her face. She withdrew her hand from Aymee's and stepped back, bumping against the bed. Where would she go? She had nowhere, no place she belonged. "I-I don't..."

Aymee held up her open palms in a placating manner. "Shh, I know. And we'd never force you out of here without somewhere to go. My parents have a couple open rooms, if—"

Kronus clasped Eva's hand, his hold firm but not painful. "She will stay with me."

"What?" Eva breathed, turning her wide eyes toward Kronus. Had she heard him correctly? Had he just...

He held her gaze. "You will stay with me, female. In my den. My...*house*."

"Oh, um," Aymee cleared her throat. "Are you okay with that, Eva?"

Eva searched the swirling depths of molten gold that were his eyes, and her heart beat faster. The hand holding hers was warm, comforting. Stable. Kronus was her rock. Though she hadn't known him before the attack, he'd been there from that moment, remaining strong and true even when everything else in her life fell apart. He'd kept her grounded when all she'd wanted to do was float away.

The expectancy and vulnerability in his gaze were accompanied by hope — but the light of that hope seemed muted, guarded, wary.

"Yeah," Eva said softly, squeezing his hand. "I would like that."

She *wanted* that.

It was a surprising realization. Only a couple weeks ago, she'd been joined with Blake, content with her life. What did it mean that she was so ready to stay with Kronus, that she secretly craved even the smallest of his touches? Did that make her just as bad as Blake?

No. He left *me.* Discarded *me.*

It had been Kronus who'd stuck by her, not Blake. The days she'd spent with Kronus had been difficult, had contained more than their share of discomfort and pain, but they'd been *real*, and he hadn't given up on her. He'd taken Eva at her worst and hadn't even batted an eye. It was only natural that she'd develop some feelings for the kraken.

"Okay," Aymee said, pulling Eva's attention away from Kronus. "That's...that's good!" She glanced at the ochre kraken and grinned knowingly before looking back to Eva. "Let me show you how to remove the prosthesis and care for it, then we can get you some breakfast."

Eva tilted her head down and listened as Aymee went through the steps, demonstrating how to release the pin and disconnect the limb, how to remove the liner, and how to put it all back on again. As Aymee spoke, Eva glanced up to find Kronus watching raptly. When Aymee pushed up Eva's gown a little higher, Kronus's gaze followed her hand to Eva's exposed flesh. Fire gleamed in his eyes when they met Eva's again.

Her breath fled her, and desire bloomed in her core in response under the intensity of his stare.

What have I agreed to?

Surprisingly, she found that her anticipation greatly outweighed her fear.

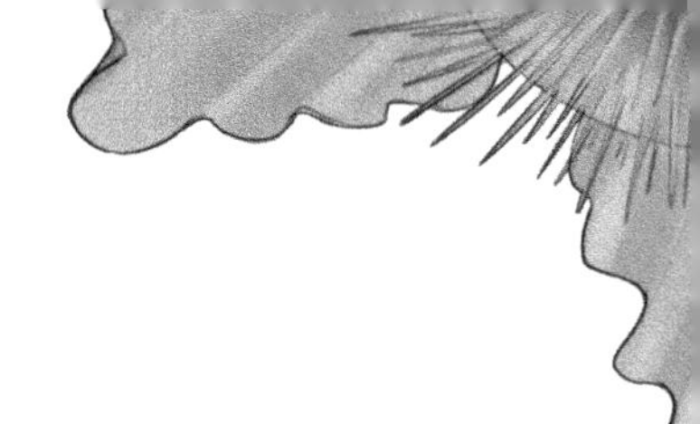

CHAPTER 12

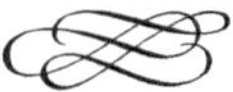

THE EVENING SUN CAST GOLDEN LIGHT THROUGH THE SEA-FACING windows of Kronus's dwelling, creating long, deep shadows in contrast to the pure, powerful illumination. The quality of the light only emphasized how unprepared he was to care for a human.

His furnishings were sparse. He had no need for anything beyond a bed and a table, and the upright cabinet a human would've used to hold clothing served as storage for the few weapons and tools he'd accumulated over his time in The Watch — a harpoon gun with a few harpoons and a single tether line, a spear, several knives and carving tools he'd yet to use, a small net, and a few sturdy sacks.

Kronus wasn't sure where to start.

Did Eva have clothing, or would he need to obtain some? What sort of plants could humans eat? More importantly, which plants did she prefer? His isolation had taught him little regarding such matters. He knew humans were as capable and varied as his people, that they had immense capacity for hard work, cooperation, and kindness while at the same time being susceptible to their own prejudices, but that was nearly the extent of his knowledge.

He began at the most logical point — he cleared the cabinet of his tools and weapons, so she'd have a place to store her belongings. Once that was done, he removed his blankets and bedding from the bed and set them up in the corner, creating a nest-like spot for him to sleep. Then he opened his wooden storage chest and pulled out all the spare bedding it contained. Macy had insisted he take it all when he moved into this den, just in case he ever needed it. He'd not understood the reasoning behind it, but he'd accepted, if only to end the uncomfortable conversation before he said something to cause conflict. As he arranged it atop the bed now, he finally understood. Though it had taken time, the extra bedding finally had a purpose.

With the bed made as neatly as he could manage, he slid the table against the wall beneath the seaside window. The sunlight, now more orange than gold, fell on the little carving laid atop the table — the one-legged human female.

A strange sensation crept through him, making his chest tight and his stomach hollow. The wooden figure seemed alone and out of place; naked, vulnerable and fragile. A precious thing to be protected.

Kronus poured through his mind for a word Arkon had once explained to him, a word that meant something was being used to represent another thing, even if there wasn't a direct connection or correlation between the two things.

Meta...metaphor?

He shrugged off both the word and the feeling. Arkon was much better suited to such thoughts. Kronus had a purpose, the completion of which would directly affect Eva, which meant there was no time to ponder unimportant matters. His den needed to be prepared for her. He needed to be able to provide everything she wanted and required.

And he couldn't determine what she'd require on his own.

After exiting his den, Kronus paused to glance seaward. The setting sun lit the water with a brilliant golden-orange glow, highlighted by shimmering sparks of white that contrasted the darker patches woven throughout. All of it was in constant motion, bound only by the distant horizon. The beach below the rise was peaceful and undisturbed; undoubtedly, the presence of razorbacks in the coastal waters was keeping the people who dwelled in the nearby houses from enjoying the beach where they so loved to swim and play.

Regardless, the scene was beautiful, and the sound of gentle waves against the shore was soothingly familiar to Kronus. He'd never stopped to appreciate beauty before. Instead, he'd voiced doubts about Arkon and Jax for their pursuits of it, whether through art or exploration, because that was not the kraken way.

And now, Kronus was going to ask Jax for help.

Because I finally found something beautiful. Something of my own.

He turned away from the sea and moved along the path that linked all the dwellings on the ridge. Jax and Macy lived in the next-to-last building of the row relative to Kronus's den.

Some of the people from the nearby dwellings were outside; Kronus silently acknowledged their greetings as he passed them, grateful that most had given up on engaging him in conversation months ago. He harbored no ill will toward any of them — he simply had little to say and found what humans called *small talk* to be tedious and largely without a point.

At any other time, for most any other reason, Kronus's last shreds of pride would've prevented him from asking Jax and Macy for any assistance, no matter how dire the situation. He'd already caused them so much suffering and heartache, and he couldn't look at them without being reminded of everything that had transpired — without recalling the blood that had been spilled because he'd pushed and pushed beyond reason. What right did he have to ask them for anything?

Their dwelling came into view farther down the path. It was built with the same wood and stone as his own, with a similar design, but theirs was larger; it was sized not to accommodate a lone kraken, but a family. A family that wouldn't have come to exist if Kronus had had his way. A pang of shame pierced his chest. All he could do was grit his teeth and continue forward.

He truly had no right to ask *anything* of them, but his pride and misgivings, his discomfort and guilt, had no choice but to bow before Eva's needs. For her, he would ask, and he would pay any price necessary.

The younglings Sarina, Eros, and Jace were playing in the grass in front of the dwelling. Kronus slowed as he neared them; he'd seen them at play more times than he could count since he took his den nearby, but he still found it a strange sight. Before coming to The Watch, he'd only had contact with a single youngling who was not being trained as a hunter — Rhea's headstrong, adventurous daughter, Melaina. Male kraken only dealt with male younglings who were of age to learn how to hunt. All others were entrusted to the care of adult females and kept sheltered in a different portion of the Facility.

Macy emerged from the dwelling, stopping in the open doorway with a hand on the doorframe. Her clothing molded to her form, revealing her rounded stomach; she'd have a third youngling soon enough.

"Eros, don't pull Sarina's hair!" she called, her tone somehow gentle and commanding at once. She turned her head toward Kronus, who was only a few body-lengths away, and started. Once her initial surprise faded, she smiled.

Part of Kronus longed to find deceit in her eyes, or veiled hatred, or disgust. In some ways, it would've been easier to deal with than the warmth of her expression. Her loathing would've been less unsettling than her forgiveness.

"Is there something you need, Kronus?" Macy asked.

His throat felt suddenly constricted. "I… Is Jax here?"

"Not yet. He went to the dock with Randall a little while ago, but he should be back soon."

A squeal of laughter sounded as Sarina raced toward Kronus with Jace following close behind. Her tentacles flowed over the grass with speed and grace exceeding her age. She ducked behind Kronus.

"He's going to get me!" she cried, peering around her cover.

Jace stopped just outside the reach of Kronus's tentacles and grinned at Sarina — it was a wicked expression, promising mischief. Like Sarina and Eros, Jace was a kraken-human mix. All three children favored their fathers and would have passed for full-blooded kraken were it not for the hair on their heads and their more pronounced noses.

Kronus stared at Jace, who glanced up to meet his gaze.

Eyes narrowed, Jace lifted a hand to point a small, claw-tipped finger at Sarina. "She's mine."

Tilting his head, Kronus regarded the small male. Jace was only a few years old, but young kraken developed quickly — at least twice as fast as their human counterparts, it seemed. Still, he was too young to have been sent to learn with the hunters. Was his claim on Sarina part of a game the younglings were playing? Males did not choose females according to kraken tradition.

Haven't I broken that tradition?

The realization struck him hard. He'd known since the events in the Facility two years before that the old ways would not last, *could* not last, unless they were essential for the survival of their people. Though he'd been enraged at the thought of kraken males mating with human females, it had become clear in the time since that humans — not all of them, but most of them — were a good thing for his kind.

With so many more females available, was it wrong for a male to be forward in his pursuit of them?

"Sarina, Jace, come away and leave Kronus alone," Macy said, beckoning the elder younglings as she scooped up Eros. He wrapped his small tentacles around her arm.

Kronus eased himself down to get nearer to Jace's eye level. "She is yours?"

Jace lifted his chin higher and nodded once.

"What does she say about that?" Kronus asked.

The boy's confidence wavered. His gaze flicked past Kronus, who turned his head to see Sarina behind him, watching Jace.

"So, what do you say?" Kronus asked the girl.

Sarina frowned slightly, but didn't seem to have an answer, either.

"You are both very young," Kronus continued.

"I would make a good protector," Jace declared.

Kronus turned back to Jace. Macy stood in the background, a hand covering her mouth to hide her grin. The seriousness on the youngling's face was astounding, but Kronus's surprise diminished when he reminded himself that this was Arkon and Aymee's child; of course he was intelligent and headstrong. But he was still so young, so inexperienced.

"Do you have a mate, Kronus?" Sarina asked.

Frowning, Kronus dipped his chin. He'd claimed Eva already, and she belonged to his hearts, but did she see it that way? As intelligent as many of them were, humans sometimes seemed oblivious to simple truths. Had she understood the weight of his words on the beach? Had she understood that his claim on her life had been real?

If she hadn't yet, she would before long.

"I do," he replied.

Sarina's little hand settled on his shoulder. "And are *you* a good protector?"

A wave of confused emotion swept through Kronus,

twisting his insides and nearly stealing his breath. Younglings were precious, the future of their people, the ones most worthy and needful of protection. The knowledge that his old attitude would've prevented the birth of this little girl — of *both* these younglings — suddenly fell upon him with the weight of the entire world, crushing him.

He swallowed thickly. "Not as good a protector as I should be." Kronus lifted his face to meet Macy's gaze, making no effort to mask the guilt that had taken hold of his hearts, making no effort to mask the regret sinking like a boulder in his gut. She lowered her hand to her chest, and her smile faltered. "I came to ask your parents if they would help me learn how to do better."

"My daddy is a very good protector," Sarina announced.

"Your mother is, too," Kronus said.

Warmth entered Macy's eyes, and her smile returned — if a bit softer than before.

A chirruping call drew Kronus's attention to the grass, where he saw Ikaros, Randall's prixxir — a four-legged, scaled creature of land and sea — bounding toward them. As Kronus rose, he spotted Dracchus, Randall, and Jax following a few body-lengths behind the excited beast.

"Ikaros!" Eros called, wiggling in his mother's hold. Macy chuckled and lowered him to the ground. The youngling darted off toward the prixxir, and Jace turned to join him.

Kronus clenched his jaw, his eyes shifting to the approaching males. He'd come to ask Jax for help, yes, but he'd not expected Randall and Dracchus, too. They just needed Aymee, Arkon, Rhea, and Dracchus's mate, Larkin, to show up and nearly all the people Kronus had wronged would be gathered together. His skin heated, but he held back the instinctual color change.

He'd fought Jax and Dracchus in numerous challenges.

And he'd never once emerged the victor.

At the edge of Kronus's vision, Eros and Jace reached Ikaros. Giggling, the little kraken pounced on the prixxir, and within moments were riding atop the beast, which had flattened the spiny fin on its back. Randall, grinning, jogged toward Ikaros and the younglings.

Sarina hurried to her father when Jax and Dracchus arrived, launching herself off the ground to wrap her arms around his middle. Jax caught her easily and spun her around; her laughter filled the air.

In direct contrast to that laughter was Dracchus's scrutinous stare at Kronus, which broke only when Jax ceased his spin, and Sarina scrambled from her father to Dracchus. The black kraken brightened immediately as the youngling latched onto his arm.

Jax moved to Macy and took her in an embrace, settling a hand on her stomach. After kissing her, he turned his head toward Kronus, brows low. "What are you doing here?"

Macy frowned at Jax and jabbed her elbow into his side. The gray kraken grunted and gave his mate a questioning look.

"Be nice," she said.

Jax released a heavy sigh and turned back to Kronus. His lips drew back in a forced smile that displayed his pointed teeth. "What are you doing here?" he repeated in a slightly higher pitch.

"Jax!" Macy shoved his shoulders.

Kronus battled the urge to curl his hands into fists. Each of his tentacles threatened to writhe on the ground of its own accord, and he had to still them all individually. He needed to avoid any movement that could be considered confrontational or threatening, no matter what he *wanted* to say or do in response to Jax's tone.

He understood Jax's attitude; even when unthreatened, Jax had always been very protective of his mate and younglings. Kronus understood now more than ever — now that he had Eva.

"I am here to ask for your help," Kronus replied.

Jax and Dracchus stared at Kronus in disbelief. Their silence was total, allowing the sounds of Ikaros, Randall, Eros, and Jace at play to take prominence.

"Is something wrong?" Sarina asked, brows drawn in confusion as she looked between the males. She lifted a hand to Dracchus's face and guided his gaze toward her. "Is Kronus okay?"

Dracchus frowned, seemingly unable to answer.

"He's just fine, Sarina," Macy said, smiling. She shifted in Jax's hold to face Kronus. "What do you need?"

Kronus refused to allow guilt to overwhelm him again. He had this evening and the next day to prepare his dwelling for Eva, and he didn't want to waste any more time. "The human who was injured by the razorback is going to share my den," he said, "but I…I have no idea what food humans need, what items they require for comfort, or how to obtain any of it."

The disbelief on Jax and Dracchus's faces became something closer to shock.

Macy glanced at them, chuckled, and extracted herself from Jax's suddenly slack arms.

"Did I just hear him right?" Randall said, coming up from behind Kronus.

"Kronus has a mate and would like some advice," Macy said.

"A *human* mate," Jax said.

Randall walked past Kronus, eyebrows raised as he regarded him. "Really?" He stopped beside Dracchus and Sarina. "*Him?*"

Kronus clenched his teeth and fought back the red tint slowly overcoming his skin.

"Okay, that's enough," Macy said, glaring at the other males. "We've *all* made our own mistakes, and we can afford to cut Kronus some slack after what he did to atone, can't we?"

"Macy, we—" Jax began.

"Don't you *Macy* me. I'm going inside to gather some things for Eva, and you all better treat our *guest* kindly." She looked at Sarina and held out her hand. "Come help me please, Sarina."

Sarina pecked a kiss on Dracchus's cheek before clambering down to the ground. She extended a tentacle and brushed it over one of Jax's as she passed him, rushing to follow her mother inside.

Kronus watched until Macy was gone, amazed that she had defended him — especially against her own mate and close friends. Though he did not feel worthy of her forgiveness, he was grateful for it. And yet the guilt remained at his core. Eva's words floated up from his memory.

Because they won't forgive you, or because you won't forgive yourself?

Was there a way to forgive himself? Was that possible?

"Eva?" Randall's brow furrowed. "That's the girl who survived the razorback attack, right?"

"Yes," Kronus replied. "Her human male abandoned her... and now she is mine."

Randall chuckled. "Damn. Good for you. I mean, you're an asshole, but you're not a bad guy. Hope it works out well for you. What do you need for her?"

Once again, Kronus was taken aback by the response. It wasn't exactly *nice,* but he didn't need nice. The honesty meant more. "Everything," he replied after a few moments. "Food. Furnishings. Clothing?"

"You could have acquired that anywhere," Jax said. "Why did you come to us?"

Kronus met his gaze and held it. "Because I do not know what she needs, and even if I did, I do not know where to get it. But *you* do. You are part of this place. All of you."

"As are you, Kronus," Dracchus said in his deep, rumbling voice.

Kronus shook his head, unable to hold in a scoff. He shifted his gaze away and immediately hated himself for the display of weakness.

Dracchus moved closer, his huge frame impossible to ignore.

When he was within arm's reach, he stopped. Kronus looked up at him.

"None of us has forgotten the things you said, Kronus, nor the things you did. It is the latter that speaks loudest," Dracchus said. "What you started spiraled out of control and became something you did not intend. I understand that. I have swum those waters myself. But when it came down to action, what did you do?"

"You stood with us," Jax said. "You risked yourself to come back and warn us, and then stood with us when you were given a chance to save your life."

Randall cleared his throat. "We won't forget that. If you hadn't have come back that night, things would've gone a lot different than they did."

"Your earlier actions were made in fear, and I cannot fault you for that," Dracchus continued. "You realized you were wrong, and you changed your course. I have been wrong, too. I should have made it clear to you that you are welcome wherever there are kraken. If you cannot feel at home in the Facility, I should have made you feel at home here."

"I should have, also," Jax said. Something in his tone called Kronus's attention to him; the gray kraken wore a troubled frown, and his brow was creased. "I should have made an effort. I've learned at least that much from Macy."

"I, uh…I think I've already made my stance clear," said Randall. "You're not easy to get along with, Kronus, but whatever issues we had with each other are dead and buried by now. Shit happens. Just have to learn to move on."

Kronus's chest constricted, and his throat burned. What was *this*? He'd come to help Eva, not to see that old conflicts were resolved. This was unnecessary, unbidden, unexpected…and it was overwhelming.

"You waited two years to tell me this and yet called *me* an *asshole*?" he said.

Randall's brows rose, and an instant later he burst into laughter. Jax grinned widely, and even Dracchus, whose mouth seemed locked in a permanent frown, smiled.

Jax and Randall came a little closer as Dracchus moved aside, forming a loose ring with Kronus. There was something casual about it, something…friendly.

"Have you mated with Eva yet?" Randall asked.

Kronus narrowed his eyes at the human. "I do not see how that is any of your concern."

Randall raised his hands, palms displayed in surrender. "I just thought you came here for some advice, but if you don't need it…"

"What are you on about, human?" Kronus demanded. "Your females are not *that* different from kraken."

Dracchus and Jax shared a look, the meaning of which Kronus could not decipher.

"*Are* they?" Kronus asked.

Grin lingering, Randall cleared his throat. "We could just let him find out for himself."

"That may be best." Jax glanced over his shoulder toward his den. "For us, at any rate."

Dracchus nodded with a grunt.

Kronus scowled. "All three of you are *assholes.*"

"Yeah," Randall said with a chuckle. "Guess we may as well start a club."

Kronus tilted his head. "What do you mean?"

"It's a figure of speech," Randall said as all three kraken looked at him questioningly. "You know, because we're all— You know what, never mind. It's not funny when I have to explain everything."

"So speak plainly, human," Dracchus grumbled.

"What were you going to say about human females?" Kronus asked.

Randall sighed. He also glanced toward Jax's den before shifting his gaze to his own home, which was the next down.

What was this hesitancy? Were they afraid of their females for some reason?

Was there some secret they were not meant to share?

Randall leaned closer and lowered his voice. "Human women have something called a *clitoris*." He raised a hand with two fingers pointed down, like a triangle missing its bottom. "This is their…" His cheeks reddened just slightly as his eyes flicked toward the houses again. "You know."

"Their slit," Kronus said.

"Yeah. Right. That's as good a word as any."

"It is *the* word, is it not?"

"There are many," Jax said.

"Humans have more words for that than pretty much anything else," Randall said.

"There are many words for cock as well," Dracchus replied. "More, it seems."

Randall lowered his brows. "Guys, we're getting sidetracked here. Focus, Kronus, because I'm only saying this once." He lifted his other hand and pointed to the point between his two fingers. "Right there, human women have a little nub called a clitoris. You'll want to pay *extra* special attention to it."

"But not all at once," Jax said. "You have to *build* to it."

"Build?" Kronus shook his head. What good were answers that only raised more questions?

"It's really sensitive, so you have to start off easy most of the time." Randall was speaking faster and faster, eyes shifting to Jax's den repeatedly. "You can use your fingers — just watch those claws — or your tongue, or whatever, okay?"

Kronus's brow rose. "Tongue?"

"You just give it some attention…"

"The tongue works *very* well," Dracchus said. "And the taste…" He growled low in his chest and turned his head as though searching, but unlike Jax and Randall's, there was only eagerness on Dracchus's face.

The thought of using his tongue was intriguing; though he'd mated with several kraken females, they'd never used their mouths on one another. He knew humans were fond of kissing, but he'd only seen them do so lips-to-lips — or to other spots on their heads.

"I am not sure I understand all this," Kronus said.

"You will," Jax said.

"It's not complicated," Randall added. "You'll be fine, and it will make her *very* happy."

"But—"

A series of excited chirrups from Ikaros called everyone's attention toward the prixxir. Eros and Jace chased after the animal as it darted toward a trio of approaching females — Rhea, her daughter Melaina, and Larkin, who was both Dracchus's mate and Randall's sister.

"Ikaros!" Melaina shouted, her tentacles lashing over the grass in her rush to meet the prixxir.

"Melaina's here!" yelled Sarina, who bolted out of the house and across the grass like a silver darter. Macy stepped outside behind her, smiling as she looked toward the other females.

Larkin grinned at Dracchus and ran toward him, crossing the distance swiftly. She leapt at her mate, and he caught her with a growl, slamming his mouth against hers. Kronus watched as Dracchus carried Larkin toward their dwelling.

Larkin tore her mouth away from Dracchus's. "Wait! Wait!"

Dracchus growled again and halted. "I've waited long enough, huntress."

"My, you're frisky. Wonder what got into you." Larkin grinned.

"I am more interested in what is about to get into *you*, female."

"Oh my God," Macy said, cheeks flaming. "Dracchus! What did I say about talking that way in front of the kids?"

Dracchus's eyes narrowed under his falling brow. "Why must we delay?" he asked Larkin.

"Rhea has something amazing to tell everyone," Larkin said, her grin broadening.

Kronus swung his gaze to Rhea, who had taken a place beside her mate. Randall had his arm around her shoulders, and she had hers around his middle.

Randall looked at Rhea, brows raised. "What is it?"

She smiled widely, took his hand, and placed it over her abdomen.

For a moment, Randall's features were drawn with confusion, and then his eyes widened. "You mean… We're going to…"

"A youngling," she said and reached up to caress his cheek. "Ours."

"I'm going to be an aunt again!" Larkin yelled with a whoop.

The ensuing excitement and celebration were overwhelming to Kronus; he'd only seen a similar situation once before, after the kraken had come to The Watch to make peace with the humans. This was far more intimate. He felt like an intruder on the moment, but he cast that aside.

A new youngling was *always* a cause for joy. Rhea was a fierce mother, and Randall, despite being physically slower and weaker than a kraken, was a skilled hunter and an unwavering protector of his mate and her daughter. It had never seemed to matter to Randall that Melaina had been sired by another male.

A warm, tingling sensation sparked in Kronus's chest and slowly spread outward. It took him several moments to guess at its nature.

He *wanted* this. He was watching *family*, a group of people who'd come together under less than ideal circumstances and forged bonds stronger than any kraken ever had before. They…

loved each other, would fight and die for one another if necessary, would support each other without hesitation or fail.

What would it be like to have Eva as his mate, his mate *forever*, to share in this companionship and passion and joy? What would Eva look like with her belly rounded with his youngling?

"Now can we return to our den?" Dracchus asked.

"You are now free to have your wicked way with me," Larkin smirked.

Kronus hadn't realized just how quickly kraken could move on land until Dracchus sped off with Larkin. Dracchus had been searching for something while they were speaking of human females, and now Kronus understood what — *who* — he'd been looking for.

Anticipation burned in Kronus's belly; though he still had many unanswered questions, he'd been given a starting point. The thought of exploring his female, of discovering her *clitoris* and every other spot she liked to be touched, was exhilarating. His blood heated; he wanted to please his female the best he could — no, even *better*.

"Kronus?"

He shook off his thoughts abruptly and turned his head to see Macy standing nearby, wearing a patient smile.

"When is Eva supposed to join you?" she asked.

"The day after tomorrow."

Macy nodded. "Let me know before you leave, and I'll grab the basket of stuff I threw together before Larkin and Rhea showed up. I'll bring more by your house tomorrow morning, and if you want, I can go with you into town and show you where to get anything else you need."

Gratitude swelled in his chest, but the words to express it — those deceptively simple words —lodged in his throat. He swallowed thickly and forced them out.

"Thank you," he said gruffly.

It suddenly felt like a weight had been lifted off him.

CHAPTER 13

Eva stood back as Kronus opened the door to his home — *their* home. Her arms and legs were sore after the trip from the clinic; it was by far the longest distance she'd walked since the attack, and she was grateful for her choice to take both crutches well before she'd reached the halfway point. Her prosthesis was amazing, and she was beyond happy with it, but her body needed time and practice to adjust.

She was essentially learning to walk all over again.

A pair of Kronus's tentacles latched onto the inside of the doorframe, and he drew himself inside, twisting his torso to fit the basket containing her belongings through along with him. He hurriedly set the basket down and turned toward her.

Eva stepped closer to the threshold and paused. This was it. As soon as she entered, her old life was gone forever. Whatever waited for her beyond this point would be new, unknown, and...*exciting.*

Nervous, she met Kronus's gaze. His brows were drawn, and there was a frown on his lips. What was he thinking?

If you would throw away your life, then I will claim it as mine.

She wasn't entirely sure of what he'd meant by those words.

Though they made her belly flutter in anticipation, she wasn't quite ready to explore their depth or reflect upon their implications.

One step at a time.

Eva snickered. That phrase didn't really simplify anything anymore, did it?

Planting the crutches on the ground just outside the doorway, she stepped through. But as she took her next step, the foot of her prosthesis caught on the threshold. She attempted to adjust her crutches to salvage her faltering balance, but the tip of one caught on the door jamb, and she teetered through the doorway.

Kronus was an orange blur, darting forward to catch her in his powerful arms before she hit the floor. She followed her immediate instinct and abandoned the crutches to throw her arms around him and anchor herself; they clattered loudly on either side of her as they fell.

He clutched her against him, one large hand spanning over the center of her back and the other over her backside. The familiar scent of land and sea enveloped her, and Eva closed her eyes to breathe him in, absently squeezing him a little tighter.

"I guess I need more practice," she said.

"I think you have had enough for today," he replied. His warm breath tickled the side of her neck.

"I agree."

He rose slowly, drawing her upright along with him. One of his tentacles slid beneath her long skirt to brush over her right shin. She barely suppressed a pleased shiver.

Without further delay, Kronus swept her into his arms, pushed the door closed with a tentacle, and carried her deeper into the house. Eva looped her arms around his neck and studied his profile. As usual, it was hard to guess at his thoughts. He hid his emotions behind a seemingly displeased mask, but she'd caught glimpses of warmth through the cracks.

Kronus turned and gently sat her on a wooden chair with a soft cushion on the seat. She sensed reluctance in him as he drew back.

"Are you all right?" he asked after several moments.

"Tired, but otherwise fine," Eva replied distractedly as she studied the room.

It was a modest space, with everything contained in one room — save the bathroom, which looked to be through a doorway near a corner. She was sitting at a table, which itself was situated beneath a window that looked out on the ocean. For a moment, she stared at the rolling waves, the sound of which set a faint but unmistakable undertone even inside. She'd have that sound lulling her to sleep each night.

The bed was positioned against the wall to her right; it looked freshly made. The front door was straight ahead, with a fireplace, counter, and cabinets in the corner to the left of it. A narrow door at the end of the counter likely opened on a pantry. Immediately to her left, an armoire stood against the rear wall. A large, rectangular woven rug covered the floorboards in the open central space. The furnishings were sparse, but it was…cozy.

Kronus lingered nearby, the tips of his tentacles flicking restlessly. For once, he seemed nervous instead of agitated, and that difference piqued her curiosity.

"What's wrong, Kronus?"

"Nothing is wrong," he replied, a tad too quickly. He shook his head. "I just…" He scowled, and his brow fell low over his eyes. "Is everything to your liking? Should you require more…"

Eva reached out and placed a hand on his forearm. His muscles twitched beneath her palm. She looked up and met his gaze. "I like it."

"We can put your clothing in that," he said, gesturing toward the armoire with his free hand. "Macy gave me extra clothes she thought would fit you, if you need them. And *hangers*, too."

"You asked someone for clothes for me?" Her gaze caught on the harpoons and spear leaning against the wall between the door and the fireplace. Wadded netting and at least two canvas sacks lay on the floor beneath them. The objects had the look of things set down by someone who didn't know where else to put them. It warmed her heart to know he'd gone out of his way to accommodate her, that he'd displaced his own belongings to give her room.

When she looked back at Kronus, he nodded, his lips pressed into a tight line.

She could only imagine how uncomfortable he must've been doing that; Kronus didn't come off as someone who asked for anything, but he'd done so — for her.

She tugged on his arm, silently requesting him to lean down. He obliged. Reaching up with one hand, she cupped his jaw, shifted forward, and pressed her lips to his cheek. They lingered there before she placed another kiss next to the corner of his mouth.

"Thank you, Kronus," she said, releasing him.

He didn't straighten; he remained still, pupils dilated to black, fathomless pools and face slackened by awe. His gaze dipped to her lips. Before she realized what he meant to do, his hand was on the back of her head, and his mouth crashed down upon hers.

Her eyes flared at the suddenness of it, but her surprise swiftly faded as fire ignited within her. She moaned, her eyes fluttering shut as she leaned into the kiss, her hands sliding over his shoulders to wrap her arms around his neck. His lips were firm but yielding, savage but gentle, and the clumsiness of his efforts were more than made up for by his eagerness and passion.

His other hand curled around her hip and tugged her closer until she had no choice but to spread her legs and allow him to wedge himself between them. Her hardened nipples rasped against his chest through her shirt, sending tingles of pleasure straight to her core. Her lips parted in a soft exhalation. She nipped at his bottom lip, first capturing it between her teeth, then soothing it with her tongue.

A long, low groan resonated from his chest, vibrating into her. His hands tightened; the sting on her scalp and the pricks of his claws on her waist only heightened her desire for him. Liquid heat flooded her, dampening her underwear, and her sex clenched with need. She kissed him harder, tasting the sea upon his lips, and beckoned him with her tongue to open his mouth.

She wasted no time when he parted his lips, sliding her tongue between them to dance delicately, teasingly, along the peaks and valleys of his teeth.

But Kronus seemed to be nothing if not a quick learner. He swiftly took charge and reciprocated her attentions; soon, his tongue was exploring *her*, moving with strength and confidence. What would that tongue feel like elsewhere on her body? This kiss alone had her on the edge of an orgasm, and the thought of his head between her legs nearly sent her over.

Her skin prickled, craving more of his touch. Then she felt it — the gentle kisses of his suction cups as one of his tentacles brushed the inside of her thigh, having worked its way under her skirt. She panted against his mouth as the tip of his tentacle moved higher, until, finally, it settled over her sex. The thin layer of fabric separating his skin from hers made no difference when his suction cups moved over her clitoris.

Her climax was swift, overwhelming, *delicious*. To *feel* again — to be *wanted* — after all she'd been through was more exquisite than her wildest imaginings. Eva cried out, tearing her mouth from his as her body stiffened. Her arms and legs tightened around him as though she could draw him into herself. All she could do was breathlessly cling to Kronus until the final, blissful tremor subsided. And yet her body thrummed, eager for more.

"I need more of you, female," he growled as a second tentacle slid up her leg to join the first. His hold on her was firm; she could sense his restraint in the tension of his muscles. He dipped his head and pressed his lips to her neck, flicking his tongue over her skin. "I made my claim on you. Do you accept it?"

The tentacles between her legs stroked her sex as though fighting each other for access. The tip of one wriggled beneath the fabric, delved through her wet folds, and entered her.

"Yes!" Eva rasped, hips bucking against him. She didn't think — *couldn't* think — not when her mind and body were floating on a euphoric high.

"Your *scent*, female." His voice was a low rumbling in his chest.

Two more of his tentacles rose and shoved her skirt up, exposing her legs, and he dropped both hands to her thighs. His palms were scalding hot as they moved up to her pelvis. His claws slipped into her underwear. There was pressure, and the waistband bit into her skin for a moment before the fabric tore. All the while, the tentacles at her sex never stopped, never slowed, stroking her inside and out. Eva's nails sank into his skin, and she bit her lip as another climax stirred within her.

"Kronus," she moaned, tilting her head back.

His hands shifted to her backside, and his tentacle suddenly withdrew from her sex. Her eyes flashed open, and she was about to protest when Kronus pulled her off the chair and *onto* him. She gasped as his cock sank deep inside her. He stretched her, filled her, and that sharp bite quickly turned into something *more*, something tantalizing and pleasurable.

She met his feral, heated gaze and held it, losing herself in its depths.

He coiled his tentacles beneath her and slid his hands to her hips, providing her strength and support as he raised her and slammed her back down. Eva released a choked cry. He pumped again and again, impaling her deeper and deeper with each upward thrust. Blistering pleasure speared her, building ever higher, but she kept her eyes open and locked with his.

"Give me *everything*," he growled, lips drawing back to bare his teeth. The points of his claws pricked her flesh, and his movements grew more powerful, more demanding.

Eva was helpless but to obey. Sensations both agonizing and rapturous surged through her, stealing her breath, her sight, her very self. Her cries filled the room as her body tensed. She writhed upon him and clawed at him, desperate to get even closer as her sex contracted around him, flooding them both with liquid heat. Something stroked her clit; each flutter created a fresh wave of pleasure, prolonging her climax.

Several of Kronus's tentacles curled upward to grasp Eva's waist and legs as he pulled her down a final time; he burst in that moment, releasing a roar as his body hardened and his hot seed filled her. He maintained his hold on her as, with ragged breaths, he shallowly pumped his hips. His cock thrummed inside her. Whatever had been stroking her clit continued to do so, its movements more leisurely but no less pleasing. She shuddered and moaned, resting her head upon his shoulder.

As she caught her breath, Eva brushed her fingertips over Kronus's velvety skin and listened to the strange, rapid rhythm of his heartbeat. Her left leg ached, and her limbs were weak. Her clothing clung to her, irritating her sensitive skin, and sweat trickled between her breasts. His tentacles idly stroked her bare flesh, leaving those little kisses in their wake.

She waited for the guilt, the regret, for the feeling of *wrongness*…but none of them came. This moment felt…*right*. Being with *Kronus* felt right.

She wasn't sure how much time had passed when he finally drew back from her. His movement reminded her that he was still deep inside her.

His eyes dipped. "Next time, these will come off, too," he said, tugging the fabric of her shirt and skirt with his hands.

Next time.

The way this had happened, the way they had come together, was unreal to her. Given everything that had occurred over the last couple weeks, sex had been the furthest thing from her mind when she came here.

But that's not true, is it? I've been looking at Kronus...noticing him. Wanting him.

Despite the unexpected nature of their lovemaking, it was exactly what she'd needed — the perfect way to make this place feel like home. It was proof that Kronus accepted her, completely and undeniably, as she was.

She grinned at him, feeling suddenly bashful, which was absolutely insane since they'd just had sex and his cock was *still* inside her with whatever-they-were stroking her sex.

"Yeah, they will," she said. What would he think of her body once it was bare? She hadn't even fully seen *him*; his cock certainly hadn't been visible before.

His lips curved upward in a smile — only the second real one she'd seen from him. It paired well with the passion smoldering in his eyes. She stared at his mouth, raised a hand, and brushed her thumb across his lower lip.

"You should smile more," she said. "I don't think you do it enough. It suits you."

"I have had little reason to before you," he replied.

The raw honesty in his tone pierced her heart; what kind of life had he lived prior to their first meeting? "I can't imagine your time with me has been all that joyful."

Kronus trailed his claws through her hair. "You are a worthy female with a strong will and a strong heart. I can imagine little as fulfilling as helping you see that." He settled his hands on her hips. "Come. You have had a long day, female. I will bring you food, and then you may rest."

Before she could answer, he rose; gravity pushed her down on his erection, which didn't seem to have diminished at all, and elicited a startled gasp of pleasure from Eva. He gently lifted her off him, sliding his shaft free. She felt immediately bereft. His tentacles guided her feet to the floor, but he did not release his hold on her even after she was standing upright. His seed, combined with her essence, ran down her inner thighs.

"What would you prefer to eat?" he asked. The pads of his fingers trailed over her skirt at her hips. "We have fish and krull meat, and many plants I do not know the names for."

She squeezed her thighs together to slow the flow of liquid. "Um…can I clean up first?"

He tilted his head and lowered his brows as though she'd asked the strangest question in the world. "What do you need to clean up?"

"Um…"

She glanced down, meaning to look at the slick on her thighs. Instead, her eyes trekked along Kronus's muscled torso, past the point near his waist where his skin darkened and caught on his exposed erection. Her heart leapt.

That had been inside her?

His shaft extruded from an open slit at his pelvis. It was long and thick, the dark coloring at his base matching his stripes while the skin at its rimmed tip was a shade lighter than his normal ochre. He lacked a scrotum, and his cock seemed to be secreting its own lubrication, but it was the four two-centimeter-long tendrils around the base that made her eyes flare with true surprise.

Those were what had been stroking her as they made love.

Eva squeezed her thighs together even tighter. She could almost feel the touch of those tendrils, caressing her most intimate flesh.

He followed her gaze downward and grunted softly. "You must rest before I take you again, female."

Eva's head snapped up, and she met his gaze. Heat suffused her cheeks; there was a predatory glint in his eyes that spoke of ecstasy to come.

She cleared her throat. "I, uh, still need to clean up."

He frowned slightly, confusion again creasing his brow. He leaned closer to her, nostrils flaring, before one of his tentacles slid up from her right calf to brush the inside of her thigh. She inhaled sharply.

Understanding eased his expression. "I did not realize. Kraken usually perform such acts in the water." He relinquished his hold on her, shifted aside, and pointed toward the bathroom.

"Thank you," Eva said. She lifted her foot, took one step, and her knees buckled.

Rather than fall to the floor, she fell into the wall of flesh and muscle that was Kronus. She didn't understand how he could move so fast — it seemed almost unnatural — but she was grateful for it. His arms slipped around her only long enough to adjust her position before scooping her up.

Eva slid her arms around his neck and buried her face against it. His skin muffled the laughter that bubbled out of her as her shoulders shook.

He paused halfway to the bathroom. "What is wrong, Eva?"

"Nothing," she replied, folding her lips inward and biting them to keep her laughter contained. But it was no use; she couldn't stop it.

He was silent until she calmed somewhat. "What is amusing?" he asked in his *serious* voice, which sent her into another burst of giggles. "Female, are you broken?"

"What?" she managed to squeeze out.

He frowned. "Is something wrong with you?"

Eva took several deep breaths, attempting to calm herself. "I was just thinking about how you're the one who helped me walk again...."

"And that is *amusing?*"

"Well, yeah, because you just sexed me so hard that I can't walk now."

His eyes widened with sudden alarm. "I will bring you to the clinic," he said, tightening his hold on her and hurrying toward the front door.

"Kronus, no!" She raised her head and took his face between her hands, forcing him to look at her. "No. I'm *fine*."

Perplexation mingled with the slowly fading panic in his expressions. "But you said I—"

"You didn't hurt me. You just…made my knees weak." She glanced away from him, skin flushing. "It felt good. *Really* good."

The tension in his muscles eased, and he relaxed his hold. For a few moments, he remained in place, within arm's reach of the front door. Then he turned around and headed to the bathroom.

"Why does your kind seem incapable of speaking plainly?" he muttered.

Eva narrowed her eyes at him. "What's that supposed to mean?"

He twisted his torso to carry her carefully through the bathroom door. "Everything from humans is always…*metafords* and double-meanings. It is confusing."

"*Metafords*? What is— You mean *metaphors*?"

Kronus frowned deeply, narrowing his own eyes. "I mean what I said."

His tone nearly had her laughing again; had her correcting him bruised his ego? Fortunately, she held it in this time. "Well, most people aren't as blunt as you."

"There would be a lot less pointless *small talk* if they were," he grumbled. Despite his gruffness, he was nothing but gentle as he sat her atop a stool in the corner, just in front of the toilet.

Nonetheless, his words caused a small pang in her chest. Did he view all their shared conversations as pointless? Was she nothing more than an annoyance to him?

"So…you'd rather not talk to me?" she asked quietly, folding her hands in her lap.

His frown intensified. His lips parted as though he meant to speak, but only a soft breath escaped him at first. He shook his head and dropped into what she now thought of as the *kraken squat* — tentacles splayed and torso low.

"You are the *only* one I want to talk to," he replied, voice just as quiet, as he cupped the back of her prosthesis and lifted its foot off the floor. He raised her skirt with his other hand, exposing the prosthetic limb in its entirety.

"Even if it is pointless small talk?"

Kronus pressed the button that released the pin holding her prosthesis in place. He slipped the artificial leg off and carefully propped it against the wall. "It is not pointless with you." He lifted his gaze to meet hers. "If I can learn even a tiny…*something* about you, it is never pointless."

Her stomach fluttered. Everything about Kronus was intense; his actions, the way he spoke, even the way he looked at her. It had never been like that with Blake. Their relationship had been a whirlwind of excitement and instant attraction — though that whirlwind seemed more a breeze now, compared to what she had with Kronus. The more distance she gained from her joining with Blake, the more she realized there'd been no substance to their relationship, no depth…

And if she knew that after only a couple weeks of reflection, she had no doubt the love between her and Blake had been fleeting. Hell, it probably was never love at all. It had been lust sprinkled with some adventure. She'd been hurt when he broke their union, but most of that pain was because she'd been left with nothing — she'd lost her leg, lost her friends, and then lost her only source of support. At heart, her suffering hadn't been about losing Blake; it had been about being alone. She cared about him and was glad he'd come to no harm, but what she felt for him had never been love.

She *knew* that now.

But what did she feel for Kronus? Was it simply gratitude?

He'd been there from the beginning of this new phase of her life, and she'd always be thankful for all he'd done, but it wasn't that. Gratitude didn't make her heart pitter-patter at the thought of seeing him, didn't make her stomach twist into knots when he was near, didn't send a rush of heat through her when their eyes met. It sure as hell wasn't what made her crave the feel of him inside her even now, when her knees were too weak to hold her upright.

His hands slipped under her skirt, and his fingertips brushed over the slickness coating her inner thigh. Eva's breath caught. Kronus stilled, keeping his eyes locked with hers for several seconds before hooking his fingers under the woolen sock covering her stump. He drew it off, folded it, and tucked it in the top of her prosthesis. He returned his hands to her thigh to peel off the liner, holding it delicately to avoid scratching her or damaging the material.

She placed her hands upon his, stopping him before he could remove the liner completely. "I…I can do this."

His hands stilled, but he did not pull them away. "I know you can. But *I* am tending to you now."

Why had everything been okay while she wore the prosthesis, but now she could barely look at her leg, much less allow him to see it uncovered?

Because with the prosthesis, I can pretend it's real. That I'm whole.

Maintaining her hold, she pressed her lips together and stared at her leg.

He resumed the movement of his hands.

"Kronus, please, I can do it," she said, tightening her grip. She couldn't keep her desperation from seeping into her voice. They'd just shared something wonderful, and she'd felt beautiful and desired for the first time in weeks. She didn't want this…*deformity* to taint that.

Her struggles did not deter him; he slid the liner off, exposing her stump. She removed her hands from his, grasped the hem of her skirt, and attempted to pull it down over her leg, but he caught her wrists in his tentacles and stopped her. Tears blurred her vision as she turned her face away from him.

Kronus cupped her jaw with one hand, directing her attention toward him. "What is this?" he asked. "Speak plainly. Help me understand, Eva."

She blinked, allowing the tears to spill down her cheeks. "I don't want you to see it."

"I have already seen it. Many times."

"I don't want you to see it *now*. Not after we…" She closed her eyes and fought the trembling in her lower lip. "For a moment, for that wonderful moment with you, I felt whole. I felt…beautiful."

"And why should that be any different now?" His thumb slid across her cheek, wiping away the moisture. "What have I done to make you feel otherwise?"

Eva opened her eyes. "You haven't done anything. You've been…perfect. You *are* perfect."

Something subtly softened in his expression. His other hand slipped under her left knee, and the pads of his fingers drifted lightly across her skin. "As are you, Eva. What has been taken away from your body does not take away from *you*."

Her chest warmed and tightened with emotion. "But it's…ugly."

"I have seen ugly," he said, his hold on her strengthening infinitesimally, "and there is nothing about you that could ever be such." Raising her leg, he bent down and placed a gentle, lingering kiss just below her left knee. His eyes never once faltered in holding her gaze; they shone with adoration and pride like she'd never seen.

Eva brushed her fingertips along the side of his face and around the outer rim of his siphon.

"Whatever people see when they look at us outside these walls," he said, shifting his hand from her jaw to the back of her head as he rose and tipped his forehead against hers, "however we may feel out there…in here, we are just ourselves. Nothing more or less. You will never be judged here. You will never need to hide. Not from me. Just *be*."

She caught his face between her hands and kissed him. Her tears continued to fall, but she focused solely on him. His fingers slipped into her hair, claws lightly grazing her scalp, as he returned the kiss.

Pulling back, Eva rested her forehead against his and grinned. "Now, if we're done with all this small talk, we should get cleaned up."

He withdrew uncertainly, brow furrowed once again. Eva made no effort to contain her laughter this time as she brushed the moisture from her cheeks.

Kronus's mouth curled into a smile that glittered in his golden eyes. She didn't know if he'd understood her humor — he was serious almost all the time and seemed to have trouble telling when people were joking — but it didn't matter. The happiness on his face was genuine, and she was glad for it no matter what had brought it about.

Without speaking, he moved his hands to her right foot, removed her shoe, and set it aside. Eva held his gaze as he grasped the hem of her shirt and slowly raised it. His fingers trailed tingles in their wake as they brushed over her skin. She lifted her arms when he pulled the garment over her head. His eyes fixated on her bared chest.

"I *should* have removed your clothing," he muttered as he draped her shirt over the top of her prosthesis. Splaying his fingers and stretching the webbing between them, he covered her left breast with his palm.

Eva released a shuddering breath and reflexively arched into his touch. Her nipple hardened.

He shifted his hand to take her nipple between the pads of his forefinger and thumb. He lightly pinched, stroked, and squeezed her sensitive flesh, sending a thrill straight to her core. Her breath quickened with every brush of his fingertips. Fire sparked low in her belly, and her sex clenched in need.

"Take off the rest," Eva heard herself say before she could stop.

She yelped as he suddenly slipped his hands beneath her backside and rose, lifting her off the stool. Tentacles coiled around her legs, supporting her weight, as he shifted his hands to her waist. He hooked his claws into the fabric of her skirt and already tattered panties and tore them apart with ease.

"Kronus!" Eva braced her hands on his shoulders as he pressed her back to the cold wall.

"You have other clothing," he growled. His hand settled over her breast again to resume its prior movements. Lifting her higher, he dipped his head and closed his lips over her other breast.

The heat of his mouth made her gasp. She closed her eyes and settled her hands on his head, moaning at the suction as his tongue rasped over her sensitive nipple. His tentacles moved along her legs, warm and strong, and she could no longer tell how many of them were there.

He lifted his mouth and growled against her breast. "Your scent already has me starving for more of you, female."

"*Now*," she rasped. "I want you now."

His hands fell to her backside again, gripping handfuls of flesh, as his tentacles positioned her legs to either side of his torso. He slid her down his body, her exposed sex brushing over his sculpted muscles until her legs were around his waist and the head of his cock pressed to her entrance. Without hesitation, he pulled her down and thrust deep inside her.

She dug her nails into his shoulders and opened her mouth in a silent cry that was cut off by a dominating kiss. His lips claimed hers, his breath filled her lungs, and his body branded her with searing heat.

Kronus lifted his hands and closed them around Eva's wrists. He forced her arms up over her head and pressed them against the wall, shifting his hands up to twine their fingers as much as possible, palm-to-palm. Not once did his quick, powerful thrusts slow.

Kronus growled, breaking the kiss. "Look at me, female."

Eva opened her eyes and met his burning gaze; its intensity had built to a frantic gleam.

"You are *mine*," he snarled. "Nothing will take you from me. *No one* will take you from me. Do you understand me, female?"

"Yes," Eva breathed. She cried out as his tentacles angled her hips upward, making his cock sink even deeper.

He leaned closer, pressing his chest against her breasts, and brushed his flat nose against her cheek. "Tell me who you belong to."

"You." She gasped when he nipped her ear, the prick of pain adding to the growing pressure in her core.

"Louder," he commanded. "Tell me who."

The tendrils at the base of his cock fluttered around her clit, stroking it each time his pelvis met hers. Eva whimpered as she felt the first tingles of an oncoming climax. She fought against his hold, tightening her fingers on his. She was trapped against Kronus and the wall, forced to take everything he deigned to give, and she relished every moment of it.

"Tell me!" he bellowed.

"You!" she screamed. "Oh God, you!" Pleasure burst through her. Her sex clamped down, her inner walls quivering so intensely it almost hurt. Her moans rose in pitch as euphoric waves struck her like the ocean crashing against the seaside cliffs.

Kronus's roar reverberated in the bathroom, filling up all the space that wasn't occupied by their intertwined bodies. His heat blossomed inside Eva as he ground his hips against her pelvis, pushing his cock as deep as their bodies allowed. Her sex greedily drew him in, craving more.

Time passed as Kronus held her limp form. They breathed heavily, unmoving but for their heaving chests.

Eva rubbed her cheek against his shoulder and inhaled in his scent. "You, Kronus," she whispered. "I belong to you."

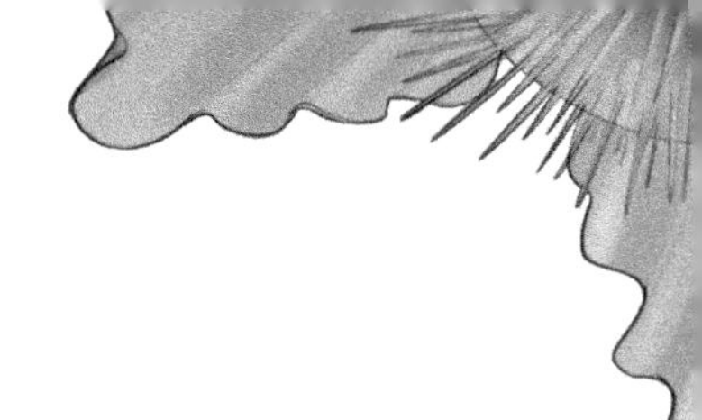

CHAPTER 14

KRONUS TURNED HIS HEAD TO THE RIGHT AS HE FLOATED OUT OF sleep. Grayish early dawn light filtered into his den through gaps in the front window curtains. Though he'd risen around this time on most days, he considered it too early now — why leave bed when Eva lay tucked against him, enwrapped in his tentacles? Her body heat was blissful, and though the bed had been sized for a single kraken, it wasn't crowded or cramped. He enjoyed the feel of her skin against his.

She'd spent three nights with him, and they'd shared the bed during each, savoring one another's closeness and exploring each other's bodies with hands, fingers, and tentacles.

His eyes roamed around the room once they were adjusted to the faint illumination. The furnishings, which remained sparse, were blanketed in a calm, comfortable gloom. Many of the shadowy forms were familiar sights upon waking, but the few additions and rearrangements made the space feel new and exciting. Knowing the cabinet — which she called the *armoire* — contained her clothing now, or that the pantry was stocked with abundant food suitable for a human, was an unexpected source of satisfaction to him.

Eva had been through two full days in his den now. Though she was still somewhat clumsy, she managed to move about with little assistance — even without her prosthetic leg, she'd regained enough strength to walk using only one crutch.

He'd faced two struggles, neither of which should have surprised him. The first was a struggle to avoid mating her constantly; the dwelling wasn't large, and they must've come together in nearly every possible place within by now. He had to remind himself often that she was human; even were she not still recuperating from her injury, she needed rest sometimes.

Her own seemingly insatiable appetite for him didn't help his self-control.

His second struggle felt less immediate but proved no less difficult. He found himself instinctually compelled to help her with *everything*. Oddly enough, the conflict was in part between those instincts and his pride — both in himself and in her. She was a female whose capability had been diminished by her wound, but she was not helpless. There was a difference between lavishing her with pleasure and coddling her, a difference between providing for her needs and treating her as a helpless creature. Sometimes, those distinctions seemed uncomfortably subtle.

He tightened his hold on her slightly. Her head was resting on his shoulder, and her slow, steady breath was warm across his chest. Absently, he trailed the tip of a tentacle along her calf, relishing the slightly salty flavor of her skin.

The speed with which she was adjusting to her new life, her new situation, was astounding, and he was proud of her for it. She smiled often, even through some of the difficult moments. Kronus found himself smiling more in turn. He'd noticed her wistfully looking out toward the sea on a few occasions, and he could only guess at her thoughts in those moments, but she always perked up when she turned her attention to him. Her rapid adaptation put him to shame; even after nine months, he still wasn't fully adjusted to life in The Watch. Eva was an example worthy of emulating.

Despite Kronus's best efforts, he knew he was sometimes terse, knew he let frustration color his speech when he felt overwhelmed or uninformed. Those instances occurred most frequently when discussing human matters. Eva responded to his gruffness in two ways — she gave it back to him tenfold or joked and teased until she coaxed a smile onto his face. In either situation, she never backed down.

A new side of her was awakening a little more every day — cheerful, playful, and sometimes carefree. He'd not seen her in such good spirits before. Upon reflection, he realized it must've been how she was before the attack; this wasn't a *new* Eva, though she'd undoubtedly been altered by her experiences — muted, perhaps, but not broken. Not anymore.

Kronus turned his eyes back toward her. More of his tentacles were moving now, gliding over her smooth, warm skin, his suction cups gifting her with what she called *little kisses*. She stirred, burying herself more snugly against him, and drew in a long, deep breath that she released as a sleepy, contented sigh. Her tousled hair tickled his arm and chest; despite how strange hair had been to him since he'd first seen Macy years before, he'd found that he enjoyed the feel of Eva's hair.

She did not wake, and he was willing to let her sleep a while longer.

If he'd ever known happiness, it must've been during his earliest years of life, before he was sent to live with the hunters, who turned even play into training and lessons. Such was well beyond the power of his memory. The first glimpse he could recall of happiness had been from Jax and Macy. In hindsight, that might have been part of why he'd so strongly opposed her presence in the Facility; he'd been jealous of the happiness the couple shared.

But now, he finally knew what it felt like firsthand. He had Eva to thank for that.

Every day, she grew a little stronger, he grew a little prouder, and they grew a little closer.

Kronus trailed a tentacle farther up her leg, running its tip along her inner thigh. He'd known hunger before; the hunters who supplied food to the kraken were skilled and dedicated, but they did not always meet success. Their people had endured lean times. But the sort of hunger he felt for Eva was unlike any he'd ever experienced. Tastes of her left him constantly wanting *more*; his appetite for her was insatiable.

His tentacle worked its way to the apex of her thighs to brush over her folds. Her scent and taste flowed across his suction cups; feminine, sweet, and alluring. He groaned softly. Though his suction cups picked up her flavor well, their touch didn't feel intimate enough, didn't feel *real* enough.

Kronus's mind leapt back to the conversation he'd had with the other males before Eva came to share his den. Dracchus's words resonated above all else.

The tongue works very well. And the taste...

When he increased the pressure of his tentacle, Eva released a whimper and squeezed her thighs together around his limb. Her scent intensified.

He wasted no time in consideration; he'd not yet tasted her directly, but he would remedy that now. He would see just how well his tongue worked for her.

Carefully, he disentangled himself from Eva and the blanket that had somehow twisted around them. He managed to do so without waking her; Eva's features were drawn for a moment, as though in confusion or mild distress, but she rolled onto her back, and her expression relaxed again. He anchored his tentacles around the posts at the foot of the bed and drew himself down slowly, unable to pry his gaze from the majesty of her naked form. No matter how she saw herself, she was perfect in his eyes. It took all his willpower to keep from running his hands over every bit of her body.

Not now. Not yet.

He positioned his torso over her legs, propping himself on his arms, and stared down at the patch of hair on her pelvis. Leaning on one hand, he parted her thighs. They fell to either side with little coaxing. Her sex lay open to him, its petals pink and wet, perfuming the air with her scent.

Kronus closed his eyes and inhaled. Fire blazed through his veins, and his cock strained against his slit, blocked from emerging by the bed. As much as he longed to enter her again, he wanted this taste of her more.

When he opened his eyes again, he lowered his head between her thighs and slid his tongue into her folds. Her salty-sweet flavor swept through his mouth, momentarily obliterating his memory of all other tastes; none could compare to hers. Nothing could come close. Sliding his hands under her backside, he lifted her pelvis off the bed and pressed his mouth to her sex. He greedily lapped her nectar as he worked his way up to flick his tongue over her clitoris.

"Kronus," Eva rasped breathlessly. She moaned and reflexively squeezed her thighs together, but Kronus wrapped his tentacles around her knees and pulled them wider apart, further opening her to him.

He glanced up, looking over her body and through the valley between her breasts to watch her face. Her eyes were closed, and her lips were parted. She panted softly with every stroke of his tongue as it explored her slit. Eva's sounds and reactions only aroused him more. Nectar flowed from her, and Kronus groaned, savoring every drop.

Her taste was delectable, but he needed more of her, needed to *feel* more of her.

He draped her legs over his shoulders and slid his hands up her back, lifting her off the bed. Most of his tentacles swept forward to support and caress her, encircling her waist and coiling around her breasts. Her back bowed, and she gasped as his suction cups latched on and kissed the hardened buds of her nipples.

Wrapping his arms around her thighs, he sucked her clitoris into his mouth and swirled the tip of his tongue around it.

Her entire body tensed.

"Kronus!" Her hands fell upon his head, and her nails bit into his skin. "Oh fuck!"

She gyrated her hips, grinding her sex against his mouth. A fresh wave of sweetness flowed out of her, washing over him like the tide rushing ashore. She writhed in his hold, and her hands fell to clutch his wrists as though they would better ground her.

He thrust his tongue deep inside her as her inner walls contracted, gifting him with more of her essence, and drank deeply. He lapped, nipped and sucked until she was mindless in his grasp, reduced to pleading and calling his name. He only stopped once her trembling thighs went slack, and she lay quivering and limp in his hold.

As he removed his mouth from her, he licked her nectar from his lips and groaned appreciatively. His cock — fully erect, extruding, and seeping with oils — throbbed achingly.

He lowered Eva to the bed and withdrew his tentacles. Leaning over her, he braced himself with his arms to either side of her head and gazed down. Perspiration coated her rosy skin, hard nipples were reddened from the attention they'd received, and her eyes, dark with lust, were glassy and half-lidded as they met his.

"This will happen often, female," he said.

Eva chuckled huskily. She raised a hand and trailed her fingers down his chest, her nails grazing his flesh as they moved toward his abdomen. "And what of you?"

Kronus arched a brow. "What of me?"

Eva wrapped her fingers around his cock. He hissed, gritting his teeth, as his hips jerked.

"Would you like my mouth on *you*, Kronus?" Eva asked, pumping her hand along his shaft to elicit a shudder from him.

It took Kronus a moment to realize what her words implied; just as he'd never considered using his mouth on her until his talk with the other males, he'd never considered the reverse being a possibility. With a female kraken, it remained an unlikely prospect — unless a male didn't mind having his cock shredded. But what threat could Eva's blunt teeth pose to him? He already knew the pleasure she could create with her mouth and tongue from her kisses.

The feel of her hand on him already had Kronus on the verge of a climax. His entire body thrummed, but he fought it back, too intrigued by her question to allow himself to come.

Eva released his cock. Kronus clenched fistfuls of the bedding, nearly snarling at the pleasure-pain left in the absence of her touch.

"Lie back," she commanded, shoving against his shoulders.

He obeyed; the promise of her touching him again was too enticing a motivation to resist.

Straddling the central pairs of his tentacles, she leaned over him and grabbed his cock. She kept her eyes locked with his as she lowered her head. He watched, captivated, as her lips wrapped around the head of his shaft. She sucked, taking him deep into her mouth. Her tongue slid over his sensitive skin, its texture creating delightful friction.

His eyes widened at the feel of it; it was unexpected, overwhelming, and intensely pleasing. He gritted his teeth, dug his claws into the bed, and bucked his hips involuntarily. She bobbed her head up and down, sliding her lips along his shaft and making maddening circles with her tongue.

"Eva!" Kronus snarled and reached up to take hold of the bed frame before he did any more damage to the bedding.

As easily as he'd plunged her into mindless pleasure, she enslaved him to his own.

With a few flicks of her tongue, Eva became his master.

"Where are you taking me?" Eva asked, watching her footing as she picked her way over the rocks. Briny wind tugged at her clothing and blew her hair around her shoulders. The sound of waves rolling onto the shore grew more soothing as they progressed, becoming a steady, sighing rise and fall.

Kronus remained close to her, holding one of her hands to offer support; he was more solid to her than the stones under foot.

"This way," he replied.

She rolled her eyes. "I meant beside the obvious."

He turned his head to face forward, looking toward a place where the rocks fell away into the ocean. "The tide is low this afternoon."

Eva followed his gaze. "So it is. That still doesn't answer my question."

Lifting his free hand, he pointed to the long, wide outcropping of low rocks ahead that extended from the coastal cliffside along which they were moving. Calm water glistened in the late evening sunshine amidst the stone. "There are pools here that only exist when the tide is this low. I think you will enjoy them."

She eyed the rocks skeptically; they'd already crossed several rough patches through which she'd struggled, and it seemed there would be more before they reached the level area awaiting them. Her legs were already sore and tired.

"I don't know if I can make it, Kronus."

Tensing his arm to strengthen her support, he helped her over a jutting stone. By her estimate, they had at least another thirty or forty meters of this before they reached the pool.

"Do not start whining at me again, female."

"I am *not* whining."

"That is what people always say when they whine," he replied. "Push yourself through this, and you will be stronger by the end. I will be with you throughout."

Eva looked at Kronus. She understood him a little more each day. Though he was gruff and standoffish most of the time, there was a thoughtful, considerate, caring male beneath that rough exterior who was afraid to let his guard down. The vulnerable moments she'd been gifted were rare, and she treasured them because they were only for *her*.

That he'd be with her meant a lot, but it didn't take away her longing to be able to do it on her own. She was still growing accustomed to her prosthesis, still learning how to balance herself and slowly building the muscles that would power her forever-altered stride.

She still experienced moments of unbearable pain. It was during those times that Kronus's mask slipped to reveal the concern perpetually hidden beneath. Though the boosters Aymee administered had helped hasten her recovery, Eva knew she'd never be the same. Only time could determine how severe those changes would be.

Kronus stayed at her side, allowing her to lean on him as they walked. His tentacles flowed over the rock like water, and she couldn't help a touch of good-natured jealousy; she was stuck with a leg and a half, while he had eight. That hardly seemed fair.

After some more grunting and straining, they crested a low rise and paused. A large, natural pool stretched out before them. Its surface shimmered orange with reflected light from the setting sun. The stone surrounding the pool was crusted with splotches of purple, red, and green — strange sea creatures Eva had never seen before. Beyond the rocks lay the open sea, its waves rolling tirelessly to and from the horizon.

"Wow," Eva breathed. "This is beautiful."

Immediately after losing her leg, she'd been filled with hopelessness. She'd always enjoyed exploring the world around her; after her injury, she couldn't see how she'd ever be able to do that again. How would she climb mountains, hilltops, and trees? How would she dive from high cliffs into pure blue waters? How would she trek through dense, sweet-smelling jungle foliage to discover new places as beautiful as they were dangerous? Coming to The Watch with Blake had been a step on that journey, the opening of a door to a new place, to new things, but she'd felt like that door had been slammed shut after the attack.

This spot, this pool, however small in the grand scheme, held as much meaning to her as the ocean held water; it meant she wasn't done. Things might never be easy again, but she wouldn't be stopped by her injury.

"The tide is not often this low," Kronus said. He raised a hand and gestured over the rocks before them. "All this is usually covered by the sea. But for now, for this little while, it is yours."

Eva looked at Kronus and couldn't prevent tears from blurring her eyes. "Thank you." She wrapped her arms around him and pressed a tender kiss to his lips.

He returned the kiss, and when he drew back, he wore a soft smile. "Come. We are not quite there. You can rest at the pool, if you wish."

She raised her hand and traced his smile with the tip of her finger. She'd grown used to the differences between them. But it was so much more than comfort with his appearance; she found Kronus appealing. And in this place, in this moment, with his golden eyes shining down at her and his face relaxed and *happy*, he was the most handsome man she'd ever seen.

And he is mine.

"Teach me to swim again," she said.

He dropped his gaze and trailed the tip of a tentacle over her ankle. "I do not know how to swim with those. With legs."

"You didn't know how to walk with them either, but you helped me learn to walk again anyway."

Kronus nodded slightly in acknowledgement. "Then I will help in the same way. By being an *asshole*."

Eva laughed, and Kronus's smile widened.

He helped her down from the rise and, finally, onto the relatively even rock. She stood still, one hand on his shoulder for support as he bent down to remove first the shoe from her right foot, followed by her prosthesis, sock, and liner. Once he set everything aside, he peeled off her outer layer of clothing. The touch of his strong hands sent thrills across her bare skin.

He hooked a finger beneath one of her bra straps and lifted his gaze toward the nearby beach. "Were it not for the chance of other people drawing close, I would remove these as well."

She arched a brow. "Your females don't wear these things. I didn't think it'd matter to you."

"It matters because you are *mine*, Eva, and I will tolerate no male looking upon you."

His words sent a bolt of desire straight to her core.

My kraken is possessive.

She was pretty sure she was wearing a pleased, goofy grin.

Kronus leaned down and kissed her again; one of those soul-searing, claiming kisses that left no room to question his statement. He was *hers*, and she was without a doubt *his*.

By the time he raised his head, Eva was panting, and her sex throbbed in need. One of his tentacles had coiled around her leg, the tip teasing her inner thigh.

"We'd better get in that water before I strip and demand my kraken mount me right now, onlookers be damned," she said.

A long, low groan escaped him, and his tongue slipped out from between his lips for an instant. His brief hesitance suggested he was prepared to skip the water just to have her.

But he finally stooped, slipped one arm behind her shoulders and the other behind her knees, and lifted her off the ground. He carried her to the edge of the pool and entered the water smoothly.

It was refreshingly cool compared to the hot evening air, especially welcome after the exertion of the journey to get here — they'd left their house and descended onto the beach, following the cliffs around to this spot. The distance hadn't been great, but the terrain had proven difficult for Eva. The sand, especially, had proven bothersome for her prosthesis, and her crutch was useless on it.

Kronus held her, and they drifted lazily through the water together. The pool was surprisingly deep, and when Kronus stilled, she caught glimpses of tiny sea creatures through the sparkling surface. He assured her that none of the creatures were dangerous, and she didn't question him. He'd earned her trust far more than anyone else.

She broke away from him and began the clumsy but freeing process of learning how to swim with nearly half of one leg missing. Kronus remained nearby, tugging her over the surface when she floundered, but she didn't require his help often. Though she wasn't graceful by any means, this would do. With a little adjustment to her stroke, she moved through the water without assistance.

Soon, they were swimming side-by-side at a leisurely pace. Kronus was quiet, but his unwavering presence gave her all the strength she needed.

Kronus drew himself to a halt and turned to look toward the ocean. "This is what I truly wanted you to see," he said, lifting his chin toward the sea.

Eva followed his gaze with her own. The sun hung low over the horizon; it was red-orange, its glow staining the ever-moving seawater in the same shade, which was contrasted by the deep blue and violet of the shadows beneath the waves' crests. Flecks of pure, sparkling white shined everywhere, glittering with more brilliance than all the stars in the sky at night.

He took gentle hold of her and swam to the edge of the pool farthest from the sea, where he leaned his back against the stone and positioned her to lay atop him. His arms banded around her, holding her close, and she rested her head on his shoulder. He settled his cheek upon her hair.

They remained like that as the sun slowly disappeared behind the horizon. Violet chased away the reds, pinks, and oranges staining the sky, and the shimmering color on the ocean's surface shrank until only a narrow strip of vibrancy remained.

"I have watched the sun set over the ocean almost every day for nine months," he said. "I had never seen it before coming here. Not like this. Not from…*above*. And I never understood how beautiful it is until I met you, Eva. You opened my eyes to this. To everything that's always been around me."

"How have I changed that for you?" she asked, running her fingers over his forearm beneath the water.

"Because yours is a beauty I could not ignore," he said. His voice sounded slightly strained, as though the words were difficult for him to get out. "Once I saw you, I could not help but see everything else…could not help but compare it to you and find it lacking, or wonder if you would appreciate it as I do."

Eva raised an arm, reached back, and cupped Kronus's cheek as she turned her face to look up at him. "And you never found me lacking?"

His tentacles coiled around her legs and waist, offering an almost full-body embrace. "Never."

She closed her eyes and pressed her forehead to his jaw. The simple answer meant so much because his actions often transcended the need for words.

Warmth spread through her body, and little wings fluttered in her belly. When she and Kronus came together, it was as though the whole world fell away; all her troubles, worries, and struggles ceased to exist, and there was only the two of them with their passion and caring for one another. He'd been there for her during her lowest moments, had pulled her from the deepest, darkest despair, had been a shining beacon that guided her ashore from a sea of blackness.

"Thank you, Kronus," she said, lifting her head and opening her eyes to meet his gaze. The final rays of sunlight had faded, but his eyes burned with a light of their own. "For never giving up on me, even when I gave you reason to."

She turned in his embrace, and his tentacles loosened, allowing the movement. The water lapped just beneath her breasts as she straddled him and cupped his face between her hands. "I haven't said it yet, but you deserve more than anything to hear it. Thank you for saving me that day, and every day that followed. Thank you for teaching me to live again."

His skin changed to a violet as deep as that of the sky, making his eyes seem even brighter in comparison. "I have only tried to give you what you deserve, Eva. And I have failed that task time and again."

"Why would you say that?"

"Because you deserve *everything*, but all I can offer is all of me."

"Who is to say what I deserve?" Eva leaned closer, skimming her lips over his cheek and placing a light kiss on the corner of his mouth. "What you're offering is what I want, Kronus. All I want…is *you*."

He smiled, and his skin shifted again, though she could no longer determine its color in the deepening twilight. "Then I am yours, Eva. And when the sea tries to finally claim me, I will fight it off to have more time with you."

His words sparked a sudden, bone-deep fear in her; she'd already lost so much. She couldn't bear even the *thought* of losing Kronus, too. Tears filled her eyes as she threw her arms around him and squeezed him tightly. "The sea can't have you. Not you."

"It already knows it cannot take you," he replied, enfolding her in his arms and tentacles. "You are *mine*."

Eva pulled back just enough to press her mouth against his in a fierce kiss, closing her eyes. He kissed her in return just as fervently. Their lips meshed, nipped, and caressed as they breathed life into one another. His hands moved over her back as he clutched her, holding her as close as possible, but even that wasn't close enough for Eva.

After what might have been only a single moment or an eternity, she became aware of a gentle glow through her eyelids. Eva opened her eyes to find Kronus bathed in blue light. With a startled gasp, she broke the kiss and drew back to look him over. His stripes were glowing, casting a soft blue luminescence over the two of them and reducing the rest of the world to far away, unimportant darkness.

"What is this?" she asked, awed, brushing her fingertips over one of his shoulder stripes.

"My light," he replied. "Tonight, and forever to come, it is yours. You need never suffer in darkness again."

Eva smiled, her eyes locking with his. "You've been my light since the moment you saved me." She brushed her nose across his cheek, moving her mouth closer to his siphon. "Make love to me, Kronus," she whispered. "Here, now. I don't care if anyone comes. I just need to feel you. All of you. I need you inside me."

He answered with a growl and a kiss even more passionate and possessive than the last.

CHAPTER 15

KRONUS PULLED OPEN THE DOOR AND STOOD ASIDE TO ALLOW EVA through. She paused long enough to wave at Doctor Rhodes before stepping out of the clinic. Kronus fell into place beside her. According to the doctor, she'd improved faster than either he or Aymee had expected. He'd made some adjustments to her prosthesis, given her another booster shot, and sent them on their way.

In the five days since their rocky journey to the tidal pool, Eva had pushed herself steadily harder; as of three days ago, she'd decided she no longer needed crutches. Her pace was sometimes slow, and she moved with a slight limp that grew more pronounced on inclines and declines, but she was *walking* on her own, and she shone even brighter because of it.

They turned and followed the short road into the town center, which was bustling with activity. Midday meal in The Watch meant many of the townspeople took a break from their duties to eat and converse for a little while. Today, there was music being played on the other side of the square. Kronus's siphons twitched, and he cocked his head.

The music grew louder as they crossed the town center. The

crowd was thicker near the source of the music, with clusters of people speaking in boisterous voices to hear one another over the music. Other people were moving — *dancing* — with one another, laughing and smiling. The humans making the music were at the center of the crowd, banging and strumming instruments with delighted expressions. One of the music makers had a long, thin piece of wood raised to his lips; it produced high notes as he blew into it and moved his fingers over the holes along its length.

Eva grabbed Kronus's hand and turned to face him with a wide smile. "Dance with me, Kronus."

He shifted his attention back to the nearby crowd, which was at its thickest perhaps five or six body lengths away. Their spirits seemed light, their moods merry, but dancing meant something different to kraken. It was no carefree act for Kronus's people. A dance was a purposeful thing, meant to assert dominance, to attract a mate, to establish prowess. It was not done for entertainment.

"Come on," she insisted, tugging him toward the dancers.

Kronus scanned the crowd; there were at least four other kraken present, including — to his surprise — Ector, one of the kraken elders. The old kraken was closer to the town hall, conversing with a group of humans.

He looked back at Eva's expectant face. Joy sparkled in her eyes. She wanted this, wanted to dance with him in front of everyone, showing the town that they were a mated pair. And Kronus found that he wanted them all to know she was his.

Bringing her hand to his lips, he pressed a kiss on her knuckles and led her toward the dancers.

"Eva?"

Kronus and Eva turned their gazes to the male who'd spoken her name.

Blake.

The human male stepped closer, his gaze traveling up and

down Eva's body. Something white hot sparked in Kronus's gut and spread through him, devouring everything in its path.

Eva withdrew her hand from Kronus's and faced Blake. The man's hair was shaggy and disheveled, his face unshaven, and the flesh beneath his eyes had a purple tint.

"You're…*walking*." The astonishment in Blake's tone matched his stunned expression.

Eva nodded and grasped the sides of her skirt. "I am."

Kronus clenched his jaw and resisted the instinctual urge to flare red and challenge this male.

"How?" Blake blurted.

"Aymee and Arkon made me a prosthetic leg," Eva said.

"You look…" Blake's gaze trekked over Eva again, "good." He chuckled and rubbed the back of his neck. "*Really* good."

"Thank you. Now, if you'll—"

Blake reached out and caught her arm before she could step around him. He raised his other hand toward her face, but Kronus clamped his much larger, orange-skinned hand on Blake's wrist, halting the motion of the human's arm. Just a little pressure in the wrong direction could cripple the man.

The thought was not unappealing.

"Release her," Kronus growled.

"What the hell?" Blake started and glared at Kronus. "You better get your hand off me."

Kronus leaned closer, lips curling back to reveal pointed teeth. "Release your hold on her, human, or I will tighten my hold on you."

Blake bared his own teeth but released Eva.

With a shove, Kronus relinquished his grip on Blake and inserted himself between the man and Eva. Blake stumbled backward, clutching his wrist. He looked past Kronus to stare Eva.

"What is this? What's he doing?"

"You no longer have the right to touch her," Kronus said.

"She's *my* wife," Blake snapped. "I can do whatever the hell I want."

"No, I'm not," Eva said.

"What?"

"I'm not yours. Not anymore."

Blake glanced between Kronus and Eva. The anger on his face morphed to shock, then disbelief, and back to anger again.

"You're mine, damnit!" he exploded, stepping forward, only to come to a halt when Kronus pressed a hand against his chest. He jerked away quickly. "Don't touch me!"

"Make no mistake, human," Kronus replied, forcing himself to breathe slow and even, "I *will* break you if you threaten my mate."

"*Your* mate?" Blake looked at Eva. "You… You're…with this *creature?*" The human shuddered before inhaling and shaking his head. "Eva, you're joined to me. You're my wife. I will forgive—"

"I was no longer your wife the moment you walked out of the clinic, abandoning me when I needed you most," Eva said.

"I made a mistake, Eva. I—"

"You rescinded your vow to me, Blake. You ran away and left me, just like you left all of us in the water."

"It wasn't my fault!" Blake yelled.

Kronus glanced toward the crowd; despite the music and the revelry, Blake's raised voice had called the attention of several other humans. "You are a coward," Kronus growled through clenched teeth as he turned back to the man, "and you are unworthy of her."

Blake spared a hate-filled glance at Kronus before turning his eyes back to Eva. "Come back home, Eva. I miss you. I didn't mean what I said. We can work it out, and we can go back to normal. You'll get over it."

Nostrils flaring, Kronus clenched his fists. His claws bit into his palms, but it was all he could do not to strike Blake. He could no longer keep the crimson from his skin; were it another kraken treating him in such a manner, this situation would already have descended into violence.

He was being insulted in front of a crowd, was being insulted by a male he could *destroy*, was being insulted in the presence of his mate. It was unacceptable, intolerable. And his lack of a real response was humiliating.

But he knew Eva enough to understand that she would not appreciate such a display. How would watching Blake get beaten near-to-death benefit her? She wouldn't feel better about herself, wouldn't appreciate Kronus more. There was a strong chance it would frighten her. He could not bear the thought of her fearing him.

"*I'll* get over it? You left me no choice but to get over it," Eva said. "And you know what, Blake? I did."

Eva stepped around Kronus and placed her hands on his chest, pressing herself against his body. He put an arm around her shoulders, a flare of pride rising through the haze of rage and possessiveness; she had chosen Kronus. In front of everyone, she was making her choice clear, and she would not back down.

"I got over you," she continued. "I will always remember our friends, and I will always remember you…and I'll remember how you ran. The first moment things got hard, you *ran*. And Kronus was there for me. A stranger, someone we thought of as a creature because of how he looks, saved me, and *saved* me, and *saved me*, and you were *gone*."

Tears filled Eva's blue eyes, but fury burned behind them.

"You were gone, Blake," she said, "but Kronus was there. He showed me what it means to care for someone, to never give up on them, to *love* them. You and I had a good time while it lasted, but it was never that. It was never love."

"What are you saying?" Blake's chest rose and fell with quick, shallow breaths. "I loved you, Eva! I still do. I was hurt by all this, too, and it's not fucking fair for you to lay this at *my* feet!"

Eva turned to face Blake fully and stepped toward him. Kronus let his arm fall away; it took all his willpower to keep from grabbing Eva and dragging her back against him, from shielding her from any and all harm with his body. This was her time. Her fight. That did not diminish his rage, but he could not act upon his own feelings.

"Do *not* talk to me about *fair*," she growled, jabbing a finger into Blake's chest. "You blamed me for *everything*. If you had just stuck by me for a little while, I could've helped you through it, too. We could've made it together, but you left, forsaking me, Blake, and there's no coming back from that. And now that I can look back on it…I'm glad you left. Because it's led me to something, to someone, so much better."

"You can't mean that! Damnit, Eva, I—" Blake moved closer, grabbed Eva's face, and slammed his mouth over hers.

Kronus darted forward as Eva jerked her head back and swung her hand, slapping Blake across his face. Blake reeled from the blow; the opening was more than enough for the kraken to seize.

Thrusting his arm out, Kronus clamped a hand on Blake's throat, just beneath he man's jaw, and lifted him off the ground.

Blake's startled cry was cut off by a grunt. He grasped Kronus's forearm with both hands, kicking his feet in the air as though it would earn his freedom.

Eva gripped Kronus's extended arm. "No, Kronus, don't!"

Rage-fueled strength coursed through Kronus's muscles; he trembled with his fury, and his skin felt as though it were ablaze. He'd tolerated a lot of disrespect thus far, but he would not allow anyone to treat his mate that way.

"I told you not to touch her," he grated through bared teeth. All he had to do was squeeze, and he would crush the man's throat.

Blake's struggles grew more desperate as his face reddened.

Eva's fingernails dug into Kronus's skin, but he did not release his hold. He drew Blake closer and looked directly into the man's eyes. "She is mine. You will regret it should you wish to challenge me, human. You gave her up. You left her behind. I have claimed her, and she has chosen *me*."

Soft, small hands grabbed Kronus's face and tugged his head down. He snarled instinctively, skin bristling, only to find Eva between him and Blake; she flinched at his reaction. A pang of guilt and shame pierced his burning cloud of rage.

"Kronus, stop. Don't do this. Please." She brushed her thumbs over his cheeks. Faint tremors coursed through her hands. "You need to calm down. You're hurting him."

It wasn't the fact that he was hurting Blake which lead him to release his grasp, but that his actions were hurting Eva. When Kronus opened his hand, Blake dropped to the ground, falling backward to land on his backside. The kraken paid him no more attention; all Kronus's focus shifted to Eva alone.

"Thank you," she said softly. "As angry as I am with him, I don't want him hurt or…killed." She glanced at Blake over her shoulder before meeting Kronus's gaze again. She stroked his cheek. "He isn't worth…*this*."

Kronus's awareness of his surroundings rushed back to him. The music had stopped, and there were people gathered all around, staring at Kronus. Some of their expressions were judgmental, some were confused, but the fearful faces struck him hardest — especially those of the human younglings who clung to their parents with wide eyes.

Blake coughed and staggered to his feet. He held a hand at his throat as he slowly backed away, staring at Kronus. "He tried to kill me!"

"That's enough!" called a male human as he wove his way through the crowd. He emerged nearby, his face pink and his eyes wide. Kronus had never spoken to the man, but he knew him as Walter Bailiff, the head councilman of The Watch.

Ector moved to a place beside Walter, wearing a troubled look on his face. Whispers rippled through the crowd, too low and indistinct for Kronus to decipher. The immediacy of his fury had diminished, but he was still aflame inside. He could not help but turn his head to glare at Blake.

"I understand that this little…occurrence was, uh, *unsettling*," Walter called, tongue slipping out to wet his lips, "but there's nothing to be frightened about."

"He was choking Blake!" someone shouted.

"Blake was kissing the kraken's woman!" another person yelled from the opposite side of the crowd.

Kronus couldn't locate the speakers, but he probably didn't know them anyway. He put his arms around Eva and drew her closer, as though he could hide her from the crowd within his embrace. His eyes shifted to meet Ector's; he could not read the elder kraken's expression well enough to guess at the thoughts behind it.

Walter raised his hands in placation. "Now look, a lot of us overhead what was going on, and considering the, uh…the unfortunate incidents that have led up to this point, I don't think it's the place of any of us to judge."

"He tried to kill me, Walter," Blake said, turning his angry gaze to the councilman.

"If I meant to kill you, you would already be dead," Kronus responded.

Another ripple of whispers spread through the crowd, this time with a slightly more alarmed tone.

"If I may," Ector said, raising his voice to be heard clearly over the crowd as he moved forward. "I know that all the people here, human and kraken alike, socialize with one another frequently. Information has a way of moving through our community with great speed. Most of us know what happened to Eva and her friends, and we were all deeply saddened by it. Most of us also that her mate abandoned her afterward—"

"That is none of your damn business!" Blake shouted.

"It isn't," Walter said, nodding, "but it *is* public knowledge, Blake. You know that… Well, that sort of thing is news around here, for better or worse, and…"

"And it has been known for some weeks now," said Ector. "Kronus has taken Eva into his den — his *home* — to shelter her and protect her."

Blake looked at Eva, aghast. "You're living with that thing?"

Eva glared at him.

"She shares my den, and she is my mate," Kronus declared. *Let them all know it. I will face* any *challenger to my claim.*

"Amongst our kind," Ector continued, "it is considered the primary, defining purpose of a male to protect his mate for so long as she chooses to keep him. Though the nature and…*tenure* of those relationships have changed thanks to our friendship with humans, that tradition of protectiveness has not altered. If this woman is Kronus's mate, and she was threatened, he was simply fulfilling his duty to protect her."

"That's not the way we do things here!" a human called.

"Please. Please!" Walter raised his voice, for the first time seeming exasperated. "It's not ideal, no, but…but the fight is over now, and how many of us can say that we'd behave much differently if we were in that position? A lot of us have gotten into a scuffle or two. It's part of life. But we pick ourselves up and carry on. Now, unless we all want to spend the time to organize a…a public hearing over this, I don't think we need to worry on it much further. These folks'll keep away from each other if they can't get along because they're all decent people.

"Now come on. We've got lots of food left, and Jon and the rest of the band probably have two or three more songs they know how to play, at least…I mean, depending on whether they've played one or two by now." He cleared his throat, his cheeks burning bright red. "Guess I ought to leave the humor to our more charming citizens. Come on, everyone! Back to it!"

The crowd moved slowly, drifting back toward the other side of the town center, where they'd been gathered before. There was a buzz of conversation in the air, and Kronus didn't miss the occasional over-the-shoulder glances cast his way. He searched for Blake, but the human had either lost himself in the crowd or fled.

Eva gently withdrew from Kronus's hold and met his gaze. "Let's go home."

He nodded; his insides churned with unexpressed anger, and fire blazed through his veins. He understood that Eva and Blake had been mates before; though he couldn't help his jealousy over it, their prior relationship was nothing to brood over. But *this*, this blatant disrespect of both Kronus and Eva, this *public* disrespect…

Even if the immediate situation had passed, Kronus could not release the feelings it had sparked within him.

Before he could lead Eva away, he noticed Ector approaching. Kronus's muscles tensed; he'd always held the elder in high esteem, but Kronus's actions over the past couple years had not necessarily conveyed that. He knew his skin was still red, but he couldn't find the will to revert it to normal.

"That was unfortunate," Ector said, shaking his head. His lips were downturned in a small frown.

"I was not—" Kronus began, but Ector waved a hand dismissively, silencing him.

"I lay no blame upon you, Kronus. What good would it do for me to say I expect better of you when dealing with humans? I do not know a kraken who would not have hurried to defend his mate in that situation." Ector's frown shifted into a gentle smile as he turned his attention to Eva. "I am Ector, one of the kraken elders. We are…something like your councilmen. I have heard much about you, Eva, although I would rather our first meeting have been under more pleasant circumstances."

Eva offered a tight, forced smile. "It's nice to meet you, Ector."

The elder nodded and looked at Kronus again. "She's helped you find balance, it seems. The Kronus I once knew would not have been quite so restrained as you were."

Embarrassment temporarily heated Kronus's skin, but his lingering fury proved too great to allow his color to alter.

"Our lives with the humans are peaceful, calm," Ector continued. "Quite unlike what we've known before. But we must always remember that, despite our many similarities, we are different. We were shaped for a different world, and it shaped us in return. Sometimes…our ways are not the best ways. In this world, our instincts may sometimes mislead us. But you seem to have an excellent guide." Ector glanced at Eva again, briefly, before nodding to Kronus. "I will not keep you longer. We each have our lessons to learn, and you, Kronus, have already learned more than most."

The elder reached out and placed a hand on Kronus's shoulder; it was firm, and stronger than his years belied, but gave no hint of confrontation or aggression. The gesture confused Kronus. Male kraken rarely touched save for when they were fighting one another. Strange how Ector's touch was unsettling for its unfamiliarity while Eva's, from the very beginning, had been soothing, familiar, and thrilling all at once.

Lowering his hand, Ector turned and moved away, joining Walter and a few other humans.

Kronus turned his head toward Eva. His rage would have remained a towering fire if not for Ector's gesture throwing him just off-balance enough to disturb the flames. Anger was a simple emotion, easily understood. Everything else…

If it weren't for her, Kronus would have no idea where to begin.

He extended his arm, holding his hand to her palm-up. Eva took it without hesitation.

"I will not let anyone stop us this time," he promised.

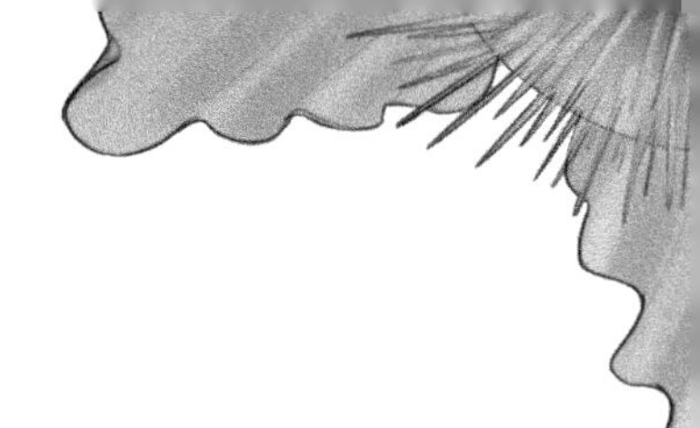

CHAPTER 16

Eva's limp was more pronounced as they entered their home. The long trek to and from the clinic had left her legs sore, and the tremors coursing through her after the confrontation with Blake refused to subside. She'd known she would run into him eventually; they lived in the same town, and there were only so many places to go. But she hadn't expected…*that*. The last time she'd seen Blake, he'd looked happy, carefree, had already been moving on with his life.

She'd seen a different Blake today; he looked like he'd gone to hell and back.

Aymee had told her everyone experienced and expressed grief in their own way. Had Eva given up on him too soon?

No.

Eva shoved aside that twinge of guilt as quickly as it had come. Whether or not she had Kronus, it didn't change the fact that Blake had left her, spurned her, had chosen himself and his own desires over her without a backward glance. He'd placed the blame at her feet — *foot* — looking at her injury with open disgust. That wasn't how a person was supposed to treat their loved ones. Regardless of what he'd said in the town center today, his actions immediately after the attack spoke loudly about how he really felt about her.

She'd been right to say they hadn't loved each other.

Eva made her way across the room and sat in the chair near the window, coming down more heavily than normal. Her hair, left loose, fell around her face as she massaged her thigh.

Kronus sank down in front of her and placed his hand on her leg to mimic her massaging, his fingers strong and confident.

"What may I do to aid your comfort, Eva?" He kept his voice low; there was still a slight red tinge to his skin, and he'd been stiff and brooding throughout their return trip.

"Could you take it off?" she asked. Though she'd accepted the loss of her leg, she preferred having the prosthesis on, if only to maintain the illusion of normalcy. No matter how many times she and Kronus made love, no matter how many times he'd seen the rounded end of her stump, she was still self-conscious of it.

Nodding, he drew back slightly. He raised her skirt over her knees and cupped the back of her prosthesis with one hand, straightening her leg as he lifted it. With his other hand, he pressed the release; the pin disconnected with a soft click.

Eva watched him silently for a time, her eyes moving over his bent head, along his muscled arms, and down to his webbed and clawed hands — hands capable of such violence and destruction, hands that could maim or kill with ease, hands capable of such gentleness and care, hands that could soothe and caress.

"What did Ector mean?" she asked as Kronus removed her prosthesis. "When he said you've learned more than most? That I helped you find balance?"

His hands stilled, and his shoulders rose with a deep inhalation. After a few moments, he carefully slipped off her sock and liner, keeping his eyes on his task. "When Jax first brought Macy to the Facility, Dracchus made him present her to our people. Dracchus and many others were swayed by her, especially when Jax declared she was his mate...but I could not forget the history that had been taught to me since I was a youngling."

Eva frowned. "What history?"

"We were kept as slaves by the humans who once dwelled in the Facility," he said, folding the sock and liner. "We were not people to them, but tools, ideal for the harvest of halorium, some sort of crystal that made their machines erratic or inoperable. Halorium holds great power, and they were eager to have it. But they were cruel to our ancestors. They...they had *created* us, had given us life and purpose, but they did not acknowledge the intelligence they had designed within us.

"My ancestors rose against those humans, generations ago. And they killed every last one of them to claim the Facility as our home, our sanctuary. The lesson we held to afterward was simple — humans could not be trusted. They were our enemy, and they would seek either to control us or destroy us. But, for whatever reason, they never came. So we kept to ourselves, and saw to our own people, all the while struggling to overcome the things they did to keep us under control. They built us to...to die out, without their intervention."

"What do you mean?" Eva asked, eyes wide. *Die out?* Was... was something going to happen to Kronus? To the others?

"Macy and Arkon have accessed many files in the Computer. There are records detailing the way we were designed by the humans who made us. Our females have great difficulty conceiving young, and when they do, they rarely birth more females. It was a simple means to control our population. They wanted us to reproduce, to maintain their workforce, but they did not want more of us than they could control. It mattered little for them, in the end."

After setting her prosthesis and its accessories aside, he finally lifted his gaze to meet hers. "When Macy came, that is what I saw. Our ancestors fought to take our home from her kind, and she had no place there. Even if she was not a physical threat, there was always a chance of her contacting other humans, of her revealing the location of the Facility. Of revealing *us*. And for all our strength, we knew we could not match human numbers and human cleverness. We had grown up around the things humans had built. We knew their weapons. If enough humans came, our kind would have been doomed.

"So I raised my voice against her. I denounced her presence and demanded she be cast out into the sea to fend for herself. When more humans were brought to the Facility, I could scarce contain my anger — especially when two of those humans were hunters who had come for the sole purpose of finding our kind and killing us." He clenched his teeth, causing the muscles of his jaw to bulge. More color rippled through his skin, red and brief, pulsing flares of purple. "There were other kraken who felt the same as I. That humans had no place amongst our kind. That those who had embraced the humans were traitors both to our people and to the legacy of our ancestors.

"I fought. I challenged Jax and Dracchus on several occasions, and every time, I was forced to submit. No matter my fury, I could never best them. But I took the pain and pushed on. I wanted them *gone*. Away from our home, from our people, so that we could be safe. Because I believed that we would never be safe so long as there were humans amongst us."

He dropped his gaze to his hands, which lay palm up atop his tentacles, and curled his fingers. "Even after Macy gave birth to Sarina and Aymee to Jace, two younglings who were, by most measures, kraken, I fought. Despite those younglings being a glimmer of hope for our kind. Because what did that mean for *our* females? If humans could bear kraken young, would our females be abandoned? Would they be unimportant? Everything we had held to be true, everything we had been taught, was being threatened, and I could not allow our ways to be destroyed because they were *all that I had*.

"One night, one of my supporters crept into a den shared by a kraken female and her human mate and attempted to kill the human. Rhea was wounded defending her mate, and her youngling, Melaina, was present during the attack. I knew then that things were spiraling out of my control. I was furious over Rhea choosing a human male when there were so many kraken males she might have selected, and I did not want humans in our home…but I could not support harm coming to females and younglings. I said nothing when judgment was passed on Volk, who had carried out the attack. He was banished.

"More hunters came, and they captured three of our kind. One of those three was a kraken who supported my stance. He was called Neo. Though all three escaped, Neo clung to his experiences aboard the human ship, clung to the pain and suffering they had inflicted upon him, and returned to us filled with hatred for humans." Kronus raised a hand to his forehead, slowly trailing his palm back over his scalp. "I thought it should have been obvious to all our people after that. Humans were the enemy. They were cruel. We could not accept them.

"But some of my followers had grown dissatisfied with my leadership even before Neo's return. They felt I should have done something to protect Volk, that I should have spoken in his defense. They thought my lack of action against the humans was cowardice. But the humans had Dracchus on their side, and Dracchus… He is the largest, the strongest, the most respected of us all. Even the elders looked to him as a leader."

Kronus lifted his gaze to meet Eva's again. His features were strained, and his coloring had taken on an oddly muted tone. "I wondered more and more what I had begun. Was it worth the turmoil amidst our people?"

Eva reached out and brushed her fingers along his jaw. "What happened?"

He leaned slightly into her touch, expression softening infinitesimally. "There came a day when Neo called for a hunt. It has always been our way that the male who declares the hunt should lead it. Any who disagree or dispute the leader's methods may challenge him for that right. He led us far from home, insisting we hunt using traditional means though Arkon had devised new tactics that made our hunts faster. During that hunt, human ships came upon us. Neo insisted we attack. Both myself and Dracchus disagreed.

"But the hunters knew we were there. A battle ensued, and during the battle, I was struck by a harpoon." He moved a hand to his abdomen, to one of many scars Eva had caressed on many occasions. "I was run through, and the humans were pulling me toward their boat. Neo fled, saving himself."

They shared a meaningful look. Eva knew they were thinking about the same thing — the way Blake had left her to die. All along, Kronus had known what it felt like to be abandoned by someone he'd relied upon in his moment of need.

"It was Randall, the human who'd originally come to hunt kraken, who saved my life. Randall, whose death would have brought a smile to my face. Despite the danger to himself, he would not leave me behind...because he had accepted the kraken as his people. All kraken, even those of us who did not want him.

"When we returned to the Facility, we discovered that several of the females and younglings had been poisoned."

Eva gasped, covering her mouth with a hand. Kronus inhaled deeply, giving her a fleeting glance before averting his gaze again.

"Despite all the things I had said, despite the hatred I had spewed toward her, that was the first time Macy attacked me. Because her friends and family had come to harm. Because her *child* had come to harm...and she blamed me. And as I looked upon those younglings — younglings who were saved largely because of Aymee, another human — I knew it *was* my fault.

"I had never called for them to be poisoned. I had known nothing about the plot. But I knew I was responsible, nonetheless. That was the result of all that I had said and done — several younglings nearly killed. Neo had arranged it. He and the others had worked without me to obtain the venom of the blue needler to taint the humans' food supply, then he called the hunt to ensure that as many of us were away as possible. But Jax and Arkon had refused to go because they were having a… I do not know what it is called when people sit together on a blanket and share a meal."

"A picnic," Eva whispered.

Kronus's brow knit, and his lips were downturned in a deep, troubled frown. After nodding, he bowed his head, squeezed both his hands into fists on his lap, and swallowed thickly. "It was decided afterward that all those who'd followed me would be banished. I was given a chance to stay after speaking out against Neo and denouncing what he had done, but… I could not deny my responsibility in all of it. And I did not feel as though I had a place in the Facility any longer. In my desire to protect our people, I had betrayed them. I accepted banishment along with the others.

"I was left with *nothing*, and I could blame only myself for it. I could not return to the Facility without risking death, and I faced the same if I attempted to join the kraken who had once followed me. I had been wrong, *so* wrong…but Neo and the others…" He shook his head again. "They had cast honor and tradition aside just to pursue their hatred. That wasn't what I'd wanted, but I enabled it. I could not let it go, could not allow myself to forget and move on.

"I followed them, unseen, for two weeks. And when they decided to attack the Facility, to kill Dracchus, Jax, Arkon, Rhea, all the humans, and the younglings, I could not remain idle.

That was *not* what I had fought for. So…I went back to the Facility, knowing it meant my life was forfeit, to warn them. I did not expect to leave alive. To be honest, I…I did not *want* to. It would have been a good way to die, I thought. A small act of redemption, and then…nothingness."

Tears spilled down Eva's cheeks. She slid off the chair, down to her knees, but before her weight settled upon them, Kronus caught her and pulled her onto his lap. He raised a hand to her cheek and stared into her eyes.

"I fought alongside the people I had sought to remove from the Facility. I bled for them, and I killed kraken who I had known all my life. And if I could cry…I would have." He touched the tears on her cheeks and rubbed the moisture between his thumb and forefinger. "Tears became another thing for which I envied humans."

Eva wrapped her arms around his neck and cradled his head in the palm of her hand. She held him close, and he embraced her in return.

"You can't blame yourself for what happened," Eva said. "You might have given voice, but they already knew that hatred in their hearts. You…you didn't know true hate. You sought to protect those you cared for."

"I knew hate, Eva. First for the humans, and then…for myself. And when those I had wronged offered me forgiveness…I could not accept it. I did not know how." His hold on her tightened. "Not until something more important came along. Not until *you*."

Eva's breath caught, and her heart skipped only to begin beating rapidly an instant later.

He drew back to meet her gaze again, leaning his forehead against hers. "I came to The Watch because there was nowhere else for me. No place I could fit in, no place where I could look around me and not be reminded of what I had set into motion, of the blood that has stained my claws. But this place *never* felt like a home to me until you came into my life."

She sobbed, unable to hold back fresh tears. "How? How could I have made such a difference? I was…" She shook her head. "I didn't even see you as a person, either. I railed at you, hit you, *hated* you."

"You were broken, Eva. I knew that was not you. From the moment I took hold of you in that water, I knew the sort of person you were."

"What was I?"

"Selfless. Your leg was shredded, and your blood was misting the water, and all you wanted was to go back for your friends. All you wanted was to save *them*."

I have you, female. You are safe.

M-My friends Please! We n-need to save my friends!

Eva closed her eyes as the fragmented memory arose in her mind — Kronus's words, followed by her own. The desperation and pleading in her voice had been clear, and even now it made her stomach clench with dread.

"When I carried you onto the beach, you tried to crawl toward them." Kronus cupped her chin and tilted her face toward him. She opened her eyes to meet his golden gaze. "You had lost so much blood, teetered on the edge of death yourself, yet you spared not a thought for your own safety. *That* is who you are at your core. That is the female I wanted. That is the female I fought to save. All I did was help you remember who you have been all along." He caressed her chin. "A worthy female. More than I deserve…but I could not keep away from you."

Warmth blossomed within her. She recognized the feeling in her chest — it was overwhelming, consuming, breathtaking. It was joyous and painful, and everything in between. She'd only felt a fleeting hint of it before Kronus, a shadow, but *this*…she knew what it was now.

Eva framed his face with her hands. "You *are* worthy, Kronus. Everything you've gone through has made you into who you are now. It's shaped you, made you stronger, just as you've done for me. You fought your way up from the depths to rise above it all. You are worthy. *So* worthy. And you are the male I want. The kraken I love."

"Love," he repeated. He'd heard the word exchanged between the other kraken and human mates, had heard it from Eva, but it had never been directed at him. Though he had no prior experience with *love*, he somehow knew it was the correct word. It encompassed all the simplicity and complexity of what he felt for Eva; as mysterious as it was powerful, consuming and fulfilling. It was *everything*.

She was everything.

"I love you, Eva," he said, and it felt *right*. "It was not long ago that I did not understand what that meant, but I do now. I love you."

Eva made a small sound, something between a whimper and a sob, and brought her lips to his. She kissed him hard, desperately, as though she needed him in order to breathe, and Kronus returned it, dropping his hands to wrap his arms around her waist to pull her close.

"Join with me, Kronus," she pleaded against his mouth. "Be my husband, my mate, in every way, and never leave me."

"I will *never* leave you." His hearts thundered, and his blood ran hot through his veins. "I am yours, Eva, in every way possible."

Her hands smoothed down his back, and she clutched at him. "I need you. Now."

Kronus cupped her backside with his palms, arms pressed along her outer thighs. He rose, lifting her along with him, and she wrapped her legs around his waist as he carried her to the bed. He laid her on the covers and followed her down, holding himself aloft with arms on either side of her.

Her eyes opened and locked with his. She skimmed her fingertips down his chest and abdomen. His arousal was instant, and as soon as her fingers stroked his slit, his cock extruded into her waiting palm, aching and throbbing with want for her. She closed her fingers around his shaft and slowly moved her hand, up and down, twisting in the way she knew he liked. His hips pumped in time with her strokes.

Kronus bared his teeth and growled. Each stroke flooded him with sensation, threatening to steal his strength. Her touch was too much pleasure for him to bear for long.

Dropping a hand, he caught her wrist and stilled it. "Not yet."

He needed to be inside her.

Eva pulled her hand away and shifted, forcing Kronus to draw back. She turned onto her hands and knees, crawled farther up the bed, and peered at him over her shoulder. Her eyes were dark, their blue nearly engulfed by her pupils.

"No waiting." She tugged her skirt up over her waist. "Now. Take me *now*, Kronus."

Kronus fixed his eyes on her backside. This position was new. Her underwear molded to her slit, and the dampness of the fabric served as a visual confirmation of her arousal — not that he could miss her scent.

He stretched out his tentacles and drew himself up onto the bed, positioning himself behind her. She parted her thighs. He hooked a claw on either side of her underwear and pulled. The band offered only a moment's resistance before tearing. He tossed the tattered fabric aside and shifted his gaze to her glistening sex, releasing a low groan. She'd been right; there could be no waiting.

Keeping one hand on her hip, Kronus reached between her thighs and touched her scalding flesh, mindful his claws, to seek the little bud that provided her so much pleasure. She moaned and closed her eyes as he stroked it. Her hips undulated, grinding against his hand. He listened to her quickening breath and her soft sighs and soon felt the trembling in her thighs that signaled she was close to her peak.

Before she reached it, he pulled his hand back, bringing it to his mouth to lick her nectar from his fingers. Her flavor burst on his tongue and made him crave a deeper taste, but his need to be inside her was stronger. He needed to feel her sex clench around him, to feel her heat, to feel *her*.

Whether it lasted for a second or forever, he needed her to be the *only* thing to exist in his world.

"*Kronus*," she rasped.

He took his cock in hand and pressed the tip to her entrance. She eased back, taking that little bit of him inside her. He growled, set his hands on her shapely hips, and thrust into her as deep as she could take him.

Eva gasped as her body rocked forward with the force of his entry. Blissful heat surrounded his shaft; her tight walls squeezed him, drawing him deeper still. Pleasure spiraled up his spine. He drew back and looked down at where they were connected, and another wave of pleasure speared him. His cock glistened with their combined oils.

Kronus watched, enrapt, as he pushed forward and fed his erection into her body. He groaned again; this new position had altered the angle of their joining completely, creating stimulation he hadn't imagined before. Gripping her hips tighter, he raised two of his tentacles and coiled them around her legs. He swept the tip of one over her sex to tease her clitoris as he gradually increased the pace of his thrusts.

Eva grasped fistfuls of the bedding and inhaled sharply. Her body suddenly tensed as she came, her inner walls fluttering around him as a rush of liquid heat flooded her. She leaned down, hiding her face and muffling her cries. But it wasn't enough.

He slid two tentacles forward, slipped them beneath her shirt, and pulled them outward, ripping the fabric from her body and baring her back to him. He bent over her and caught the front of her throat in his hand, thumb and forefinger pressing against her jaw to tilt her face upwards. Wrapping his other arm around her middle, he pulled Eva back and forced her to lean against him in a kneeling position, adjusting the angle of her hips to allow him to push even deeper into her. She lifted an arm and cupped the back of his head.

Kronus pressed his face into her hair and skimmed his lips over her neck. "You are mine, Eva," he said huskily, nipping her ear as he moved a tentacle up her chest to cover her breasts, caressing her nipples with his suction cups.

He quickened his thrusts. "You are my mate."

His building pleasure was so concentrated that it formed immense pressure inside him; it nearly hurt, but it felt *so* good. *She* felt good. "You are *my wife.*"

Panting through parted lips, Eva tilted her head back. Her pulse ran wild beneath the pads of his fingers as she gripped his arms, blunt nails biting his skin.

"And I will *never*—" he pounded into her as deep as he could go "—*ever*—" another powerful thrust "—let you go."

He slammed his hips forward on each of those last three words, and the final thrust was the one that sent him over. The pressure within him burst with enough force to lock up all his muscles while simultaneously sapping all his strength. He threw back his head and groaned low, loud, and deep. His seed pumped into Eva as she was swept away by her own release. Her sex quivered around him, and Kronus willed his seed to take root, to fill her womb with a youngling of their own.

Dropping his hand from her throat, he pressed his palm over her heart — her solitary, human heart. It thumped rapidly. Her head lolled back, coming to rest on his shoulder, and he tightened his hold on her, inhaling deeply to draw in her scent. When she smiled, his eyes dipped to her lips.

Withdrawing from Eva, Kronus guided her body to turn and face him. He swiftly peeled off her remaining clothing, leaving her naked; her skin glowed with pleasure, softly pinkened and beaded with sweat. Then he lifted her again and lowered her onto his cock. He laid her on her back and propped himself over her, catching her lips with his.

He made love to her slowly this time, savoring her softness, relishing the taste of her sweetness on his lips, and thrilling in the subtle tremors that coursed through her limbs. Eva's hands roamed over his body, trailing fire in their wake, as his tentacles rose to caress her skin in response.

He was driven by an overwhelming need to possess every bit of her, to sear each moment they shared, each touch, forever into their memories, and to give himself over to her wholly.

Her throaty sighs filled the room, rising in pitch as she reached another peak. Kronus followed, baring his teeth in a growl as pleasure ripped through him and spilled into her.

Breath ragged, Kronus looked down at his mate, his beautiful Eva. His hearts constricted with emotion — with *love*. Her hair was a dark golden halo, her cheeks rosy, and her lips red from his kisses. She exhaled heavily and met his gaze, eyes sparkling with unmasked love.

Eva reached up and cupped his cheek. He turned his face into her touch, kissing her palm.

Everything he'd done had brought him, ultimately, to *her* — no matter the nature of his decisions, each had played a part in leading him along this path. Despite the hardships, despite the suffering, he would not have changed any of it. He didn't care if it was selfish; so long as they led to her, he would swim those waters again and again.

CHAPTER 17

EVA TORE AN EAR OF CORN FROM THE TOWERING STALK AND dropped it into the basket in front of her, repeating the process for the next stalk, and the next. She'd fallen into a steady rhythm as she made her way along the row. Tabitha, the woman who was carrying the basket, walked backward silently, hurrying off to empty the corn into the wagon nearby whenever the basket was full.

The field was blanketed with the sounds of rustling leaves, snapping stalks, and friendly conversation as at least two dozen townsfolk assisted the harvest. Eva kept her focus on her work.

She relished the burn in her limbs, the sweat rolling down her skin to dampen her hair and clothing, relished the sunlight and the scents of vegetation and rich earth. Her left knee and stump ached and throbbed, but she appreciated even that. After four weeks spent indoors apart from the few outings she went on with Kronus, this was a welcome change.

But it was bittersweet.

She'd no longer hear Addison's delighted squeal when Samuel snuck up behind her and kissed her neck or pinched her backside. Samuel would never make another silly joke, and

Hailey could never utter another snarky remark. But they were all safeguarded in Eva's memories, and she would always carry them with her.

A shrill whistle snapped Eva out of her thoughts.

"Time for break," Tabitha said, offering Eva a smile as she set the basket down. "Great work."

"Thanks. You too," Eva said, returning the smile.

As the two women walked toward the edge of the field, another group passed them, heading to pick up where the workers going on break had left off. It was a constant rotation that kept people in the fields all day without wearing anyone out.

Traversing the soft, lumpy soil presented difficulties for Eva, especially after a full morning of work, but she grew stronger and more confident each day. That was all because of Kronus. He'd pushed her to challenge herself from the start, refusing to accept *I can't* as an answer. He'd known what she was capable of long before she realized it.

Eva's heart quickened at the thought of her mate — her *husband*. Though they'd only been apart since the first rays of dawn touched the sea, she missed him and knew it would be a long day for them both. She drew comfort from the knowledge that she'd be in his arms again that night.

Once she emerged from the tall corn stalks, Eva made her way to the water table. She smiled and thanked the elderly woman who filled a cup of water for her. The woman chuckled when Eva guzzled it down and asked for more.

There was another table nearby set with food — sandwiches, fruits, vegetables, and small muffins — where several of the workers were already lined up to fill their bellies before their next rotation.

Eva stepped into line and pulled her braid over her shoulder, letting the breeze cool the back of her neck. When she reached the table, she plucked up her share of food and stepped away to find a place to sit and rest until her next shift.

She chose a spot beneath a winefruit tree. It was about twenty meters from where the other workers were gathered, but she couldn't resist its shade.

Though walking over the solid ground was easy, sitting on it was not. Holding her arm against her chest, she piled the food atop it and used her other hand to hold the trunk for support, slowly easing herself down. She released a slow exhalation once she was fully seated. She'd taken Kronus's presence for granted; he was usually there, lending her a hand or simply picking her up and setting her down somewhere comfortable. It was nice to be independent, but she had to admit, she took delight in his thoughtfulness and pampering.

Her stomach growled as she set the food on her lap. She unwrapped the sandwich, took a big bite, and closed her eyes, breathing slowly as she chewed. Before she knew it, she'd devoured both the sandwich and the muffin. She was peeling a violet-skinned winefruit when a pair of legs entered her peripheral vision.

"Hi, Eva," a familiar voice said.

Eva looked up to see Macy standing nearby. The blonde woman smiled. She bore her own armful of food.

How many times had Eva seen Macy as they'd worked in the fields since coming to The Watch? Likely more times that she could count. She had known *of* her then but hadn't *known* her — many townsfolk still talked about Macy and the events surrounding her even years after they'd occurred.

After hearing Kronus's tale, Eva wanted more than anything to get to know this woman, the one who'd brought the humans and kraken together.

"Is it okay if I join you?" Macy asked, gesturing to the ground next to Eva.

"Sure. I'd like that."

Eva studied Macy in silence as she lowered herself to the ground and unwrapped her sandwich. Macy seemed a little older than Eva, but not by much. Her skin was lightly tanned from the sun, and her hair, which was pulled back into a messy bun, was golden blonde. Her brows were dark, resting over wide blue eyes. Eva's gaze dropped to her slightly rounded stomach.

Unbidden, Hailey's words flitted through her mind.

Just the thought of one of those things squirming inside me makes me want to vomit.

"What's it like?" Eva asked before she could stop the words from escaping. She inhaled sharply, eyes flaring as they shot up to meet Macy's.

Macy chuckled. "What's what like?"

Eva cleared her throat, glancing away. Her cheeks burned with embarrassment. She looked down at the partially peeled winefruit in her hands.

Well, I've already asked. Might as well find out.

"Carrying a kraken baby," Eva said. "Does it…feel strange?"

"Honestly, I wouldn't know."

Eva looked back up at Macy, who wore an easy, unoffended smile. "What do you mean?"

"I've never conceived a human baby, so I don't know the difference. To me, they simply feel natural."

"So no…squiggling?"

Macy laughed and shook her head. "No. No squiggling. Here." Macy folded the wrapper over her sandwich, set her food aside, and leaned back. The change of position tightened her shirt around her middle. "He's quite active right now, if you'd like to feel?"

"Really?" She'd never touched a pregnant woman's stomach before. "You don't mind?"

"Not at all."

Eva gently placed her hand upon Macy's stomach. She

watched and waited, ears straining as though there were something to be heard. Her brows lowered; what was she meant to feel?

Something bumped against her palm, making her gasp. It was such a small, gentle touch, but it was the most amazing thing she'd ever felt. Her gaze flew to Macy's.

"The baby?" she asked, awed.

Macy nodded, her smile widening.

Eva returned her attention to Macy's belly as the baby nudged a few more times. She couldn't help but wonder what it would feel like to carry her own. To carry…Kronus's child. The thought sent a rush of excitement through her.

Could she be pregnant even now? She'd received a contraceptive shot when she'd joined with Blake, but it had likely worn off by now. She and Blake hadn't been ready for children. But after feeling this wonderous thing, Eva couldn't wait to share this part of life with Kronus. She grinned. He'd be such a protective father.

"It's a boy?" Eva asked.

"I'm not sure. We won't know until it's born." Macy laid a hand on her stomach next to Eva's. "Sarina is hoping for a sister."

"How many do you have?"

"This will be our third and final. At least for a while." She smiled wistfully. "They grow so fast in the beginning."

Eva withdrew her hand. "Thank you for that."

"Of course," Macy said, righting herself and picking up her sandwich.

They ate in companionable silence, listening to the drone of conversations and rustling of cornstalks around them. There was an easiness about Macy that Eva liked, and she wondered if a friendship could form between the two of them in time.

"I was attacked by a razorback once," Macy said, breaking the silence.

Eva turned her rounded eyes to Macy. "What?"

"While I was in the Facility, a young kraken girl, Melaina, went missing. She was a wanderer, much like my mate, Jax. She loved to explore, but she never quite understood the danger." Macy's fingers idly brushed over the sandwich wrapper. "I didn't understand the danger either, but it didn't stop me. All I could think of was how terrified she must've been. That she could've been killed at any moment, and how that would've broken her mother's heart. It reminded me so much of my family, and how we lost my sister that I just…acted. I didn't waste time waiting for one of the males to return or hoping one of them would find her. I *knew* how I could find her, so I just acted.

"I was wearing one of the diving suits when it happened. I remember the crushing pressure and the pain when its teeth finally broke through it. I've never been so terrified in all my life. I was able to kill it before it did any more damage, but I'll never forget those moments. The fear, the pain, the feeling of loss when I realized I might never see Jax again. And had I not been wearing that suit…"

Macy reached down at pulled up her pant leg. Pale, jagged scars ringed her calf, nearly in the same place Eva had been bitten.

"Thanks to Arkon's quick thinking, I got patched up pretty quick, so I wouldn't bleed to death…but an infection set in," Macy continued. "I would have died had Jax not risked himself and his people by bringing me back here."

Lowering her pant leg, Macy placed her hand atop Eva's. "I'm so sorry for what happened to you and your friends, Eva. If you'd ever like to talk, or just hang out, you're always welcome in my home."

Eva turned her hand and squeezed Macy's. "Thank you. That means a lot to me."

Macy smiled. "You have *no* idea how happy I am for Kronus.

When Aymee told me what he was doing for you, it seriously blew my mind. I didn't believe her. Kronus and a *human*." She shook her head, chuckling. "I didn't think I'd see the day. But I am happy. For both of you."

They talked until the whistle blew, announcing the next rotation. Macy followed Eva into the field and worked alongside her. Time slipped away as their conversation continued. Although Eva's body felt as though it would collapse at any moment, she pushed on to the final whistle.

Anticipation thrummed within Eva, though she knew it was likely too early for Kronus to be home yet. The sun had dipped, painting the sky orange and gold, and ushering in cooler temperatures that felt wonderful on her sweat-slicked skin. She stared at the sunset for a time, wondering if Kronus was looking at it and thinking of her, too.

She and Macy walked side-by-side through town, chatting easily with one another. Eva's leg pained her, worsening her limp, but she didn't care. It was wonderful to feel so carefree. To feel *normal*.

Macy was in the middle of a story about how Jax thought she was going to die after she drank fresh water when Eva was brought up short by someone grabbing her arm. Eva's laughter died.

She spun on her right leg and stumbled, nearly losing her balance until she was pulled securely against a broad chest. She gasped, startled; her arms were caged between her body and the man holding her. A familiar scent tickled her nose, mixed with alcohol fumes.

No, not now! The day was going so well!

"Eva—"

"Let me go, Blake," Eva said stiffly.

"Please just let me ta—"

"She said let her go," Macy said, her sweet voice turned hard.

Blake tensed, his arms tightening around Eva for a moment

before loosening. He drew back from her, but took hold of her upper arms, keeping her in place.

"Eva, please come home," Blake pleaded. "I miss you. It's…it's not the same without you. Other women aren't the same—"

Eva jerked out of his grasp, catching her balance by slapping a hand against the side of a nearby building. "After everything you've done, after I've moved on and found *happiness*, you really have the nerve to ask me to go back to you?"

Blake stepped closer, but his advance faltered when Eva held her hand up and retreated.

"No, Blake," she said.

He pressed his lips together and frowned. His hair stood on end, his shirt was rumpled, as though he'd just thrown it on after picking it up off the floor, and there were dark circles under his eyes. Eva had no reason to feel guilty. He'd chosen his path when he walked away from her, when he renounced her. But deep down, she still cared for the man who had once been her husband, who had once been her friend.

"Blake," she said softly, "you need help. You…you might not have shown your pain in the beginning, but now… I think you should talk to someone."

He shook his head and stepped closer. "I just need you, Eva. Let's start over. Remember how we used to be? How we couldn't keep our hands off each other? We could have that again. I wouldn't even mind your…" his eyes dropped to her left leg, and he cringed, "deformity. I can learn to ignore—"

"That's enough," Macy said, moving to Eva's side.

"This is none of your business!" Blake snapped, glaring at Macy.

"She's right, Blake," Eva said. "That's enough. I am not coming back to you. I belong to Kronus now."

Blake flinched as though she'd slapped him. "That…that *creature*? You're really *fucking* that thing?"

Eva narrowed her eyes. She could ignore his remark about

her *deformity*, but she wouldn't stand here and let him insult Kronus. "He is my mate. My *husband*. We've joined, and I love him."

"*No!*"

"Yes. You and I are done, Blake," Eva said with finality, then softened her voice. "We're done."

Eva turned away from him and forced her legs into motion. They were stiff, and fire blazed through her left leg, but she kept putting one foot in front of the other without looking back. Macy remained beside her and quietly offered Eva her arm, giving her a shoulder to lean on. For that, Eva was thankful. She didn't know if she could have continued on her own.

"Are you okay?" Macy finally asked once they'd followed the path through the jungle and the row of clifftop houses was in view.

"I'll be fine." Eva turned her head, meeting Macy's concerned gaze. "Thank you."

"Of course." She rubbed the back of Eva's hand. "I'm sorry you had to go through that. He...doesn't look well. I'll talk to Dr. Rhodes tomorrow to see if he'll pay Blake a visit. I think whatever guilt Blake's holding onto is festering inside him."

Eva frowned. Had Blake remained by her side, everything would have been different. They might have pulled through the entire ordeal together...or they might not have. She'd never know. Perhaps it made her heartless, but she was glad for the way things had turned out. She'd discovered true love — it was both selfish and unselfish, unwavering, powerful. Everything that had happened had brought her to Kronus.

Macy remained with her until they reached the home Eva and Kronus shared. Before the woman could leave, Eva caught her and pulled her into her arms, holding her tightly. Macy returned the embrace without hesitation.

"Thank you so much, really," Eva said. "For everything."

"Anytime," Macy replied.

Macy drew away and made a shooing motion. "Get inside and take care of that leg. You worked hard today, probably more than you should have. Rest up."

Eva laughed, brushing the moisture from her eyes. "I will."

Once Macy was gone, Eva went inside and moved to the window. She gazed out toward the sea, searching the beach below for any signs of Kronus. Though she knew she wasn't likely to see him until after dark, she couldn't help her hopeful anticipation. She touched her fingers to the glass.

Soon.

Stepping into the bathroom, she pulled off her filthy clothes and tossed them in the dirty clothes basket. Her stomach felt hollow, but the thought of food nauseated her. All she wanted to do was clean up and crawl into bed.

After removing her prosthesis, sock, and liner, she grabbed her crutches from their place against the wall nearby and stepped to the shower. She set the crutches aside and turned on the water.

Cold blasted her, making her hiss. It made her cherish those few hot showers she'd been blessed with at the clinic all the more. She washed quickly, soaping up her body, shampooing her hair, and rinsing off without pause. By the time she was done, she was shivering.

Plucking the towel off its hook, she hurriedly dried herself and wrapped it around her body before pulling her crutches closer. After brushing her hair and teeth at the sink, she made her way back into the main room.

Standing in the center of the room, Eva looked around. Everything was so still, so quiet and lonely without Kronus. So *empty*. It was their home, and yet...

This *place* wasn't home, *he* was.

Whenever he was near, everything felt right in the world. When he wasn't, this place was nothing more than wood and stone. She wouldn't care if it burned to the ground so long as she still had Kronus.

Eva plucked a sleep shirt out of the armoire's drawer and pulled it over her head, letting the towel fall. She caught the towel on her stump and flung it aside. She maneuvered over to the bed, turned, and plopped down on the edge. A relieved sigh escaped her; it was lovely to finally be off her legs.

She propped her crutches against the bottom corner of the bed and glanced out the window. The sky was a deep violet, with only a sliver of sunlight on the horizon. She smiled knowing Kronus would return soon.

Scooting herself farther onto the bed, she laid down and closed her eyes. Every one of her muscles felt like it was made of rock, heavy and unresponsive, and her whole body ached from the day's work. Before she knew it, weariness tugged at her consciousness, dragging her into the depths of slumber.

It felt as though she'd just closed her eyes when the bedding dipped behind her and a body pressed against her back. She must have turned onto her side in her sleep.

He's home.

Eva smiled, humming sleepily as a warm hand fell upon the bare skin of her hip. It slid upward, bunching the hem of her nightshirt as strong fingers smoothed over her belly and toward her breasts. Her skin tingled with awareness. The palm cupped her breast as forefinger and thumb caught her nipple and pinched. A bolt of arousal shot through her, but something about this touch felt *wrong*.

She pushed past her grogginess, forcing herself to alertness. The hand touching her was rough, calloused, and not once did she feel the delicious scrape of its claws.

Eva's eyes shot open, and her entire body jolted when a hard cock, restrained by clothing, ground against her backside. There was a deep, throaty groan from behind her.

"Fuck, Eva. I missed you so much," Blake said, brushing his

lips against the back of her ear and trailing them down her neck.

"What the fuck!" Eva screeched, kicking her leg and reaching for the edge of the bed to pull herself away from him.

Blake grabbed her, yanked her closer, and rolled her onto her back. He loomed over her, a dark shadow in the night, and captured her wrists in his hands, securing them on the bed beside her head. Eva thrashed beneath him.

"Stop it, Eva! Quit fighting me!"

"Let go of me!" she screamed.

"Shh! Be quiet! I don't want anyone—"

Blake's word cut off in a pained grunt as her thigh connected with his groin. His hands loosened, allowing her to escape. She pulled herself out from beneath him and crawled across the bed toward her crutches. She reached forward. Her fingertips brushed the cool wood of her crutches when Blake's hands fell on her hips, pulling her back.

The crutches clattered to the floor.

"Damnit, Eva! Why are you doing this?" Blake growled, picking her up. "Why are you fighting us?"

"Let go! Leave me alone!" she yelled, shoving against him.

"Eva, stop! Damnit, stop fighting me! I can't let you keep fucking that monster. You're *my* wife!"

Eva pulled back her fist and struck him. She felt the scrape of his teeth against her knuckles as he flinched, reflexively dropping her.

She wasn't expecting it. She fell, striking her head first on the corner of the bed, then the floor. Pain exploded within her skull, and a wave of dizziness hit her. The floor was cold against her cheek. She tried to lift her head, but it was too heavy. Whimpering, she stretched her arms and curled her fingers, seeking purchase to drag herself away.

"Fuck!" Blake snapped, stomping his foot. He growled, then released a frustrated yell. "Damnit, Eva, why did you have to fight me?" His footsteps neared until he stood right next to her. Sighing, he slipped his hands beneath her, lifted her body off the floor, and cradled her against his chest.

Eva's stomach lurched, and black spots swam before her eyes. Her head hurt so much...

"Let's take you home," Blake said softly.

"No... I'm—"

"Shh," he soothed, caressing her face, his finger pausing when it met something wet on her cheek. "I'll take care of you this time, Eva."

No. No! I want... I want Kronus!

But she couldn't give voice to her pleas; her eyes drifted shut as darkness claimed her.

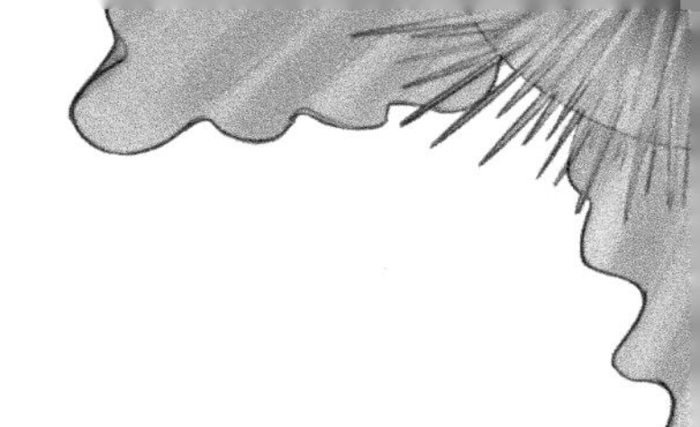

CHAPTER 18

KRONUS WATCHED THE RAZORBACK GLIDE THROUGH THE WATER below, shafts of evening sunlight creating wavering patterns across its spiny back. The pair of harpoons jutting from the creature's side had not been fired today; they were reminders of what had happened near the dock four weeks ago.

This was the razorback that had escaped.

He adjusted his hold on his spear, shifting its haft to run along the outside of his harpoon gun's barrel. It wasn't an ideal arrangement, but the spear was too large to hold in his tentacles as he swam without impeding his movement. He flicked his gaze ahead. Dracchus swam in the lead, the spearhead of their hunting party. He was flanked by Randall and Larkin, both dressed in sleek diving suits from the Facility. Vasil, Kronus, and Brexes formed the middle row — Kronus in the center — with Charos and Mareus immediately behind. Jax swam at the rear, the diamond point immediately opposite Dracchus.

Kronus's hearts thumped. Razorbacks were dangerous beasts, but it was not fear that sped his hearts. He could not deny the thrill of being on a hunt again, the thrill of swimming alongside his people — human and kraken alike. Locating the other razorback that had attacked Eva and her friends was an unexpected but welcome bonus.

And still, he found he would rather have remained with Eva. The pride of providing for and protecting his people was great, but it could not compare to the joys he shared with his mate, could not compare to the happiness he'd finally tasted.

This is for her as much as for anyone else.

The reminder strengthened his resolve; a mate meant the gaining of new responsibilities, not the abandonment of old ones. These hunts for razorback would mean food, but, more importantly, they would make the coastal waters safer for *everyone.*

He split his attention between the razorback and Dracchus, awaiting the latter's signal. The water teemed with countless schools of fish, which often swam between the hunters and their intended prey, obscuring the most direct lines of attack. That the razorback was not feasting on the abundant sea life was telling; the migration had brought so many fish to these waters that even razorbacks, normally ravenous beasts, could easily eat their fill.

A long stream of fish passed, their tight formation resembling a shimmering silver ribbon waving in the breeze. The fish flowed above the razorback in an undulating line. Once they passed, the water was suddenly clear. Kronus swung his harpoon gun to the ready.

Dracchus raised a hand and flashed yellow. A moment later, his skin flared red, and he curled his fingers into a clenched fist. No one had any doubt of what his sign meant.

Kronus squeezed the trigger. The rapid thumps of nine harpoon guns firing pulsed through the water. The razorback's leisurely movements grew suddenly frantic as all nine harpoons struck.

Tether lines went taut as the creature attempted to flee. Panicked bubbles churned the water, accompanied by wispy tendrils of blood. Kronus tensed and flared his tentacles to battle the creature's strength; it seemed none of the harpoons had done enough damage to be immediately fatal. The muscles of his arms strained to maintain his grip on the gun.

Dracchus signaled again; it was time for the next phase.

Kronus passed his gun to Vasil and took his spear in both hands. The others swam in opposing directions, expanding the diamond formation and pulling the tether lines even tighter. The sudden force from conflicting directions severely limited the razorback's range of movement. Such an opportunity would not last long.

Without a second thought, Kronus darted toward the razorback as quickly as he could swim, extending the spear ahead of him. His momentum punched the head of the spear into the beast's skull, and it sank deep — at least as deep as Kronus's forearm was long. A cloud of blood blossomed on the underside of the beast's head. Kronus propelled himself clear of the razorback's jerking death throes.

The surrounding fish gave the hunting party a wide berth as Kronus and his companions hauled the huge carcass back toward the waiting boats, towing it by the tether lines.

Kronus felt lighter. A successful hunt was always a source of pride, but this one was more special than most. He finally felt like a part of his people again, he finally had a mate — a *forever* mate — and news of this hunt's prize would hopefully bring Eva satisfaction.

She'd walked with him to the dock early the previous morning, descended the steps into the sand, and looked out over the water where her life had been forever changed. With the wind tousling her hair, she'd let go. Let go of the friends she'd lost, let go of her guilt for being the one who'd lived. Tears had streamed from her eyes as she'd said goodbye to them. Kronus had taken her hand to let her know he was there with her. He'd had no words to offer in those moments, but he felt words weren't what she'd needed.

All she needed was *someone*. All she needed was *him*. Just the same as he needed her.

When the hunting party reached the boats, they quickly bundled the dead razorback alongside the largest vessel; it was too big to be brought on board any of the watercraft. The carcass would create extra drag and slow the ship, but neither kraken nor human was willing to let so much meat go to waste.

Splitting up, the hunters climbed into the boats. Kronus shrugged off the familiar sense of heaviness as he pulled himself from the sea's embrace and into open air. He wouldn't allow anything to weigh him down. The journey back to The Watch was likely to take a few hours, but once it was done, he could be with Eva again. He knew little about the work humans did to grow and harvest their plants but was eager to hear about her day.

He eased himself down onto the floor of the boat, stretching his arms along the railing. The day had been long, but his aches were well-earned.

The boat swayed as Vasil climbed in, but that motion was insignificant compared to the wild rocking when Dracchus pulled himself up and over the side. Water dripped from the trio of kraken and pooled at the bottom of the boat.

"Guess I'm the popular one today," said Camrin, the red-haired human piloting the vessel. His smile, as ever, was warm and good-natured. He was one of the younger fishermen, and his mate and their small child awaited him in town.

Despite Kronus's lingering unease with humans — which refused to cease no matter how much he came to know about them — he couldn't help but like Camrin. He seemed an honest, dependable man.

Kronus glanced at the other three vessels, each of which held two of the hunters. Bobbing atop orange-stained waters, the ships looked like they were skimming across liquid fire that licked and lashed at their hulls but could not ignite the wood. It would be dark by the time they arrived home.

Home...

He felt strange thinking of The Watch that way, but that did not change the fact — after nearly ten months of it feeling like nothing more than a place in which to exist, the town had suddenly become his home because of Eva.

"Perhaps you offer the smoothest sailing," Dracchus said. His black skin glistened in the sunset light, creating gold and orange highlights along the ridges of his powerful muscles.

Only two years before, Kronus would have bristled at having to share so tight a space with Dracchus.

Wrong, he told himself. *That was true up to a couple weeks ago.*

"I'm not sure about that," Camrin replied with a chuckle, "but I'll accept it as a compliment, all the same. Just, uh…let's not tell Breckett or my dad, okay? I don't want to test that old saying about fishermen."

Kronus turned his attention to the human, watching as Camrin manipulated the boom and rudder to swing the boat around, beginning their journey homeward. "What saying?"

Camrin laughed, cheeks reddening slightly. "Right, sorry. Sometimes I forget you guys weren't brought up around here."

That seemed an odd reply. Kronus's instinct was to seek the insult hidden in those words, but he could detect none. There was only…acceptance, an implication that the kraken were a natural, familiar part of life for Camrin.

"Anyway, I was just thinking of something my father used to say all the time." Camrin cleared his throat. When he spoke again, he did so in a gruffer, deeper voice. "*Only thing harder than an old seaman's head is his fists.*"

Kronus pondered the words. At face value, their meaning was simple, but he sensed there was more to them just beneath the surface. Humans liked saying things that contained layered meanings. When the realization came to him a moment later, he felt foolish. It wasn't merely an observation, it was a warning — do not cross the older fishermen. They were a hard bunch. He couldn't help but smirk; his time with Eva over the last few weeks had taught him to better recognize — and appreciate — human humor.

There was a bit of self-deprecation in a man who made his living by the sea admitting to hardheadedness. That was a sort of humor Kronus might relate to, one day.

"I have worked with Breckett often," Kronus said, "and thus know your words are true."

Camrin's smile stretched into a grin. He manipulated the ropes and rigging to adjust the sail, matching the speed of the boat hauling the razorback.

The blazing orb that was the sun hung just above the horizon on the port side of the boat, casting the sky and sea in brilliant reds, pinks, oranges, and purples. The coast was visible to starboard, already blanketed in deepening shadow. The gentle sounds of water in motion all around were soothing, easing Kronus's hearts back to a normal pace.

"How is your female, Kronus?" Dracchus asked.

Instinct sparked fire in Kronus's gut; he could not hold back the surge of protectiveness rising within him, could not prevent his suspicion. Eva was *his*, unquestionably, irrevocably, *forever*. Another male taking interest in her was unacceptable. Though he'd never bested Dracchus in a challenge, Kronus would not hesitate to fight. He would not relinquish her.

Dracchus has a female of his own already, riding in one of the other boats. He is just asking after Eva's health. Just...making conversation.

The thought cooled Kronus's agitation, but only slightly.

"Fine," Kronus replied.

Dracchus swept his gaze across the surrounding water. "I am glad."

No one said anything for some time. Heat crackled beneath Kronus's skin, a clear indication of his lingering displeasure and defensiveness.

"I was told to invite you and your Eva to my den," Dracchus said after a while. "Larkin wants to meet her."

Kronus and Dracchus looked at each other in that moment, gazes locking. Dracchus wore a wary but hard expression. Despite all the changes that had overtaken the kraken way of life, dens remained private places, shared only by mates and younglings. Even Dracchus, who had been one of the kraken to lead their people to embrace those changes, had not fully overcome the old way of thinking.

Clenching and unclenching his jaw, Kronus nodded. "I am sure Eva would enjoy that."

"Larkin, as well."

They held each other's stares. Camrin coughed, but neither kraken looked toward him.

"If you mean to challenge one another, get into the water and do so," Vasil said at length.

His words finally broke both Kronus's and Dracchus's focus; they turned their heads to face the gray kraken, who was positioned at the bow. Vasil's back was to them, his attention on the sea ahead.

"There is no reason for a challenge," Dracchus said.

"None," Kronus agreed, though he'd not shaken off his irritation. Part of him *wanted* a challenge, though it would accomplish nothing.

Vasil shook his head. "You inquired about his mate, Dracchus, while their relationship is still new."

Dracchus tilted his head, brow falling low. He stared at Vasil's back for many moments before his expression softened with sudden understanding and he turned back to Kronus. "I felt the same."

Kronus gritted his teeth. The same about what? About *Eva*?

He sank his claws into the wood beneath him. "Clarify your meaning, Dracchus."

The black kraken's lips fell into a deep frown, and his eyes shifted toward a neighboring boat — toward Larkin. "When Larkin became my mate, I felt the same as you."

"And how is it that I feel?"

"Guys, this is clearly just a misunderstanding…" A hint of unease colored Camrin's otherwise calm voice.

"Protective," Dracchus said.

Pressing his lips together, Kronus dropped his gaze. The emotions flitting through him were far more complicated than that single word, yet, somehow, it seemed to encompass all of them.

"Even now, after two years, I bristle when other males are near her. I trust her to take care of herself, but even this distance between us feels too great. And when she first became mine, I constantly battled the urge to crush *anyone* who dared even glance at her."

Kronus briefly flicked his gaze to the bow. Vasil had not changed his position, but there appeared to be a tension in his posture at odds with the easy rhythm of the boat.

"It is instinct," Kronus said after returning his attention to Dracchus.

"Yes." Dracchus nodded. "Instinct."

Silence settled between them again, allowing the sounds of wind and sea to rise to clarity.

"So…how about this weather?" Camrin asked cheerily, his tone so exaggerated that both Kronus and Dracchus smiled.

"The weather is better than any conversation of it could hope to be," Kronus replied.

Dracchus grunted his assent.

"Does this come naturally to you two, or is it something you have to consciously work toward?" Camrin asked.

Dracchus turned his head toward Camrin. "What do you mean, human?"

"Just that I can't imagine anyone being as grumpy as you guys without actively trying to be." Camrin's grin, as amiable as ever, softened his words considerably. "You guys need to relax a little. Aren't you supposed to be friends?"

Once again, Kronus and Dracchus met each other's gazes. *Friend* was one of those words that had held little meaning for Kronus through most of his life; it had existed amongst the kraken primarily as an artifact of their long-ago contact with humans. He understood it better now.

He and Dracchus had been rivals at best and enemies at worst, but those times had passed. Where did that leave them? What did that *make* them?

"We are not friends," Kronus said, "though we could be. The building of such a relationship is difficult when both individuals are *assholes*."

Dracchus's features darkened. For a moment, Kronus was sure he'd pushed too far, that he'd overestimated the good will extended toward him, that Dracchus was about to attack.

Slowly, Dracchus's frown split into a grin; the expression was sharp-toothed but not predatory.

Solemnity settled over Kronus's face. "For everything I did, Dracchus, for every wrong—"

"I know," Dracchus said gently. "Your actions afterward have spoken loud enough, Kronus."

"Yet I must *say* it." A strange sensation flitted through his chest, a desperate energy that threatened only to worsen. He rubbed at it absently, knowing in the back of his mind it would not be eased in such a fashion. "For all the wrongs I have done to you, to our people, I am sorry."

The smile fell away from Dracchus's lips. He leaned forward, reached out with one thick arm, and placed a hand on Kronus's shoulder. At another time, in another context, Dracchus's touch would have signaled a fight, with raking claws and thrashing tentacles. But things had changed...and Kronus was coming to see that many of those changes weren't bad.

"I am sorry, as well," Dracchus said, "for how it all happened. For each of our people who were lost along the way. Would that there had been a better end to it for all of us."

"It...took me a long while, but I think I understand now. I have an idea of what you and the others were fighting for," Kronus replied. "Had I known sooner, I would have chosen to swim with you from the start."

"You two are all over the place," Camrin said. Kronus turned to find the human shaking his head. When he noticed Kronus's stare, Camrin quickly averted his gaze. "I just mean that one moment, you're looking ready to tear out each other's throats, and the next you're about to give each other a hug. It's confusing to innocent bystanders like me."

"Yes." Kronus smirked. "We are acting more like humans with each passing day."

Camrin laughed, a rich, hearty sound that reminded Kronus of the man's father, Wade. Every time Kronus had been around Wade and Breckett at the same time, the two fishermen had joked and laughed frequently. Their light moods had always seemed to contradict the burly, sea-worn visages they presented to the world.

Dracchus and Kronus both chuckled. Even Vasil, whose displays of emotion were rarer and more muted than Dracchus's, watched with an amused smile on his face.

However strong his instinctual protectiveness and possessiveness regarding Eva, Kronus could trust these males. If he couldn't be with her, this company was tolerable, even *pleasant.* The realization did nothing to ease his impatience to be home with his mate, but it provided some comfort.

"Tell us about her," Vasil said. His voice jarred Kronus from his thoughts.

Swallowing the reflexive rebuke threatening to emerge, Kronus dropped his gaze to the floor of the boat, where the water that had run from their bodies was cooling in a pool of shadow. He loved Eva, and she loved him, but he was also proud of her, impressed by her, awed by her. Why not share that pride? Why not allow himself the pleasure of praising her, of conveying his good fortune to these males?

"I…first noticed her before the attack. She alone of her human companions looked at me as a person, with curiosity rather than judgment. When I freed her from the razorback, all she wanted was to go back and rescue her companions."

As Kronus continued to speak — about her selflessness, her consideration, her massive stores of inner strength and willpower — he fell in love with Eva all over again. In his mind, he was looking into her pure blue eyes and combing his fingertips through her golden-brown hair, and the ghost of her scent flowed through his memory. He could almost feel her silken skin against his, could almost feel her fingertips trailing lightly along the length of a tentacle or over the muscles of his abdomen. Even the recollection of Eva was enough to warm his blood.

"You are changed," Dracchus said when Kronus was finished.

Kronus reflected upon those words for several moments before replying. "No, I am not. I still often feel the urge to throttle you, for example." He smirked. "Eva has…brought out the best in me. She has broadened my understanding of a great many things and has taught me patience, but she has not made me change. She…wants me as I am."

"That's how Jenny makes me feel," said Camrin.

Only a sliver of the red-orange sun remained visible over the horizon, leaving the boats in a steadily shrinking column of fire-kissed seawater. Camrin sat with his eyes narrowed and his pupils enlarged. Though Kronus knew humans could not see well in the dark, he also knew that the fishermen of The Watch were so familiar with these coastal waters that they could navigate them despite the limited visibility.

Kronus regarded Dracchus, whose form grew increasingly indistinct in the failing light. "Why are you not riding with your Larkin?"

Dracchus turned his head; Kronus followed his gaze to the adjacent boat, where the glow of the computer displays in Larkin's facemask stood out clearly against the black water.

"She is using the suit to keep watch while helping to navigate," Dracchus said. "I want nothing more than to go to her, but I do not wish to be a hindrance to her duties. My instinct is to remain at her side without fail...but I know she is capable. I know she is fine. I trust her."

Dracchus's answer touched something deep within Kronus; he understood those conflicting drives all too well. Leaving Eva to join in this hunt had been amongst the hardest things he'd ever done — a fact made ridiculous if he paused to consider the many difficult and dangerous tasks he'd undertaken in his lifetime.

They sailed onward, steered by Camrin's steady hand, and easy conversations flowed between the periods of companionable silence. It was a strange journey for Kronus, but he welcomed the company. They were all on the water for the same goal, regardless of their species or their past relations. That was something in which to take pride; they'd come a long, long way over the last few years.

Old electric lights were illuminating the dock when the boats finally sailed into the bay. The gently bobbing structure glowed like a beacon on the dark water, a heartwarming sight after a long day of hunting.

After the boats were tied off, the kraken dove into the water and quickly saw to the razorback, removing the harpoons and spear before hooking it to the crane tethers. The fishermen on the dock hauled the body out of the water and into the air once it was secured.

Humans and kraken worked together to butcher the creature, cutting slabs of meat from its massive body to be stored for later use. Kronus remained until that work was done; the final task was to lift the bundled meat up to the warehouse using a larger crane situated atop the cliff, but the humans were more than adept enough to accomplish the task on their own.

The dual moons had risen above the town by the time Kronus and the other kraken — minus Dracchus, who chose to travel by land with Larkin and Randall — dived back into the water. They swam around the cape and along the coastline, keeping near to the surface and in formation in case of any lurking razorbacks. The journey proved uneventful.

Kronus lifted his gaze as he moved out of the water, sweeping it over the pale, silvery sand and shadowed cliffs to the dwellings atop the ridge. Lights — all produced by flames, as there was no electric power out here — burned in some of the windows, welcoming their males home.

Turning his head, he looked at the last house in the row, the house he shared with Eva. His brow furrowed; the place was shrouded in darkness, reduced to a lump of shadow atop the night-shrouded cliff.

Unease coiled its tentacles through his gut, slithering and cold. Eva should have been home already. He hurried his pace across the sand, offering distracted answers to queries from his companions that he didn't really hear in his suddenly frantic state.

This was her first day of work in weeks. She is tired and went to sleep. I cannot fault her for that, especially as I am always telling her to rest.

That was the simplest, most likely explanation.

Yet his hearts beat faster than usual, and his eyes continually drifted toward his home, even when he drew too near the cliff, and it was blocked from his view by the rock face.

Or she is visiting with one of the other females. I cannot keep her all to myself, however much I long to. Humans are a social people.

His mind leapt back to the day she'd taken herself to the beach in her wheelchair and attempted to crawl into the sea. That had been her lowest point, but she'd come back from it, hadn't she? Kronus shoved the possibility aside; she would not have done that again, not after all her progress. Not with how close they'd grown and all they'd shared. She was happy.

He waved to the others after scrambling up the rocks and onto the ridge, wasting no time in darting home. Rocks and vegetation bit into the undersides of his tentacles, but he ignored the stinging pain. Though part of him knew he was overreacting, it was just as he and Dracchus had discussed — it was instinct.

He would open the door and rush inside to find her sleeping peacefully in their bed. The noise of his entry would likely disturb her slumber, and he would quickly rinse the brine from his skin in the shower before joining her in bed, feeling like a fool for all his worry.

When he reached his dwelling, he forced himself to stop and release a long, slow breath. He opened the door quietly and slipped inside. The moonlight flowing through the windows created long patches of light across the floor. The bedding was rumpled, but Eva was not in bed. A strange smell hung in the air, mingling with so many familiar scents that he could not place it. Perhaps she'd brought home a plant to eat that he'd not yet encountered.

"Eva?" he called. His voice seemed thunderous in the small, relatively quiet space.

When she didn't answer, he moved to the bathroom and pushed the door open. He was greeted by more silver moonlight and black shadows. Within the light rested Eva's prosthetic leg.

Kronus spun about, panic flaring in his chest like a fire splashed with fresh oil. His gaze darted to the bed again; it was only from this angle that he noticed her crutches on the floor, one laid atop the other.

Heat prickled across the surface of his skin.

"Eva!" he shouted.

Kronus rushed to the bed, grasped the blankets, and tossed them off — as though she might somehow have hidden herself among them. The fabric fell to the floor over and around his tentacles. It was only then that he identified the odd smell; it was on the blankets, brushing directly against his suction cups.

Alcohol.

It was a drink many humans seemed to enjoy, but it made their minds...*muddled*. Eva had not partaken in such beverages while she'd been with him...

Dread solidified low in his belly as he coiled his tentacles around the bedding, seeking every smell, every taste, that clung to it. Most were known to him, familiar reminders of his life with Eva. But there was more — not just that bitter whiff of alcohol, but a masculine scent, stale sweat mixed with something pungent and foul.

Rage fanned the flames of his panic. Eva was gone, but she hadn't left of her own will. He wadded the blankets and hurled them aside, arms trembling with impotent fury. Turning, he stalked toward the door only to halt abruptly on the other side of the bed. His tentacle had touched something moist and sticky, something with a metallic tang.

He raised his tentacle into the moonlight. The blood coating it glistened in the silver glow.

A sudden, immense pressure in his chest stilled his hearts and stole his breath. His blood seemed colder than the air in the storage rooms of the Facility, where water turned solid. He'd tasted her blood before, when he pulled her out of the water after the attack. There was no question this was hers, too.

A thousand thoughts blasted through his mind in that instant — guesses about where his mate had been taken, about what fate might have befallen her, torrents of guilt for having left her alone, dozens of actions to consider. He rejected all of it.

Instinct, fury, and love; those were what he clung to, those were all that could help him find Eva and make her safe again. He would not allow himself to imagine what harm she might have come to, not now. Without wasting another moment, he burst out of the dwelling, nearly knocking the door off its hinges, and roared into the night.

The sound exploded from his burning chest, tore apart his throat, and reverberated through the night sky, so powerful it seemed likely to shake the moons and drown the ocean's whispers forever.

He hoped Blake heard it. Hoped the man was shaking with fear of what would be hunting him.

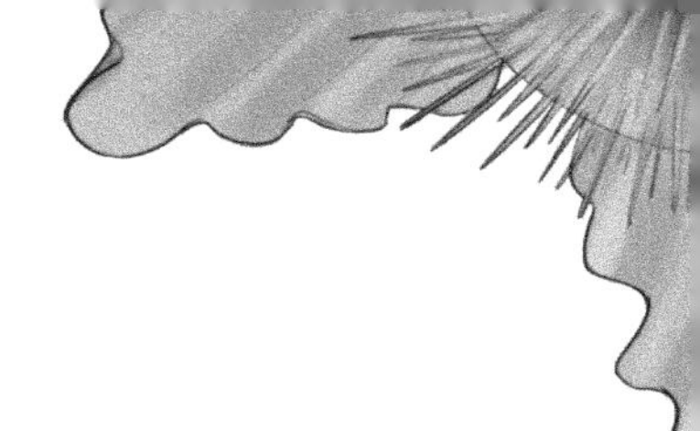

CHAPTER 19

MOONLIGHT SHONE ON THE GRASS ALONG THE RIDGE, GRANTING the illusion of countless thin, gleaming knives jutting from the dirt. Were they as dangerous as the night made them appear, Kronus would have plucked each and every blade with the intent of driving their points into Blake's flesh one by one.

Ghostly lantern lights bobbed on the path ahead, held aloft by dark figures — his neighbors, his *people*, but they were not who he wanted to see. He needed to find Eva, to take her in his arms and never release her. He needed to find Blake and draw the man into a different sort of embrace, one that would be relinquished only after the final, rattling breath escaped his frail human lungs.

But where are they? Where has he taken her? Where is his home?

A fresh wave of fury swept through him, adding to the churning sea of rage and fear inside his hearts. The Watch had dozens of buildings, perhaps *hundreds* of homes. It would take hours to locate Blake and Eva if they were even in town at all. His gaze flicked to the thicker inland vegetation, some of which cast its own soft, eerie light. Blake could have taken her *anywhere*.

"Kronus?" someone called from just ahead, raising a lantern. The light momentarily blinded him.

He growled and lifted a hand to shield his eyes. "Move aside. I must find her."

"What is wrong?" another person asked; Kronus recognized the voice as Vasil's.

"He took her, and I must go!" Kronus shouted. His skin was red, with fire coursing over its surface, and his hearts beat hard enough that they threatened to break his ribs. "She is hurt."

"Kronus, you must calm down," Ector said, hands raised in a placating manner.

"I will *not* be calm," Kronus grated through clenched teeth. "She is *mine*, and she has been taken! Now move aside."

Two more figures raced to join Ector and Vasil. Macy and Jax.

"What's going on?" Macy asked, worry etched on her features. "I heard yelling."

"Eva is gone," Ector replied with a deep frown.

"Gone? I just walked her home a couple hours ago."

"Taken," Kronus growled.

Why wouldn't they stand aside? Why were they leaving him no choice but to go through them?

"But that can't... I just saw her!" Macy's eyes widened. "Blake! We had a run in with him on the way home. He was confrontational and kept trying to grab her. He was drunk, but I didn't think he'd do something like *this*."

Kronus surged forward. Macy started and flinched back, but not before he clasped his hands on her upper arms. His muscles were tense with desperation. "Where is he?"

Macy cried out, hissing through her teeth as her features tightened in pain.

Jax moved in a blur. His fist connected with Kronus's jaw hard enough to send the ochre kraken reeling. Kronus's hands slipped from Macy's arms, but he recovered quickly; the pain on his face was distant and unimportant, little more than a dull throb.

Before he could reach for Macy again, strong arms looped around his own from behind, hauling him backward. Jax charged at him, but Macy stepped between them, putting her hands against Jax's chest. He halted as though he'd hit a cliff.

"Jax, stop!" Macy yelled.

Kronus struggled against the restraining arms, but whoever held him wrapped their tentacles around him to limit his movement further. "Release me! I must find her!"

"You do not touch my mate!" Jax roared.

Meeting the other kraken's gaze, Kronus lunged forward. The males restraining him grunted as they fought to keep hold.

"That's enough, Kronus!" Macy snapped, then turned back to Jax. "The fighting needs to stop *now*."

"He hurt you!" Jax snarled.

"I'm fine. He's worried about Eva."

"He is out of his mind. He does not get to put his hands on you, ever."

"If it were Macy missing," Kronus said, "you would be the same. You are not that much better than me, Wanderer."

Jax's eyes burned with reflected light from the lanterns. There were more people gathered now, but Kronus didn't look at them. They didn't matter.

Macy reached up and cupped Jax's face, drawing his attention back to her. "You know what he says is true. You would have fought all your people for me. In some ways…you did."

Jax pressed his lips into a tight line, brow furrowing.

"Please," Kronus said, casting his pride away. He relaxed, ceasing his struggles, knowing they would do him no good. "I need to find her. She is hurt, and in danger. I need her."

Macy turned toward him. "I can show you Blake's house, but I need you to promise me something, Kronus."

"Anything, as long as she is safe."

She approached Kronus, shaking off Jax's hand when he reached for her. "No matter what you see, or what happens, you can't kill Blake. Things are different here, and the alliance between the kraken and humans is still new. We have our own way of dealing with people who have done wrong."

Kronus clenched his fists. His claws bit into his palms, but he barely felt the pain. "If she lives, you have my vow."

Though he hadn't allowed himself to acknowledge it yet, he'd known, deep within, that Eva's death was a possibility in this situation. He didn't want to think about it, didn't have time to. But now it was there, now it was undeniable, and he could not ignore it.

His chest constricted as he leaned forward, overcoming the strength of the kraken restraining him for a moment. "If she is lost to me, I will kill him, Macy. Not you or anyone else will stop me. And once he is dead, your people may do with me as they wish."

Macy frowned and looked back at Jax briefly. "I don't believe he will kill her, Kronus. But please remember your vow. You need to choose whether your revenge is more important, or Eva."

"Take me there. Now."

She looked at Ector. "I need you to get Councilman Bailiff. His home is just behind the town hall. Tell him to go to Blake Denzen's home, and that he is possibly holding Eva captive."

Ector nodded, cast a final glance at Kronus, and hurried off; despite his age, he moved with swiftness and surety.

"No more wasting time," Kronus growled. He tugged on his arms again, and his captors released their hold on him. Rolling his arms at the shoulders, he held his gaze on Macy, ignoring Jax's glare. "Lead, female."

Macy turned and stepped around Jax, shifting her attention to Rhea, who had been observing from the grass on the side of the path with her daughter, Melaina, beside her.

"Could you watch Sarina and Eros?" Macy asked.

Rhea dipped her chin. "I will."

Macy thanked her and hurried along the path toward the jungle. Kronus followed, falling into place behind Jax, who seemed intent on serving as a barrier between his mate and Kronus. Many other kraken followed, their tentacles rustling the grass and vegetation around the path.

Just inside the jungle, they came across Randall, Larkin, and Dracchus. The trio joined without hesitation; Ector had passed them only a short time before and had explained the situation.

The group continued through the jungle, the few lanterns amongst them often overpowered by the blue glow of the surrounding plants. If the hidden creatures in the vegetation made any sounds, Kronus paid them no mind, keeping all his focus on Eva. His hearts did not slow, and he found himself bristling at the pace of travel; they needed to move *faster*.

Macy increased her speed once they emerged from the trees. The pastures passed on either side, dark and silent, and soon the group crossed onto the first of the town's paved roads. Kronus kept no track of the turns Macy led them through. The beating of his hearts grew louder and louder as he followed her, and the heat under his skin intensified further.

He'd given his word not to kill Blake.

Could he keep it?

"This is it," Macy said as they approached a small residence; it was one of several similar structures nestled along the road, with little to distinguish it from its fellows apart from the potted plants set out front — while the other homes displayed healthy green and purple plants, these were brown and wilted.

Ector and Walter arrived — along with several other townsfolk — as Kronus moved to the front door.

"Are you sure about this?" Kronus heard Walter asking. "This is an awful big ruckus to stir up without any—"

Kronus slammed his shoulder into the door, throwing all his

weight behind it. Wood snapped and splintered as the door burst inward, dangling by a single hinge.

Clothing and trash lay scattered about the place — soiled shirts, empty bottles, crumpled papers, and at least one half-eaten meal. The air was sour with the odor of alcohol and human sweat.

"What the fuck?" called a familiar voice. Blake. He skidded into the main room and looked at Kronus, the color draining from his cheeks. Fresh red scratches and welts covered his bare chest. With a curse, he fled into the room from which he'd emerged.

Kronus gave chase, ignoring the voices behind him. Grasping the door frame with hands and tentacles, he pulled himself into the bedroom only to halt just past the threshold.

Eva was sitting on the bed within, her hands behind her back and legs bound together at her knees. A wad of cloth was tied around her mouth. Dried blood matted her hair and clung to the side of her face. Her eyes widened as they fell upon Kronus, and she released a muffled cry, struggling against her bonds.

Blake stood on the other side of the bed behind her, a long-bladed knife in one hand and a wild gleam in his gaze. He held the weapon toward Kronus. "Stay away!"

Kronus gritted his teeth and advanced. He'd taken worse than what Blake could do with the knife; so long as Eva was safe, Kronus could accept a few new wounds.

Eyes rounding, Blake retreated a step. He glanced at Eva, and his eyes hardened. Blake darted to the bed, grabbed hold of her, and pulled her back against his chest. Grasping a fistful of her hair, he tugged her head back and pressed the blade of his knife to her throat. A pained, frightened cry escaped her, muted by the cloth.

Kronus stilled. That terrible, cold fear arose within him again to war with the heat of his fury.

"I said stay back!" Blake yelled. "I won't let you take her from me again. She's *my* wife!"

Eva's nostrils flared with heavy breaths. She held Kronus's gaze and carefully shook her head.

A gentle movement of air at Kronus's back told him some of the others had entered and were standing behind him. He didn't move any farther into the room, didn't adjust his position to allow anyone else entry. There was no guessing how Blake would react if he were suddenly confronted by two or three kraken instead of just one.

"Remove the knife from her throat," Kronus said, forcing his voice to be as calm and steady as possible. Only a slight trembling ran through his words.

"Back the fuck off!" Blake shouted. "Get out of here! All of you!"

Kronus raked his mind, searching all he knew about human body language and communication, wishing he'd had more interaction and had paid more attention. Slowly, he raised his hands to either side, displaying his palms. "I will not leave her, Blake."

"And neither will I!" Blake snapped, baring his teeth. His voice softened when he spoke again. "Neither will I. Not...not this time."

The tightness in Kronus's chest, the fire in his blood, demanded violence; a threat to his mate, no matter how small, could be met with nothing less.

But attacking Blake would only endanger Eva further. It could not be a solution to this situation, not now. And there was something in the man's eyes Kronus recognized, something deeper and more powerful than anger or jealousy.

"Just...just let her go, Blake. Let Eva go, and we can talk about this," said Walter from behind Kronus.

"No!" Blake's hand jerked, making Eva wince as the blade cut the fragile skin of her neck. "You just want to take her from me!"

Kronus clenched his teeth as a fresh surge of fury rose inside him. He spun and slammed his fist into the wall. The human-made stone collapsed in a crater beneath the blow, with cracks radiating outward from the point of impact. The people just outside the door — Walter included — flinched back.

"*Out*," Kronus growled at them. "Or every one of you will answer for any harm that befalls her."

"Kronus—" Macy began.

"Now!" Kronus roared.

"Just…be calm," she said softly.

His only response was a glare; he made no effort to hide his roiling emotions. Their faces were blurs to him as they shuffled out, kraken and human blending together into a featureless mob.

Scraping his claws over the wall, he slowly turned back toward Blake and Eva.

Blake was mumbling to himself, squeezing his eyes shut before opening them to look at Eva. "They're gone… I let them all die. But she's here. I…I can't… Maybe she'll forgive me? She has to. She's mine, my wife."

"Blake," Kronus said firmly.

The man's head jerked up, and his eyes met Kronus's. "What? Why are you still here? You…*touched* her!"

"I will not leave her. I care for her very much. You do, as well, do you not?"

"I love her!"

"Then you need to understand what you are doing to her."

"I'm not…" He turned his head and looked at the knife. "She's angry. I…I needed her to listen, but she kept fighting me. I just needed her to listen. To love me again. I only wanted to touch her…kiss her."

Kronus released a long breath. His tentacles writhed on the

floor, but he willed himself to betray no further sign of his agitation. Not until she was safe in his arms again. "Have you listened to *her*?"

"She doesn't know what she means. She's just angry. She'll… be better soon."

Part of Kronus's mind assessed the distance between himself and the bed, tried to judge the man's distraction, tried to estimate Blake's reaction time, but he would not allow that side to take control. This was one of those instances when instinct was not necessarily an ally.

"Eva is already better, Blake," Kronus said.

Blake shook his head. "No. She needs me. She told me. She was…crying, but I didn't listen. I am now."

"Lower the knife and remove the cloth from her mouth. If you are listening, allow her to speak."

"She still…she's still not *well*. She's still saying things she doesn't mean."

Kronus battled his urge to move closer. He wanted nothing more than to be near enough to touch her, but he understood Blake's mindset. He'd been there himself, at one point; he'd been broken, too. That did not make it any easier to curtail his impulses, but it was *something*.

"Then you are not willing to listen to her, are you?" Kronus asked.

"I'm listening, I'm listening… I'm fucking listening! But *she* won't listen!" Blake seethed, chest heaving. His hair had fallen around his eyes, and his flushed face glistened with a sheen of sweat.

Kronus dropped his gaze to Eva's face. There was fear in her expression, but there was something more there — the strength he'd recognized from the moment he'd freed her from the razorback. She flicked her eyes down once, twice, three times, until he finally followed them with his own. She was twisted with one shoulder toward him, just enough for him to see her fingers working at the rope binding her wrists together, undoing the knot a little at a time.

"She said she doesn't want me," Blake continued. "She's lying. She joined with me. *Me!* She's just mad. We belong together." He nodded. "We survived, but maybe…maybe we weren't meant to. Maybe we were supposed to die that day too." He looked at Eva, and her eyes widened. She shook her head. "We could be with them again. Addison. Sam. Hailey."

"No," Kronus growled, shifting forward before catching himself.

Blake, eyes rounded, looked at Kronus again. "*You!* You *took* her from me! This is *your* fault!"

"Then release her and make *me* pay for it," Kronus said, holding the man's gaze. "But if you care for her at all, and this is not simply a means for you to ease your own guilt, you will remove the blade from her throat. If you cared for her, if you *loved* her, you would want to give her reasons to live, not push her toward death!"

Blake's hand shook, and a strange sound escaped him, not unlike the whine of a wounded animal. His shoulders quaked with a heavy sob. "I…loved her, but I…I did horrible things. Said horrible things… I…left them, I left *her*, and I-I had sex with other women, and…"

"She is no longer yours, Blake," Kronus said, as gently as he could manage. "You have done wrong, yes, but…there can be atonement. *This* is not the way. Let her go. If you blame me, come and face me, but it will not set right what you have done. You must look inward for that."

Kronus glanced down to see the ties around Eva's wrists dangling. She loosened them further, freeing her right hand.

"I…" Blake searched her face, his expression warring with itself. "I…can't. All I feel is guilt. So much guilt. It…it would be better… I can give us *peace*, Eva. I can do that."

He leaned his face closer to hers, and the arm holding the

knife slacked. It was all the opening Eva needed. She drew back and smacked Blake's hand, knocking the knife out of his hand. It clattered onto the floor near the foot of the bed.

Kronus leapt at him.

Blake released his hold on Eva as Kronus propelled himself over the bed and crashed into the man. They tumbled into the far wall in a heap, knocking over the nightstand and the trinkets atop it to add the sound of something shattering to Blake's frantic shouts.

For his part, the human put up an admirable struggle, but even in his madness and panic, Blake could not match Kronus's strength.

Kronus caught the man's flailing limbs with his tentacles and slammed them down against the floor, shifting his body weight atop Blake's torso. He clasped one hand around Blake's throat and raised his other in a fist, ready to strike.

He hesitated for an instant, and in that instant, countless thoughts swirled through his mind. Things that had been said to him during his time here were foremost amongst those thoughts — words offered by Ector and Dracchus, Arkon, Aymee, Breckett and Vasil, but more than any other, Eva. Those words blended seamlessly with his own experiences, and he realized then that he *had* changed. He had learned, he had grown.

Even in the Facility, where insults often led to heated fights, thrown fists, and flesh shredded by claws, the worst offenses were judged by the people as a whole, under the guidance of the elders. Kraken fought one another, but they did not kill one another — not unless the situation was dire and could have no other resolution. How was this any different? Blake deserved death in Kronus's eyes, but Kronus had never been wise, had never been a great thinker. Blake had done wrong, but hadn't Kronus done wrong, also?

Kronus had ultimately been shown mercy. He'd been given a

second chance, an opportunity to try again. If his own way of thinking had been applied to those decisions, he would have been killed despite his reasons for returning to the Facility after his banishment. He would have remained a traitor to their people simply because it had once been declared so.

His fist trembled beside his head. It would be so simple a thing to kill Blake, to hammer fist into face until the human choked on his own blood. There would be honor in it; the kraken would see it as the defense of a mate — justified, if somewhat brutal. But the kraken weren't the only ones who had a say here.

He eased his hold on Blake's throat and lowered his shaking hand. Blake was broken; he needed help. Needed support. Needed his people. Perhaps they could show him the way, in time. Perhaps he would accept it — accept that Eva was no longer his and had never really been his to begin with. Kronus was willing to trust the people of The Watch — *his* people, regardless of their species — to see justice served with honor.

"Come help!" Eva yelled, her voice breaking through Kronus's thoughts.

There was a thump, followed by a grunt, and then she was there, her hands a balm as they smoothed over his shoulders to his chest before she wrapped her arms around him from behind. She pressed her cheek on the back of his neck.

"I knew you'd come," she rasped. Her tears fell hot against his skin.

More footsteps sounded within the room, accompanied by the familiar whisper of tentacles on the floorboards. Quite suddenly, the room felt full to bursting.

Kronus eased his hold on Blake only when two burly humans stooped down to take hold of the man by his arms and hauled him to his feet. They forced Blake's hands behind his back, and a third man — Randall — bound his wrists together with the same rope that had been used to bind Eva.

"I'm sorry," Blake mumbled. His shoulders shook as he sobbed. "I'm sorry. Sorry…"

"This is, uh…" Walter's voice called Kronus's attention to the man, who stood nearby, his cheeks red as he shook his head. "I don't know that I've seen anything like this since I joined the town council. It's… Hell, I don't know. This is a bit beyond the occasional belligerent drunk."

"Belligerent drunk is part of it, by the smell," Randall said as the other two men guided Blake out. The crowd parted, all eyes on Blake as he passed.

"He's sick," Eva said, "and he needs help."

"Dr. Rhodes is on his way to examine Blake," Macy said.

Kronus rose slowly, gently parting Eva's arms so he could turn to face her. She placed her hands on his shoulders and leaned against him. He wrapped his arms around her waist. "He can see to Blake *after* he checks you."

"I'm okay," Eva said.

Lifting a hand, Kronus delicately wiped away a bit of the blood welling from the cut on her throat with the pad of his finger.

"That's nothing," she said.

He frowned and moved his hand higher, touching the bloody spot on her head.

She winced.

His frown deepened into a scowl. "This is not *nothing*."

"Well, stop touching them!"

"Did he harm you anywhere else?" Kronus asked, drawing back slightly to look over her from head to toe.

"No. He…tried, but I fought him."

Kronus moved his hand from her head to rake his claws over his scalp, gritting his teeth tightly enough that they felt ready to shatter. He turned to go after Blake; perhaps mercy had not been the appropriate course.

Eva leapt at him, throwing her arms around his neck to hold him tightly. "Kronus, no. It's done. Let it *be* done."

He halted and slipped his hands to her backside to support her. Relief flooded him suddenly, unexpectedly, and he pressed his lips to hers in a desperate kiss. All those thoughts he'd cast aside earlier — all the things that could have happened — rushed back to him in that moment. He let them come so he could cast them all aside. She was safe, she was in his arms. That was what mattered. He would not torture himself over what could have been when he had everything he wanted, here and *now*.

Her lips moved over his, kissing him back just as fiercely. When she pulled back, her eyes met his. "Take me home, Kronus."

CHAPTER 20

LEANING BOTH ELBOWS ON THE TABLE, KRONUS DIPPED HIS HEAD to study the little figure, turning it delicately between the pads of his fingers. He flicked his eyes to the piece of paper laid on the table nearby. Aymee had drawn a reference of the creature based on holograms from the Facility after extracting a promise from Kronus to make a wooden carving of one for each of the younglings who lived in the houses along the ridge. He'd reluctantly agreed.

This one was both the first and the most special. He was surprised all its limbs remained intact; two more months of practice since the incident with Blake hadn't much improved Kronus's skill, but he was determined to keep to his word. Absently sliding his tongue between his lips, he carefully carved a tiny sliver of wood away from the figurine's eye.

When this carved octopus was done, it would await the birth of his coming youngling and be the baby's first gift.

He glanced at the drawing again. The tentacles and siphons were familiar, as were the pupils, but the rest of it seemed so alien and strange. Arkon had explained that these creatures — native to the same far away, impossible planet humans had come from — had served a major role in the kraken's creation. Kronus wasn't sure if he believed it or not, but he'd learned not to question Arkon on such matters.

Putting the carving tool down, he held the octopus and its curling tentacles flat on the palm of his hand and raised it to the light streaming in through the window.

Arms slid around his neck, and Eva pressed against his back.

"It's coming along," she said.

"Is not the saying *it's coming along nicely?*" he asked, emphasizing the last word.

Eva laughed. "It's coming along *nicely*." She lightly trailed the tip of her finger over one of the wooden tentacles. "It's cute."

"I intended for it to be menacing, not cute."

She turned her head and nipped at his siphon. It sent a tingling thrill across his skin. "Nothing can be as menacing as you."

He smiled, choosing to take that as a compliment. "Aymee said she would paint them when they are done. Would it be menacing if she painted this one orange?"

Eva hummed, and he could hear the smile in her tone. "It would look just like its father."

Father. It wasn't a word he'd ever thought about before humans came to the Facility; males sired younglings, that was all. But now that word filled him with equal parts joy, anticipation, and terror. It didn't seem a role for which one could prepare. As Jax had said, it was a matter of learning as you went along.

Somehow, that was more intimidating than a razorback hunt — and more exciting.

Kronus reached forward and placed the wooden octopus on the windowsill. As he did so, Eva plucked up the carving he'd made before she came to share his den — the one-legged human female.

"I still can't believe the leg broke off this by accident," she said.

"Do you doubt my honesty, female?" he asked, turning within her arms to face her.

"No," she replied, setting the figurine down and smiling at him. "I'd call it…fate."

"A suitable enough word." He raised a hand and cupped the back of her head, drawing her down into a kiss. Her body molded to his, and she moaned against his mouth as her lips parted to accept his claim.

When he finally broke the kiss, he leaned his forehead against hers. "I hunger, Eva."

"Well, the picnic is due to start soon."

"Too many people. I would rather stay here."

"You promised you would go."

He growled low in his chest. "I do not hunger for *food*." He moved his hands down her sides while sliding a pair of his tentacles up her legs, slowly lifting her skirt.

"We're going to be late," she whispered, but her gentle shiver conveyed urgency only for one thing.

As the hem of her skirt reached her mid-thigh, he rose to his full height, lifted her off the floor, and turned to face the table. With one hand, he swept the wood shavings and tools off the surface.

"Kronus," she pleaded.

He knew that breathy tone. Knew what she truly wanted.

He raised the bunched fabric of her skirt to her waist, and when his hands moved to her hips, they encountered bared flesh — no underwear. His chest rumbled with another growl. His mate had anticipated his touch. Had anticipated *him*.

Kronus sat her on the edge of the table with her legs to either side of him and pressed his lips over hers. He ravaged her mouth with lips and tongue, taking care not to hurt her with his teeth.

"Are you ready for me, my mate?" Kronus asked. His cock strained against his slit, ready to burst free, hungry for her heat. He slipped a hand between her thighs, the pads of his fingers delving into her folds. They both groaned as his fingers glided over her arousal-slickened flesh. She was hot and wet, primed for him.

It was all the answer he needed from her.

She sighed and tilted her hips, begging for more. He knew she was waiting for him to stroke that little bud that brought her such pleasure, and he would — but not with his hand.

He inhaled deeply, taking in the sweet, musky aroma of her desire, and his mouth watered.

Dropping down, Kronus curled his fingers around her inner thighs, spread her wide, and lowered his mouth to her sex.

Eva gasped, her body jolting. His shaft extruded the moment her flavor hit his tongue, pulsing in need. Her hands fell upon his head, and she moaned low and deep as his tongue trailed up and down her delicate folds, pausing to flick and tease the bud at the apex of her sex each time. He lapped at every drop of her nectar, and her cries of pleasure — soft at first but gaining in volume and passion — made the most satisfying music he could imagine.

"Oh! Kronus!" Eva panted, her hips undulating against his mouth. "I'm going to come."

He had already known she was close by the quivering of her thighs and how readily her sex gifted him with her sweetness. Wishing to hear more of her screams, he latched onto her clit and growled, sucking it into his mouth to lash it with his tongue.

She tensed, her thighs squeezing against his hold, and her heels digging into his back. Her blunt claws scratched his shoulder as she bowed over him with a choked cry. She shuddered around him and came, her cries filling the room, her essence filling his mouth. And he drank it all, ravenous for more. He did not cease the motion of his lips and tongue; instead, he eased them, allowing her to settle, leisurely lapping at her.

Eva hummed, slowly rocking her sex against his mouth as she petted his shoulder and brushed her lips across the top of his head.

"Come inside me, Kronus," she beckoned. She leaned back on the table and spread her thighs wider. "I need to feel you inside me."

Kronus flicked the tip of his tongue against her sensitive clit once more, eliciting a sharp gasp and a twitch from Eva before rising. His palms smoothed up her thighs and hips, moving possessively over her softly rounded stomach and the youngling growing within. A fierce wave of protectiveness swept through him.

This was his family. His mate and youngling, and he would tear anyone to shreds if they tried to take them from him.

Mine.

He reached down with one hand and gripped his cock, positioning its head at her entrance.

Mine.

His eyes flicked up and locked with Eva's. Hers were dark, sultry, filled with desire and love.

Mine.

Dropping his hands to her hips, Kronus yanked her to the very edge of the table and thrust into her, burying himself as deep as he possibly could.

"You are mine!" he roared. Gritting and baring his teeth, Kronus pumped into his mate ruthlessly, needing to feel her, to possess her, to stake his claim on every part of her being. His tentacles coiled around her legs, holding her in place while his suction cups kissed her flesh.

Eva panted, her breathy sounds growing higher in pitch with each thrust; he underscored them with his own ragged grunts, his mind clouded in a haze of pleasure through which he was aware only of her, of her body, of the way they fit together and the slide of their flesh. She was hot and tight, taking him in readily. His tendrils reached for her, desperate for her feel and taste, stroking her incessantly.

Eva crossed one of her arms over her chest and palmed her breast through her shirt, biting her lower lip to quiet her cries.

"Come for me, Eva," Kronus demanded, quickening his pace. He reached forward, cupped the back of her head with one hand, and pulled her face closer to his, staring into her eyes. "Let me hear you."

Her inner walls clamped around him, drawing him in deeper as liquid heat flowed from her. She cried out as he'd commanded, announcing her pleasure to him, to the room, to anyone and anything within earshot. But her sounds were just for him; he lowered his mouth over hers, muffling her cry, drinking in her breath as though taking in a piece of her for himself.

The pressure inside him soared to new, agonizing heights, threatening to tear him apart. His hands fell to the table, claws gouging into the wood. He pushed himself into her as deep as she could take him, and his seed burst from him in scorching spurts. He growled against her lips as the intensity of his release blasted pleasure through him.

Kronus wrapped his tentacles around her, holding her close as their continued connection prolonged their shuddering, blissful releases.

Breath ragged, Eva pressed her forehead to his and ran her hands up and down his back.

"I love you so much," she rasped.

"And I you," he replied.

Eva chuckled. "But really, we're going to be late."

Kronus buried his face against her neck, curling his fingers around her backside. "They can wait. I am not yet sated."

Her breathy moans were all Kronus needed to hear as he ground his cock inside her.

Eva, Aymee, Macy, and Rhea all laughed as they watched Kronus stare down at Jace, who had moved beside him. The young boy crossed his arms, squared his shoulders, and pressed his lips into a tight line. Once he lowered his brows, the transformation was complete — he was a miniature version of Kronus, blue-gray rather than ochre.

"Why are the kids so drawn to the grumpy ones?" Aymee asked.

"Dracchus is anything but grumpy around them," Larkin replied, snickering. "Oh, Jace has that scowl down pat!"

"It might have something to do with the toys Kronus has been giving them," Macy said. "Sarina adores the krull he made."

Rhea nodded. "Melaina was happy to receive the carving of Ikaros."

"Look at the way Jace is watching Sarina now," Larkin said.

Aymee and Macy groaned.

"What?" Larkin continued. "I think it's sweet!"

"They're too young!" Macy and Aymee replied in unison.

Eva grinned. She had to agree with Larkin. It was adorable how protective Jace was of Sarina. Whenever she was upset, he was the first one there, willing to do anything it took to make her smile again and glaring menacingly at anything or anyone responsible for hurting her.

It reminded her of Kronus.

She looked up to find Kronus's eyes on her. Her grin softened, her cheeks warmed, and her heart fluttered. His golden gaze was hot and possessive as it trailed over her, reminding her of what they'd done before coming to Macy's for the picnic. A lingering, phantom sensation of him, thick and hard, pulsed between her legs. Despite their recent couplings, she wanted him again and knew she always would.

Dracchus said something to Kronus, calling his attention away from her. Arkon, Randall, Jax, and Ikaros entertained the other children nearby. Delighted shrieks and laughter filled the air. Jax flopped to the sand, tentacles writhing as Eros pounced on him, growling ferociously. The larger kraken suddenly went limp, and Eros thrusts his arms victoriously into the air.

It was strange that only three months ago Eva had been ready to end her life. That she'd fallen so far it had been too painful to consider facing even one more day. That she'd lost *everything*.

But she'd gained so much since then.

Her hand fell to her rounded stomach, and her smile widened as she felt her baby moving within her, gently pressing against her palm.

She'd been gifted with a mate who selflessly remained by her side, who fought both for her and alongside her, who loved her as she was — no matter what she saw when she looked at herself. And now, they were having a baby. She couldn't be happier.

She felt like she *belonged*.

These women had opened their arms to Eva without question and had become her closest friends. She missed Addison, Hailey, and Samuel, and always would, but Aymee, Macy, Rhea, and Larkin had helped fill that void.

Blake still crossed her mind from time to time. Aymee said her father, Doctor Rhodes, spoke with Blake nearly every day to help him work through his issues. He seemed to be making progress, but he had a long road ahead of him. Though Eva was saddened by everything that had happened and wished she could help him, she hadn't visited. She had a feeling her presence would do more harm than good until he was…stable.

"Are you going to tell him?" Macy asked.

Eva turned her head. Macy was looking at Rhea, who in turn was staring at Vasil. He was next to a few of the other kraken, silently watching Melaina as she chased Ikaros.

"I think he already knows," Rhea replied.

"Does Melaina know?" Aymee asked.

"She suspects." The female kraken's tentacles curled, and she frowned. "I have been waiting for him to approach, to ask, but he has not."

"He will," Macy said, "when he is ready."

"Mommy!" Sarina called, racing toward Macy. "Can we eat? I'm hungry."

"You're always hungry," Macy said, laughing. "You need to stop growing so fast!"

Larkin cupped her hands around her mouth. "Okay everyone! Let's eat!"

The children cheered in excitement, and Eva waited until the crowd had passed before searching out Kronus. Her gaze found his, and once again, her heart sped up as she beheld her male. She moved toward him, and he opened his arms to her. She stepped into them without hesitation, brushing her lips against his.

"I find myself hungry for something a little more…particular," Eva purred, slipping a hand between their bodies. She ran a finger teasingly along his slit.

With a soft groan, he caught her wrist and glanced toward the others over his shoulder. One of his tentacles slipped under her skirt to caress her ankle. "I *have* had my fill of socializing," he said before returning his gaze to her. "But you need to eat. For you and our youngling."

"I trust my male will feed me well," Eva said, grinning, "*after.*"

"Eva?" Aymee called. "You guys coming?"

Kronus scowled, and before Eva could react, he stooped down and swept her into his arms, lifting her off her feet. She laughed, looping her arm over his shoulder and around his neck as he turned and started toward their house.

"Tired of sharing you," he muttered.

"We'll be back!" Eva yelled with a grin.

"For real?" Larkin shouted at them. "We're at a *picnic*!"

"Oh, don't act like you and Dracchus never sneak off," Macy said, laughing.

Eva chuckled and turned her face to Kronus. She traced a finger over his bottom lip, struck again by a wave of contentment.

"Thank you for dragging me up from the darkness," she said.

He paused, leaning toward her to press his lips to hers. "Thank you for guiding me home."

EPILOGUE

VASIL EASED BACK AGAINST THE DRIFTWOOD LOG AND WATCHED AS Randall sipped at his drink.

"You sure you don't want any?" Randall asked, raising the mug toward Vasil. It was not the first time he'd asked and wasn't likely to be the last, but he was never pushy, never forceful.

Vasil shook his head, and Randall withdrew the offered mug. The kraken shifted his gaze, sweeping it across the softly crackling fire, past the pale sand, and to the dark ocean waters. The sea's surface sparkled with the reflections of countless stars in the night sky overhead, reminding Vasil of the tiny, glowing orbs of halorium which sometimes rode the underwater currents. The waves rolled in one after another, their angry foam diminishing on the sand until they had no choice but to retreat and allow their fellows to continue the unrelenting assault.

Everyone else had already gone home, some carrying tired younglings; a long afternoon playing on the beach had worn out the little ones and their parents alike. Those who'd lingered after sunset had been males. Jax, Arkon, and Dracchus had eventually returned to their mates. Kronus, surprisingly, had remained a bit longer, seeming to enjoy the quiet, but he'd finally gone back to his Eva.

Why had Vasil stayed behind? Though he enjoyed company, he'd never been much of a talker. What did he have to gain here? Tomorrow would be another early morning at the docks. He needed rest.

He moved his gaze back to Randall.

Vasil knew why he'd lingered. Did Randall have a sense of it, too? Was that why he'd hung around while most everyone else left, sipping his drink as though he'd intended it to last until dawn? For a long while, Vasil had harbored suspicions, had observed things that made him wonder, but he'd never spoken any of it aloud. That wasn't the kraken way, which had suited him well enough in the past.

Yet all that had changed; he'd watched kraken society alter and shift over the last few years. The only thing that had kept him quiet was his desire not to cause trouble.

"Vasil, listen," Randall said, frowning down at his cup. "Rhea and I had something we wanted to talk to you about…"

Brow furrowed, Vasil tilted his head. "Was it that Melaina is my offspring?" he asked.

Randall's features slackened with surprise. After a few moments, he shook his head and seemed to regain his composure. "So, you *do* know."

"I was not certain of it…but it *feels* true."

"Why didn't you ask about it sooner? Rhea would have told you."

Vasil dropped his gaze to the flames dancing upon the sand. "What time I had with Rhea was enjoyable, but it was fleeting. It does not compare to what you share with her. Kraken males rarely know the children we sire. It is — *was* — not our way. I did not want to disrupt what you had."

"That's your daughter, man," Randall said. "That *means* something, doesn't it?"

"It means more with each day I spend here." Vasil's tentacles swept restlessly across the sand. "She is clever, and capable, and curious, and she may well be the one to tear down many of the traditions regarding our females. I am proud of her, but…"

"But what? She's amazing, and you're her father."

"She *is* amazing. But I am merely her sire. *You* are her father." Though he felt the truth of those words in his hearts, though he'd acknowledged them since his earliest suspicions of Melaina's parentage, they stung to a surprising degree when spoken out loud.

"Krullshit," Randall spat. He shifted his position, leaning on his right hip to jab a finger toward Vasil. "You are a good man. Or…a good *kraken*… You know what I mean. And you're just as much a father to her as I am."

Closing his eyes, Vasil attempted to sweep away the emotions sparked by Randall's words. "Does she know?"

"I don't think so, but she definitely has her own ideas. Before long… Well, I have a feeling she's going to want to know without a doubt, and once she finds out, she's going to come to you."

Vasil opened his eyes and nodded, casting a glance toward the sea; the tide was noticeably higher. It would likely cover their fire before dawn.

"It's not too late to be part of her life, Vasil," Randall said gently. He tilted his head back and drained the remaining liquid from his mug. "It'd do both of you some good."

As Randall was climbing to his feet, he paused to settle a hand on Vasil's shoulder. "Think about it, and if you want to… Let us know. We'd like you to be there when — *if* — we tell her."

For a few moments, Vasil held Randall's gaze, and he was awed by the compassion and understanding within the human's eyes. Such qualities might once have been considered a weakness in a male by kraken standards, but Vasil knew now that they were signs of deep strength and courage.

He nodded. "I will consider it, Randall."

Smiling softly, Randall stood up and removed his hand. "Night, Vasil."

"Good night."

Vasil did not watch Randall leave; his eyes were transfixed on the fire. Like the sea, it was in constant motion, but there was an immediacy to fire, a hunger it made no attempt to hide. The flames held their own mysteries, but they were not nearly as deep or dark as those of the sea. For a long while, he contemplated the nature of fire and water, wondering if they held significance beyond the obvious. If they did, he could not determine what it was.

He shook himself, willing those thoughts away. The tide was closer still; he'd lost himself for longer than he'd realized. He was in a strange mood tonight, uncertain of how to approach the situation regarding Melaina. Which was the correct course? Which course did he *want* to take?

There could be no denying that he wanted what he saw all around him here in The Watch — a family. To pass his knowledge on to younglings of his own, to see them grow and develop. He'd missed so much of that with Melaina already… knowing she was his youngling now, with no remaining doubt, could he really allow himself to miss any more?

Something flared overhead. Vasil started and swung his gaze skyward. A strange, distant boom echoed through the heavens, too succinct to be thunder. Vasil twisted to look behind him and stilled.

A streak of fire and smoke was bisecting the night sky, heading straight toward him. The object, obscured by its trail, hurtled past directly above his head, casting an orange glow across the beach. Vasil spun around to follow the thing's movement. An instant later, the sound of its passage — a roar of sizzling wind — blasted over Vasil, fading as quickly as it had arisen. He clawed himself upright and scrambled toward the water as though he could hope to match the object's speed.

The reflection of the object's fiery tail shimmered on the rolling waves. Whatever the thing was, it continued over the sea, threatening to overtake the horizon. Vasil stared after it, water splashing around his tentacles.

What was it? What was happening?

A bright, blue light flashed from far out over the water. Vasil raised a hand and narrowed his eyes to slits to shield against the light's intensity. A blue ring burst out from the center, dissipating the trail of fire and smoke. Something distant glimmered for an instant — it reminded him of moonlight bouncing off glass or polished metal. The object, made tiny by distance, vanished somewhere beyond the horizon.

From the moment the object had first lit up the sky until now, only a few heartbeats could have passed. Vasil remained in place, panting to catch his breath. The tightness in his chest only seemed to amplify the echoes of his pounding hearts. He flicked his gaze up again. The smoke, dark gray but highlighted by silver in the moonlight, was gradually fading from the landside outward.

He did not know a number high enough to count how many questions churned through his mind in those moments; they were too numerous to even distinguish one from another. The situation was mysterious, likely dangerous, and yet…

Curiosity, tempered by an oddly powerful sense of urgency, coaxed him deeper into the water.

Something had fallen from the sky, just as the humans had generations ago. If humans had come from somewhere in the stars, and they'd proven in large part to be decent, could this also be something good?

Vasil clenched his jaw. This was a foolish thing.

He dove into the surf and swam as fast as he could into the

night, keeping beneath the path of smoke blotting out a strip of the sky.

The Delver

The Hunter

<u>THE CURSED ONES</u>

<u>His Darkest Craving</u>

<u>His Darkest Desire</u>

<u>ALIENS AMONG US</u>

<u>Taken by the Alien Next Door</u>

<u>Stalked by the Alien Assassin</u>

<u>Claimed by the Alien Bodyguard</u>

<u>Saved by the Alien Crime Boss</u>

<u>STANDALONE TITLES</u>

<u>Claimed by an Alien Warrior</u>

<u>Dustwalker</u>

<u>Escaping Wonderland</u>

<u>Yearning For Her</u>

<u>The Warlock's Kiss</u>

<u>Ice Bound: Short Story</u>

<u>ISLE OF THE FORGOTTEN</u>

<u>Make Me Burn</u>

<u>Make Me Hunger</u>

<u>Make Me Whole</u>

<u>Make Me Yours</u>

<u>VALOS OF SONHADRA COLLABORATION</u>

<u>Tiffany Roberts - Undying</u>

<u>Tiffany Roberts - Unleashed</u>

ABOUT THE AUTHOR

Tiffany Roberts is the pseudonym for Tiffany and Robert Freund, a husband and wife writing duo. The two have always shared a passion for reading and writing, and it was their dream to combine their mighty powers to create the sorts of books they want to read. They write character driven sci-fi and fantasy romance, creating happily-ever-afters for the alien and unknown.

Sign up for our Newsletter!
Check out our social media sites and more!
http://www.authortiffanyroberts.com